HONEY MOUNTAiN

BY JANE TAYLOR

Published by Jane Taylor
9, Jubilee Close
Bidford-on-Avon
Warwickshire
B50 4ED

ISBN: 978-1-5272-0908-4

Cover design and illustrations by Emily J. Taylor
www.emilyjtaylor.co.uk

Designed and typeset by Emily J. Taylor and James Letherby
www.letherby.co

Printed and bound in Great Britain by SM-print
www.sm-print.co.uk

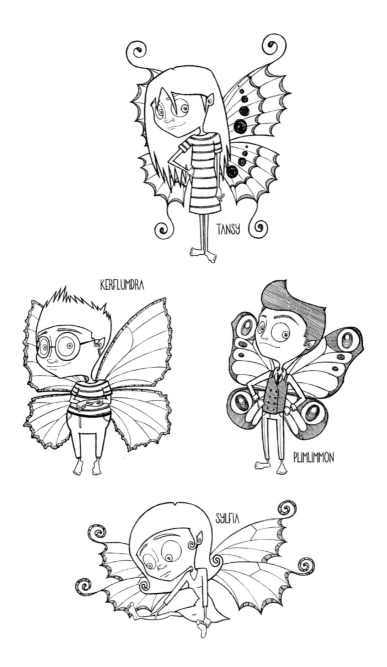

Chapter 1

On the other side of the great forest called Mulberry Wood are meadows and fields which stretch for pleasant miles until they turn into the murky Mushy Marsh and the stinking Slushy Swamp. These two damp features in the landscape have to be crossed before you can go down onto the banks of the Great Rumbling River. Crossing this wide and dangerous river is difficult and the traveller will endure great perils to get across.

On the opposite North Bank, the land rises and the country turns wild. First there is the Windy Heath, often known as the Howling Heath, and then, at higher altitudes, this turns into the Moaning Moor. Finally the traveller comes, full of fear and foreboding, to the foothills of the Blackscarp Mountains with their black, brooding peaks rising far above them. Bulzaban is the highest of these mountains and is reached by a steep climb up a path that is strewn with rocks and boulders.

All along this track there are precipitous vertical drops

on either side and at the end there is a windswept rocky outcrop called Cut-throat Crag where no trees grow and no birds sing. No birds sing songs, that is, but fierce black crows fill the air with their cawing and rasping croaks. They feed on debris thrown out by the unseen inhabitants of the mountain who dwell in the mysterious caverns beneath.

Lummock, the troll, lifted the sack curtain at the window hole of his hovel. He had been able to construct his simple home from some of the small boulders that litter the mountain side because trolls are good at dry stone walling. He was looking out because he had heard that rumbling sound again and, sure enough, another black metal wagon came clanking up the track. Like all the others, it was covered with padlocks, had no windows and was pulled by six enormous black rats with chains around their necks. The driver was an old gnome with an evil, knobbly face and a scowl that would make cheese turn mouldy. He smoked an old pipe, the noxious fumes from which made the rats' eyes water and he spat green slime onto the sides of the path. The boils on his face leaked their own putrid liquid which, once dry, encrusted his brown leathery skin with scabs and made him look even more fearsome.

At the top of the track the wagon stopped because the mountain side rose up in front as an impenetrable rocky mass. The gnome tapped out his foul-smelling pipe and jumped down from the driver's seat. He coughed loudly which was not difficult for one addicted to smoking such a vile pipe. His cough could be heard in the valley below. In response to this hacking sound, words appeared in a tidy square on the rock face. They were illuminated by an eerie green glow from within and they read, "NOCK HEER FOR ASSISSTUNS". The old gnome sighed deeply and banged hard on the square of rock. In response to his knocking a slate door, high above his head, scraped to one side but no face appeared. Instead a crackly voice called out, "Password?"

The gnome shouted back, "I dunno. Ya never tell me it."

There was a pause. Then the disembodied voice called out again.

"That's true. So, what's yer name?"

"Pustular!"

"That is correct." The voice sounded very smug.

"We knew it was you because of the smell! So what ya got this time? Wild or tame, unborn or hatched?"

"I got a nice consignment of bumblers for ya. 'Nough to keep me in the luxury to which I could very easily become accustomed," the knobbly gnome shouted up at the hole.

"We'll see 'bout that. Ya need the second portal on the right, then".

There was a grinding and scraping sound in the mountain side and a huge slab slid to one side to reveal an entrance in the cliff face.

Pustular muttered some abuse that outlined the limited nature of the gatekeeper's intelligence, flicked the chains over the backs of the rats and reined them into the blackness. His insults and curses rang in the air drowning out the squeaking of the rats as he brought down the metal links of the chain on the thin flesh of their backs.

When he had rumbled into the darkness the slab slid back and scraped into place with a sickening groan. No sign of life remained and the cold, echoing mountain-side returned to normal.

Lummock frowned, dropped his raggedy curtain and went back to the wooden bench which served as his bed. He buried his bulk once again among the tattered sacks that acted as his bed linen and pondered on what he had seen. However, his rather slow brain cells were soon exhausted and he fell back into troll slumber, dreaming of a goat pie that ran with thick onion gravy and was topped with crispy, golden brown pastry. He dribbled and drooled in his sleep.

It is a well known fact that a fairy who has been up all night at the Grand Spring Ball in Mulberry Wood must be in want of a place to sleep and that is why Tansy had snuggled inside a buttercup flower in Dingle Dell and was about to snatch a much needed forty winks. Feeling very weary, but extremely contented, she curled her deli-cate frame into the cup of yellow petals and let the gently rocking breeze quickly lull her to sleep. The soothing fragrance of wild meadow flowers filled her head and it was not long before she was dreaming of the night before; the handsome young fairies who vied for her as a partner in the dance; the pleasure of fluttering and gliding with them through the blossom laden trees; the tinkling music and the sweetly singing fairy voices.

Tansy Gospritely was unbeatable when it came to dancing. Her airy grace and supple form ensured that all of her movements were of the enchanted best and they earned her well deserved praise in the world of ethereal beings.

In her mind's eye she saw again the judges' scores, brightly illuminated by the coloured pixie lanterns hanging high in the tree tops. She had been awarded 10 – 10 – 10 – 10, a perfect score, because every move had been executed to perfection, from her double back somersault, with corkscrew pirouette, to her fleet-footed arabesque landing with exquisite grace, the tip of her toe balancing on the thin edge of the Fairy Queen's cocktail glass.

All at once her peace was shattered as a crashing sound in the long grass woke her from her reverie. A tubby, red faced fairy noisily broke cover and crawled towards her bed on his hands and knees. As he approached he felt around with his hands in the grass and muttered anxiously to himself.

"What're you doing now?" asked the sleepy Tansy, as she peeped over the edge of her flower's petals and recognised her friend Kerflumdra Penumbra, for it was he who was crawling about on the ground below.

"You're always hugger-muggering."

"Mugger-huggering? Yes, I suppose I am," her rotund friend replied. He tried to sound modest, believing that he must have done something good for a change. He did not usually earn such a fine sounding description.

"It's *h*ugger-*m*uggering, Flum. You don't know what it means, do you?"

"Well – I think – it sort of means – er – well – no, Tansy, I haven't got a clue."

Patiently, Tansy explained.

"It means that you are always causing chaos and disturbing the peace, more specifically, *my* peace."

Flum's face fell with disappointment.

"Oh, I see," he said. "Now, if you're referring to that incident last night when I was tripped in the rush for the supper table because someone shouted that they were beginning to serve honey-dipped, deep-fried, chocolate-flavoured mushrooms and I fell into that posh Purple Peacock thing – whatsisname – Pure Linen or something? – and made him spill his goblet of nectar down his new indigo velvet waistcoat – the one with the shiny brass buttons in the shape of honeysuckle flowers – well – all I can say is that the catering staff should be more organised and develop a system of queues."

Flum paused for breath and Tansy took the opportunity to ask her original question once again.

"That's all very well, my funny friend, but what are you

doing, *now*? I'm so tired I could fall fast asleep on a motorway and you're stopping me. His name is Plimlimmon, by the way. Plimlimmon fon Ffonfavor, to be precise. He's the butterfly fairy with the Purple Peacock wings"

"Is that his name? Humming blell! It takes up as much room as his ego!"

Flum got to his feet and tried walking in an aristocratic way with his hands on his hips and his nose in the air. This came to an end when he tripped over his own feet and ended up on his hands and knees once more. Tansy laughed.

"You asked what I'm doing. I'm looking for my specs," he told her.

"Your specs? Why should your spectacles be in the long grass?"

"Well, I was flying along, minding my own business just now when who should zoom across my path, without due care and attention, but that busy bee, Mrs. Humblebum."

"Oh, Flum, you mean Mrs. Bumblehum. Try not to get things mixed up. One of these days you'll get into a lot of trouble. Bees are not to be trifled with."

"Sorry, I can't help it," Flum groaned. "It happens all the time. My brain must be in back to front. Anyway, she was going at such a pace she knocked me flying. Well, I know I was flying anyway, but you know what I mean. My specs were thrown off and she lost her sacs of pollen."

"Why was she in such a hurry?" Tansy asked, uneasily.

"I don't know but I do know that I have never seen a

big bumblebee flying so quickly and in such an excited state. Her buzzing sounded like 'Out of my way! It's after me! I'm done for!' Or buzzes to that effect."

"Are you sure?" Tansy persisted with her interrogation, sounding really anxious now.

Perhaps this was not just another of his many minor accidents, thought Flum, and he decided to sit down on the grass to hear what his friend had to say about it. Immediately, he jumped up again, clutching his rear. There was a look of pain on his chubby face.

He mouthed the words "Bells hells!"

Then he spoke out loud, "I've found my specs!"

Tansy flew down daintily from her buttercup perch and landed with poise and precision beside her friend on the grass.

"We need to talk, Flum," she said.

Flum fitted his spectacles back on his nose and tried to look serious. They were now bent out of shape, and looked a bit lopsided but if he tilted his head on one side, to compensate, he could see well enough.

He was a short fairy with a round comical face and a shock of sandy yellow hair which always stuck straight up in the air and no amount of cuckoo spit would make it lie down. His eyes were large and bright blue, like the sky on a bright summer's day. He had rosy cheeks and a ready smile, was also impetuous, inquisitive and very fond of food.

He and Tansy had met at Lepidoptera Fairy College where their kind of fairy goes to learn how to look after moths and butterflies. They were in the same year but not in the same class. Kerflumdra's family was traditionally concerned with the care of moths and so his training involved a great deal of night flying and other activities after dark. This did not mean that he was inactive during the day. He was too interested in all forms of life to sleep much and anyway, some moths fly during the day.

Tansy was crossing the College Square one morning, carrying a substantial pile of text books with titles such as 'The Lives of Caterpillars', when Flum, flying like the wind to get to a lecture on 'Peppered Moths – Today and Yesterday', collided with her. He apologised profusely while retrieving the scattered books.

"Sorry, I'm such a flumsy cool. Me and my fig beet!"

Tansy translated this for herself into "Sorry, I'm such a clumsy fool. Me and my big feet!"

When she started giggling Flum joined in the laughter and they had struck up a firm friendship on the spot.

Tansy had thick straight red-gold hair and bright green eyes which sparkled and flashed like emeralds. She had a kind, thoughtful face and was honest, brave and determined. When she had graduated and chosen her adult wings she went for a striking pattern in red, orange and velvety brown with a bold eyespot on each wing. This pattern was inspired by Red Admiral and Tortoise-shell butterfly wings and indicated her bold, confident approach to life.

Flum, not to be outdone, chose the gaudiest wings that he could find in all the colours of the rainbow.

His mother had asked him why he could not be a nice conservative moth fairy and wear serviceable brown, grey or mustard yellow. He simply said that a born fool might as well look like a jester. As they sat side by side on the grass the scales on both of their sets of wings caught the rays of the sun and scattered the light, producing gorgeous patterns of colour.

Fairy wingmakers have studied insect wings for generations in order to manufacture them to such perfection. Sometimes insects, who fancied a change, would borrow a pair for a couple of days. Those creatures swore that they were just as good as their own (but none said that they were better).

Tansy bent her head close to Flum's ear and whispered "There's something going on. I don't like it. I've looked after the usual number of larvae and chrysalises this year. I hid them from the birds and kept them sheltered from the frost. I gave them the right amount of care."

"You always do, Tansy. You always work hard."

"Thanks, Flum, but when I went to check on them yesterday I could only find half of them. The others had gone!"

"Hooming blell! Are you sure that they hadn't just hatched?"

"It's too early in the year and anyway the cases would have been left behind. Now we've got bees flying around in panic and a lot of them are disappearing as well. Did you know that?"

Flum shook his head and stared at her dumbfounded.

"You say you collided with Mrs. Bumblehum?" Tansy went on. "Think now, Flum, when did a bumble bee ever collide with anything? Anyway, why did she not stop to give you a good telling off and make you gather up the bags of pollen? Bees are bossy as well as busy. She didn't, though, and she wasn't. She just disappeared! I think we need to look into this and I vote that we go and consult the wisest creature we know."

Flum thought for a minute then nodded vigorously.

"You mean Hornbeam, don't you? C'mon then. I'd like to meet him again. He's a dool cude!"

"Wait a minute. What's happened to your glasses? You need a straightening spell."

Tansy pointed her finger at Flum and her green eyes glowed. In her most strident, spell-making voice she incanted, "Uncurly-wurly, stretch and straighten, go back to normal (we are waitin')."

An arc of white light whistled from her finger and struck the spectacle frames with a 'zing'. The frames wriggled for a moment, sighed a little, then stretched out into perfect alignment. Tansy smiled a smile of satisfaction. Flum grinned with admiration.

"Thanks, Tanz. What would I do without you? I never got the hang of molecular rearrangement. The lectures were too early in the morning when I was still eating my breakfast."

Tansy laughed again as they flew off together in the direction of Mulberry Wood. They flew at a leisurely pace, side by side. Fairies have negligible mass and can fly at the speed of light, if they want to, but what is the point in getting there before the event has happened? It only leads to confusion.

Chapter 2

As Tansy and Flum flew over Dingle Dell and back towards the wood that had been the scene of last night's revels, they heard the sound of fairy laughter below. Fairies make a tinkling noise when they laugh. It's like running your finger over a row of delicate metal chimes.

The friends stopped flying forwards and hovered instead. Below them they saw two fairy figures stretched out, side by side, on a moss covered log. They were blowing rainbow bubbles.

"I love those," Tansy murmured and before Flum knew what was happening she had caught his hand and pulled him down to land on the log. The two bubble blowing fairies sat up quickly and looked a little guilty.

"We were only killing time until singing practice," the elegant male fairy told them. It turned out to be Plimlimmon, no less, the fairy with the perfect Purple Peacock wings and the expensive gear from top fairy outfitters. When he recognised Kerflumdra he said,

"Oh, it's you, Fatty. You owe me the cost of a new waistcoat."

"If you didn't stand with your nose in the air, feeling superior, you would know what was going on and then you would be able to get out of the way in time," Flum retorted.

Tansy thought how strange it was that, when he was really angry, Flum could speak very plainly without getting his words mixed up.

"Come on you two," she said. "It was an accident. These things happen when crowds gather. Please will you introduce us to your friend, Pim?"

Flum jumped when he heard his friend addressing his enemy in such familiar terms. He had forgotten that Tansy and the Purple Peacock thing had been in the same class at school.

While he and Plimlimmon had been frowning at each other, Tansy had been staring at the other bubble blower. Now Flum turned to look at her as well. He and Tansy both gazed at the newcomer in wonder. She was the most beautiful butterfly fairy that they had ever seen. She had long silver hair and her soft grey eyes sparkled like diamonds. Her shy smile was so sweet that no one could fail to fall in love with her. Her wings had a double sheen and they fluttered constantly. Sometimes they reflected a stunning purple-blue light, like the wings of an Adonis butterfly. At other angles they emitted the strong golden colour of a Yellow Brimstone which might well remind the onlooker of bananas covered with warm honey.

"Yes, of course, Tansy. May I introduce Sylfia Mellifula? She is staying with us for the rest of the summer," Plimlimmon intoned in his most aristocratic voice.

"It's lovely to meet you both," said Sylfia, shyly. Her speaking voice had the same silvery tinkle as her laughter. It was easy to imagine that her singing voice would be absolutely beautiful.

"H – hello. Meased to pleet you, I'm sure," Flum stammered.

"Me too. I mean *p*leased to *m*eet you, that is," Tansy added.

"I saw you dancing last night, Tansy. You were amazing. I was singing in the Mulberry Fairy Choir and so I had a really good view of your dancing," Sylfia told her.

"Well, thank you very much. I'm sure that your lovely voice will be an asset to the choir. I thought there must have been a reason why the singing was especially good last night. I expect you made all the difference."

Sylfia and Tansy smiled at each other appreciatively.

"Oh, here we go," thought Flum. "The 'Girls' Mutual Admiration Society.' How can a fellow compete? They're always so good at everything."

Meanwhile, Pim was looking very pleased with himself for bagging such an admirable companion. He was a very tall fairy who always stood very straight with his proud nose in the air. His shiny black eyes would flash ruby red when he was annoyed. His wings were superbly iridescent, very large and perfect copies of the wings that all his family possessed. They had the pattern of a Peacock butterfly's wings but the background colour was deep purple, like the wings of an Emperor butterfly.

His family described themselves as extremely well bred with royal connections. Centuries ago, his great uncle Pensisly had been Chamberlain at the Court of the Fairy King and his great-great aunt Peaseblossom had been an attendant of the Fairy Queen on that night when she had made a fool of herself by falling in love with an ass called Bottom. Peaseblossom had shown her loyalty by helping the Queen to keep the matter under wraps. The family had bought a mansion in The Great Royal Park, using the hush money. It was an early example of cash *with* honours.

"Sylfia comes from the Chalk Downlands near the coast. My parents met her parents last summer when they accompanied the Royal Party on a river trip to the sea," he boasted.

"Splendid!" said Tansy, without much enthusiasm.

"They should have taken you with them and forgotten to bring you back," Flum muttered under his breath and Tansy shushed him with a nudge and a frown.

"Well, we have something to do in Mulberry Wood," she said hastily. "So nice to meet you, Sylfia. I hope we'll see you again soon. Goodbye!" So saying she pulled Flum by the sleeve and they both took to the air once more.

"I hope we meet Sylfia again but as for the other one, no thanks, not if I see him first," Flum spluttered.

"Behave yourself!" Tansy giggled as they flew off together.

Mulberry Wood is a huge, ancient, magical wood and in the middle is a huge, ancient, magical tree. Inside the tree lives an ancient wood elf called Hornbeam Hardycumhandy.

It goes without saying that he is magical too, but, although he is about twice the size of our butterfly fairies, he is not huge.

He has lived such a long time that he knows a great deal about the ways of the world. He has contributed much to the education of generations of fairies and elves. He and Tansy's father taught together for a number of years in the Wood Craft Night School. In fact, he is a dear friend of the family and Tansy looks upon him as an extra grandfather. He has a leathery nut-brown wrinkled face, gnarled looking old hands, bright, twinkling eyes and a warm friendly smile.

Many people believe that fairies and elves are the same. It is not so. They are completely different races. Fairies never live alone. They like to live and work together in large fairy communities. They work hard when they are supposed to but they much prefer to get together for revels. Revels usually take place at night and involve prolonged dancing, singing, cooking and eating.

Most of the time fairies ignore humans, although it is true that mischievous youngsters are attracted to human habitations in order to tease and cause trouble. In the country they can still turn the milk sour and stop the free range hens from laying and, in town and country alike, they will enchant the toast so that it always falls to the floor butter side down.

It has been this way since the beginning of human time but now some fairies have discovered a whole range of new annoyances with which to tease Homo Sapiens. They can hide car keys for hours, crash the computer before you have saved your three thousand word essay and they can make the phone ring but give no answer when you pick it up. This is especially annoying if you were just having a soak in a hot bath.

Some really *bad* fairies can actually go over to the Dark Magic and then they turn into imps. Such fairies are never mentioned again in decent fairy society.

Elves, on the other hand, do not mind living alone and often choose to do so, especially when they reach middle age. They go on studying all their lives and, unlike fairies, they can become very wise indeed. They study everything. They study the animals and plants, the seasons of the year, the weather and the tides, the sun, moon and stars. They even study human beings. They sit for hours, very quietly and in disguise, in school playgrounds, magistrate courts, university lecture halls, bus stations, hairdressers, supermarket checkouts and beside BBC news desks.

You can spot elves everywhere if you concentrate. They do no harm and are simply learning oceans of wisdom so that they can answer any question you might ask.

Everything from "Where do all the biros go?" to "Where can I buy a really good old-fashioned vanilla custard slice like we used to get before the war?"

Everything from "Where is that pair of scissors that I had in my hand just now?" to "How close are we to discovering a Unifying Theory of the Universe?"

It was teatime when Tansy and Flum knocked on his door. The evening was chilly because it was still early spring and so Hornbeam had blown up a small glowing red fire in the grate. A kettle hung over this and he was busy toasting elf-sized crumpets. He already had six of these keeping warm in a red and white bowl on the hearth. Another dish contained curls of fresh, creamy butter, not too soft and not too hard, just right for spreading.

"Come in, Tansy! Come in Flum!" cried the elf.

"How did you know it was us?" asked Tansy. "Oh, don't tell me, I know. You had your spies out! How *are* Hootsmon and his lodgers?"

With this she gave her old friend a hug. Fairy hugs are lovely hugs. You can breathe freely throughout and up your nose you get the delightful scents of herbs like thyme, marjoram and lavender.

Hornbeam chuckled merrily. "The old bird is flown of his feet. His summer visitors are starting to arrive already and he has more bookings than ever. His fame

19

is spreading it seems. Come right in Flum and warm yourself by the fire."

Flum had met Hornbeam at Tansy's Family Wassail last Midwinter and he was still very much in awe of the wise old elf.

"Thank you, sir," Flum said, holding up his hand in fairy salute. Then he solemnly intoned, "May your loof never reak."

"I hope it won't," Hornbeam chuckled. "Pass me the plates and mugs off that dresser will you? Tansy can butter the crumpets while I make the tea."

Flum relaxed at the sight of food and began to feel more at home. When they each had a mug of steaming hot nettle tea and three or four crumpets dripping with butter they settled into comfortable old chairs by the hearth. Hornbeam threw some pine cones on the fire and they burnt up fiercely with crimson flames and the pungent woodland smell of pine filled the room.

The house occupied the inside of the trunk of the tree and so each room was roughly circular. The ground floor parlour which the fairies had entered directly from the forest floor was no exception. The fireplace was situated directly opposite the front door. To the left of the fireplace was a wonderful shiny black oven. These fire ovens are out of fashion in human houses now but anyone who has been lucky enough to taste freshly baked bread from one of them will tell you that there is nothing like it. Roast meat, cakes, Yorkshire puddings, crispy baked vegetables, rhubarb crumble, rice pudding with a crunchy brown skin on top and many other foods are a delight when produced in an old wood or coal fired oven such as this.

To the right of the fireplace stood another door which opened to reveal the bottom of a staircase. This staircase could be seen to spiral upwards to higher floors, following the curve of the tree trunk. At various points on the ascent doors led off into other circular rooms. Directly above the parlour was Hornbeam's bedroom, above that was his study and library, above that was a guest room and right at the top was his observatory and laboratory. Here at the top of his tree trunk house he would perform scientific experiments or, on clear nights, he would study the heavens using various telescopes that humans had discarded and he had renovated.

On each of the middle floors there was an en suite bathroom tucked under the stairs.

During the day sunlight could enter the house through windows on the staircase or through the front door which stood open in warm weather. At night or on gloomy winter days the house was lit by magic elfish lanterns. These produced a range of soft glowing colours and re-sponded to commands such as "luxor fortissimo", when a bright light was needed for reading or working and "luxor diminuendo" when a gentle light was required for dozing or story telling.

On the ground floor four other doors were spaced around the parlour walls. One led into a scullery which is an old-fashioned type of back kitchen used mainly for washing dishes and clothes. A second door led to a cloakroom, a third opened onto a storeroom and a fourth concealed a pantry. The storeroom contained almost every piece of domestic equipment that you could ever wish to use or choose to ignore. These included a broom, a mop, a bucket, an ironing board, a hammer, a chisel and a wrench. There was also a wonderful old rickety bicycle with a basket on the front which Hornbeam rode through the wood, bumping and rattling along, stopping frequently to collect herbs, nuts and fruit or deliver news to the other inhabitants of the forest.

The pantry, however, was his pride and joy. It was lined with shelves on which were stored jars of jam, honey, chutney, pickles and sauces. On the floor were sacks of walnuts, beechnuts, hazelnuts, barley, beans and rye. Every sort of herb hung in bunches from hooks in the ceiling. Some were to make tea, some to flavour food, some to make medicines and some were to hang up around the house to perfume the atmosphere with their delicate aromas.

The harvest of the forest and the surrounding fields was neatly stored in Hornbeam's pantry, ensuring not only his survival through the winter, but also that of many other creatures who shared this ancient habitat.

No sooner had all three settled by the fire when there was a fluttering sound and a rustling on the other side of the front door. The door creaked open in the same way as it had done to admit the fairies. A feathery head, in which were set two large, round and blinking eyes, was squeezed through the gap.

A vowel rich Scottish voice said, "How are ye ma wee feeary friends?"

"They're fine, Hootsmon," Hornbeam told him. "We're just having tea. Why don't you take a breather and join us?"

"Och aye. Ah think ah'll just dee that. Thank ye kindly. That'll be better than dustin' an' hooverin'." With that he squeezed his bulky form in through the doorway and made his way closer to the fire.

As with all birds he could get into much smaller spaces than you would expect at first glance. This is because most of their bulk is due to feathers and without them birds would be quite skinny.

Hootsmon was a Tawny Owl who had settled in Mulberry Wood after a forced emigration from Scotland. His own forest home had been demolished to make way for twenty luxury time-share cabins and an eighteen-hole golf course. Flying south he had spotted an Opportunity for High Rise Development in the upper branches of Hornbeam's ancient tree. After lengthy negotiations, and many cups of mint and blackberry tea, the pair had struck up an agreement and had formed a firm friendship.

Hootsmon was a canny business bird and offered comfortable, homely accommodation for a variety of lodgers in the higher levels of the tree. He worked hard to keep these nesting sites in good order and many local birds used his tree all year round.

In addition, summer visitors migrated there each

spring and Hootsmon had become known, far and wide, as a generous and hospitable host. Any day now he was expecting a pair of turtle doves from France and he was looking forward with impatience to their billing and cooing. They had sent word by carrier pigeon that they would like to try his accommodation this year. Hootsmon was determined to impress this exotic continental couple.

He had been busy all day, cleaning the spare nesting sites. He was hoping for a record number of hatchlings and fledglings from all of his 'wee birdies' this year. He looked forward to telling the little ones stories, as well as gossiping with their parents. Hootsmon was an excellent story teller. Baby bird eyes would open wide as the little ones heard tell of the Far North. They imagined themselves skimming over high mountain-tops, on patrol with the fierce Golden Eagles, or they saw themselves dropping feet first into deep ice-cold lochs to grab huge salmon in their razor sharp talons, just like the Ospreys.

Hornbeam and the fairies did not believe that Hootsmon had ever been near a Golden Eagle, or an Osprey either, but they enjoyed his Tales of the North, just as much as anyone else who gathered around at story telling time.

Hootsmon filled much of Hornbeam's little parlour and became an effective duvet, stopping any draught that might have reached those assembled around the fire. Very soon Hornbeam and all his friends were feeling very cosy indeed and with their tummies full of food they could easily have nodded off. Tansy, conscientious as ever, fought against this soporific feeling.

She sat up straight in her chair to say, "We have something important to tell you, Hornbeam. It may be serious. We think that bees are being chased and captured. It may also be happening to butterflies and moths. I have found that some of their eggs and pupae have disappeared. They may have been stolen by persons unknown."

Hornbeam's eyes shot wide open. "Surely you are mistaken, my dear. Do you know anything about this, Hootsmon?"

The owl blinked, lowered his head and whispered, "Och aye, ah have heard rumours but ah thought that it was just a bit of tittle-tattle from those chaffinches. They're such cheeky wee show off birds. They're always lookin' fer attention."

Tansy went on to explain what had happened that day and Hornbeam started to look concerned.

He frowned and said, "These are the insects that we rely upon to pollinate the flowers. If we lose too many it will spell disaster for the plants."

"If plants don't get pollinated there will be fewer of them," reasoned Tansy.

"If there are fewer flutterbies and moths there will be fewer eggs laid to hatch out into curry fatterpillars!" Flum chimed in, his round eyes even rounder with fright.

"Oooo!" hooted the owl. "Fewer caterpillars means less food for birds, so fewer birds!"

"Where will it all end?" Tansy gasped.

'Hoo noos?' the owl asked.

"It will end with the death of the planet," continued Hornbeam.

After further thought he added, "Humans have made such a mess of the atmosphere recently. They have been filling it with CO_2."

"See who too?" Hootsmon asked, tilting his head on one side and looking very puzzled.

"It's a gas, Hootsmon, from burning fuels. Humans have done too much of that and the CO_2 produced is making a blanket around the earth, causing it to warm up. This is another type of disaster and only plants can put it right. We have to find out who these insect thieves are and put a stop to them. Hootsmon, when you are out tonight fly extra quietly. Keep your night vision peeled. See if you can spot anything unusual. We all need to work on this."

Chapter 3

Pimlimmon stamped his foot and glowered. "That is such an irritating little moth fairy. I'd like to take his silly rainbow wings and ……"

"Swap them for your own, Pim? They are really something, aren't they?"

Pym glowered, angrily.

Sylfia's eyes followed the flight of Tansy and Kerflumdra until they were out of sight. She wished that she knew them well enough to join them. She consoled herself with the fact that it was not too long before singing practice. Then she would escape from Pim for an hour or two. To fill in the time she danced her way towards Mulberry Wood where the choir would assemble.

Pim saw another chance to show off and so he raced after her and joined in the dancing. Together they hovered, shimmered, darted, twirled and fluttered through the long grass and into the shade of the trees. As they went, Pim boasted of his recent success in the Dingle

Dell Bat Racing Gold Cup. Then he gave a blow by blow account of his underwater fight with a fierce Giant Water Beetle when he was snorkelling in the Slushy Swamp. Then he bragged that he had been chosen as Wand Bearer to HMFK (His Majesty the Fairy King) in the Midsummer Revels and told how he had already picked out a suit of scarlet silk for the occasion. It had a dozen tiny buttons that looked like twinkling silver stars.

On and on he went with Sylfia only half listening. She was wondering where Tansy and Flum had gone and what they were doing in Mulberry Wood this evening.

Once inside the wood, Sylfia turned onto the broad grassy avenue that would take her into the centre of the forest and the glade where the choir would assemble.

Plimlimmon, however, called out, "D'you want to know a shortcut, Sylfia? Follow me and I'll show you."

Against her better judgement but curious to know as much about the wood as possible, Sylfia followed Pim as he veered off at the side of the broad avenue. He pushed his way into dense undergrowth and she followed close behind him. He had to mutter plant-bending spells so that the brambles and nettles would move apart and allow them to pass through. Daylight was fading in the wood by this time and Sylfia shuddered at the thought of getting lost in unfamiliar vegetation with her sense of direction completely gone. She was just beginning to wonder if Pim actually knew where he was going when they emerged from the undergrowth and stepped onto an unfamiliar path.

"This way!" commanded her companion and she found herself following a dark and stony track quite unlike the grassy sylvan paths that she had become used to. It was damp underfoot and the ground was littered with sticks and mossy stones. They flew silently between very old lichen covered trees until Sylfia noticed that straight ahead the path ended in a gloomy clearing where rays from the evening sun were only just managing to filter through.

She had expected a broad open space, lit by pretty coloured lanterns, where chattering choristers would be waiting for the Fairy Music Master to join them. Such a space was nowhere to be seen and Sylfia began to have the uneasy feeling that Pim had lost his way. She was just about to suggest that they should retrace their flight path when her companion stopped abruptly. He had spotted a couple of figures ahead in the gloom of the clearing.

Sylfia followed his gaze and saw two very dirty gnomes standing beside a fallen tree trunk on the opposite side of the clearing. Both had unpleasant sneering expressions on their faces. One had a very large nose covered with pimples and the rest of his face was pock marked and scabby. He wore a battered old hat which was green and shiny with age and on his feet he had scuffed black hobnailed boots with steel toe caps. His name was Scabbage.

His companion had thick, matted, greasy hair and slimy skin. A scar ran down his dirty face from the corner of his eye to the edge of his jaw bone. He had no teeth and dribbled constantly from the corners of his mouth. His name was Festergum.

The gnomes did not notice the newcomers because the two fairies had stopped short of the clearing and were still in the shadow of the trees. Each gnome had a leash in his hand and on the other end of each leash was a tight collar fastened around the neck of a shiny stag beetle. The beetles reared up at the sight of each other and were obviously eager to clash horns and begin to do battle.

Male stag beetles love to fight. The idea is that they lock horns and wrestle in order to throw the opponent off a log or tree stump. The loser usually survives, unless he lands on his back and cannot get up, but he does, however, lose the respect of any female beetle looking on. The best course of action is for him to scurry away to the gym and work on his technique before the next encounter.

One other thing that all stag beetles love is a party. They gather on old rotting trees where the fermenting sugar is turning into alcohol and I am afraid to say that one or two become so intoxicated that they are unable to get up for work in the morning. This makes the capture of stag beetles a very easy matter for wily gnomes.

Each gnome held his beetle on a short leash so that they were not able to make contact with each other. Not yet that is.

"Give us yer hat," Festergum ordered.

"Not on yer life," Scabbage snapped. "Last time ah took off this hat ya filled it with sludge from the Slushy

Swamp. It were weeks afore ah got the slime out of me ears!"

"Spoil sport. It'll 'ave t'be one o' these then."

With that Festergum slouched over to a nearby holly bush climbed up into the upper branches and stole a bird's nest. He came back to the log and tipped the baby birds out onto the ground where they flapped around helplessly, shrieking for their parents.

Festergum placed the empty nest on the log.

"C'mon, coff up yer cash," he growled. "Bet yer five new silver pieces my Sizzajaws will have your Blackhorn off that log afore ya can say Jack o' Lantern."

"Nah, yer weak little bit o' beetle flesh'll be 'nialated by my mighty crusher afore ya can say Jack Frost."

Both gnomes threw their money into the nest and lifted their beetles onto the log. As soon as the collars were unloosed from around their necks the beetles locked horns and the struggle began. The gnomes set up horrible cheering, jeering and sneering noises. They punched the air and leapt up and down, pushed each other, kicked the log and danced about in an excited frenzy. The baby birds were in great danger of being trampled to death.

The two fairies watched from their vantage point among the trees and winced at the cruelty. Pim was red in the face and clenched his fists in anger.

"I've got to put a stop to this," he hissed. "We don't want this sort of thing in Mulberry Wood. It's insect exploitation and it's gambling. Both of those things are strictly forbidden under Fairy Law."

"No, Pim, please don't confront them," Sylfia pleaded. "I have a bad feeling about this. They look far too danger-ous. We should go for help."

Just as she finished speaking Pim strode out into the clearing. She was forced to hold her tongue and retreat behind a tree then she flew up into the branches and peered down through the leaves.

"You there," Pim cried. "I order you to stop that at once, in the name of the Fairy King."

"What 'ave we here then?" Scabbage snarled as he whirled around to stare across the clearing at the newcomer.

"One of them high and mighty airy fairies I do believe," Festergum snorted. "We'll have to put an end to his Hoity-Toity Highness, won't we? Follow me and do what ah tell ya."

Both gnomes swaggered over to Pim where he stood in the middle of the clearing, his hands on his hips and his head in the air.

"See here, gnomes! This is a fairy wood and your games are not allowed. Set those insects free and be on your way. Do not return if you value your freedom."

Festergum winked at Scabbage and scoffed, "Oo be yoo then, Mr High and Mighty, and why should we pay you any heed?"

"My name is Plimlimmon and I am Wand Bearer to His Majesty the Fairy King."

With mock respect and a treacherous glint in his eye Festergum made a low bow.

"Well I never, your High and Mightyness. Excuse our 'orrible ignorance."

Pim puffed out his chest and tossed his head.

"Well, now that you are aware of your error perhaps you will be so good as to obey a royal command."

Festergum snatched the hat off Scabbage's head and forced him into a low bow while lowering his own head at the same time so that he could whisper to his companion.

"Get the net," he hissed.

"Yes indeed, your hexcellence," he continued, in his mockingly polite voice. "Hif you would be so good as to walk this way we may be hable to find your himminence some refreshment. Then we will clear hup here and be hon hour way."

"Indeed you will, my good fellow. A small glass of something would be in order while I am waiting."

Pim allowed himself to be guided towards the opposite edge of the clearing. Sylfia watched in horror as Scabbage moved behind his back and collected a net from a pile of equipment that was lying on the ground. Moving extremely quickly and with the practised aim of an experienced hunter Scabbage threw the net over Pim and, before you could say Jack and the Beanstalk, he had pulled a cord tight. The cord drew the edges of the net tightly together and made a bag with Pim inside it.

Sylfia, still hidden high up in the tree had to clap a hand over her mouth to stifle a squeal of fright. Now she watched in horror as the gnomes dragged the net over to a black wagon made of iron which had been concealed in the undergrowth behind their gambling arena.

"Na' then, yer High an' Mightyness," cackled Festergum nastily. "That's what we think of yer stupid airy fairy laws! Another fer the wagon, eh Scabbage? This'll amuse 'em under the mountain. They ain't got one of these jokers. We'll ask extra fer this one 'cos he's a comic and no mistake."

Pim had recovered from the initial shock of capture and, struggling violently, he began to yell at the top of his voice. Scabbage rummaged once more in the pile of equipment and pulled out a spray gun. He pulled the trigger and clouds of green smoke blew out into Pim's face. With a moan the proud fairy ceased to struggle and crumpled into a motionless heap on the grass.

Scabbage rummaged in his pocket and produced a key with which he undid a padlock on the side of the wagon. A small door could then be opened and inside this a small cylindrical cage could be seen. The door of the metal cage was behind the solid door in the side of the wagon. The cage was just large enough to allow the unconscious body of the fairy to slide inside and then the net was removed. The cage door was closed and a bolt was shot home with a sickening thud. Finally, the door in the side of the wagon was slammed shut and the padlock was clicked back into place.

"Fetch the rest of the gear, Scabbage," Festergum chuckled. "We'll be on our way 'afore you can say Jack in the Box."

Scabbage went back to pick up what remained of the pile of equipment and he stowed it away in a box built into to the back of the wagon. Meanwhile, Festergum pocketed the money in the bird's nest and pulled the two battling beetles apart. He fastened their leashes back onto their collars and tied each to a different corner of the wagon so that they were no longer able to fight.

Both gnomes jumped up onto the seat at the front of the wagon and Scabbage shook the chains to wake up the six black rats harnessed to the vehicle. The poor worn out creatures rose to their feet, shook themselves and began to haul the wagon out of the trees and onto a nearby forest path.

Scabbage whipped the rats until they moved fast enough for his liking and then the whole caboodle rumbled away into the gloom.

The gnomes could be heard arguing about the money. Scabbage maintained that there had been no winner and that he should have his share back. Festergum insisted that he had found Sizzajaws on the log and Blackthorn on the ground which made Scabbage swear that Festergum was a thieving toad and should be cut into small pieces to be fed to the Great Water Beetles in the Slushy Swamp.

Sylfia, distraught because she had never seen anything so frightening, flew down into the clearing, shaking and sobbing as she did so. Carefully she picked up each of the trembling baby birds and gently replaced them in their nest. She flew with the nest back up to its perch high in the holly bush while the parent birds flew around her, brushing her cheeks with their wings and twittering their heartfelt thanks.

"What should I do now?" thought Sylfia. "This is the worst situation that I have ever been in. If I go back I might get lost on the way and even if I get back to a part of the forest that I recognise what can I tell them? Pim has been captured and carried off in a scary metal wagon, certainly, but where has he been taken? I don't know. I'll have to follow them. I may not be able to rescue him but I might see where he is being taken."

She flew off down the path in pursuit of the gnomes. It was now very dark in the wood and at first she could not see the vehicle ahead. She could hear the voices, though, as they were raised in argument. In this way she followed them for what seemed like a very long time. Then she noticed that the trees were beginning to thin out and what daylight remained could now penetrate the foliage. It showed her the wagon up ahead and she could see it rumbling out of the wood where it emerged from the trees into a type of countryside that she had never seen before. There were copses of trees dotted about but the terrain was composed mainly of grassland rolling up and down as far as the eye could see. On her left the sun was beginning to set over the distant hills and the sky was streaked with red, pink and purple.

Looking straight ahead, in the direction of the wagon, she could see that it would gain the top of a rise and then dip down out of sight into the next hollow, only to reappear as the rats pulled it up to the top of the next slope.

Sylfia followed at a safe distance with the sun sinking even further behind the distant hills making it even more difficult to keep the gloomy vehicle in view. She was forced to fly closer so that she would not lose the sound as well as the sight of it.

She began to wonder if there would be enough moonlight to help her to track the wagon after the sun had completely disappeared over the horizon.

Then she became aware of shapes emerging from the scattered clumps of trees that dotted the landscape. Dark bodies were flying all around her on silent wings, swooping and swirling this way and that, and only dimly visible in the eerie bluish twilight.

To her horror one of those ghostly creatures flew straight at her and she screamed as she found herself enveloped in a leathery cloak, staring up at a flat, furry face. In the face were two beady black eyes, two large flaring nostrils and an open mouth that displayed two rows of very sharp teeth. Sylfia found that she was being gripped, not by hands, but by firm bony hooks that projected from the edges of the cloak.

The hooks pulled her nearer and nearer to the gaping mouth. Her tiny frame trembled with fear but she managed to squeak in a very small highly pitched voice.

"Please don't eat me. I'm nobody's prey!"

The creature, surprised by her ability to speak, let his mouth hang open for a long moment and then closed it abruptly.

He dilated his nostrils, sniffed her all over and then emitted a series of bleeps and clicks to alert his hunting companions to the fact that he had caught an unusual flying object. As some of you may have guessed, he was a bat.

His fellow bats interpreted the code as, "Blimey, this isn't a moth. It's a blooming fairy!"

The leathery cape formed by his enfolding wings opened and Sylfia was set free. Paralysed by fear she was unable to react quickly enough to release her crumpled wings. She plummeted downwards at high speed and disappeared into a thicket of thorns where she lay, unable to move, stunned, bruised, cold, frightened and very, very lost.

Chapter 4

The iron truck rattled on making its way up and down over hillocks of velvety grass as it gradually crossed the luscious, undulating meadows.

As the sun was setting, Festergum got down from the wagon and took out a basket from under the seat. He used it to gather up glow worms and fireflies. These he transferred to glass jars with perforated lids and hung them from the front of the wagon to light the way.

Inside the wagon, Pim slept on in a deep, drug-induced coma.

Eventually, the travellers began to descend into the valley of the Rumbling River. Green meadows gave way to a reedy marsh which in turn became a watery swamp. Great care had to be taken not to stray from the road.

This highway had been constructed centuries before by ancient builders. They had sunk huge boulders into the soggy ground then smaller rocks had been piled on top in such a large number that the final layer protruded several feet above the surface. On either side of the road, all the way down to the river, there was a fen of water, mud and quicksand but the wagon moved along on a tightly impacted layer of pebbles which made a fairly smooth surface for feet or wheels to travel over.

The night was black and cold but the gnomes did not stop to light a fire, or to sleep, or to eat. They were aware of watery life all around them and the life forms were very much awake. A great deal of this life sounded unattractive and threatening as the creatures in the swamp sent up many unearthly groans, a great number of eerie cries and altogether too many blood-curdling screams as the travellers passed by. Stopping was out of the question.

When they reached the Rumbling River the sound of fresh running water came as a great comfort. The road turned west and followed the river upstream. Behind them, dawn was beginning to streak the sky with pink and orange and, when they rounded a bend in the river, they had their first glimpse of a huge waterfall that cascaded into the river upstream.

The waterfall surged over a cliff that was about one hundred meters high then plunged down into the lower river bed with a deafening roar. Spray and spume were thrown high up into the air and, on a sunny day, a magnificent rainbow would arch across the river at this point.

The highway beside the river became slippery underfoot and the rats slowed their pace to avoid sliding off it and into the river. At one point the road divided so that the traveller could choose to fork left onto a path that followed the river upstream on drier ground. The gnomes, however, kept their wagon on the slippery path which ran close to the river and right up to the waterfall.

The road seemed to come to a dead end at the rock face on the left hand side of the falling water but Festergum did not hesitate. He drove his team into the cascading torrent.

Scabbage put up a very large umbrella just in time as the rats plunged through the watery curtain. When they emerged again they were still on the road but they were now on the other side of the river. This was possible because the road had taken them behind the waterfall where a rocky ledge allowed travellers to pass behind the falling water. The ledge was just wide enough to accommodate the wheels of the wagon so they had driven through with the cascade of falling water on their right hand and a wall of green, slimy rock on their left.

Now they followed the road underneath an overhanging cliff until it turned into a path that snaked up to the top of the northern bank.

The bank on the north side of the river was much higher and drier than the south bank and it was quite a climb to get to the top. The gnomes were ready for a generous helping of fried breakfast and the rats were dropping with exhaustion when they finally reached level ground again. They headed for their usual resting place, in a sheltered spot away from the road, and there they made camp.

Before you could say Jack Spratt, they had a fire going and bacon, sausage and black pudding was sizzling and spitting in a frying pan.

Festergum and Scabbage had just settled down to munch their way through this greasy mess of food when there was a clattering sound and another black wagon, similar to their own, came rattling down the hill, following the road back to the river bank and the waterfall crossing.

It was pulled by a similar team of black rats and it was driven by our old acquaintance, Pustular. He smelled the cooking and immediately pulled his vehicle off the road. The rig juddered to a halt a little further up the hill from the campfire and Pustular jumped down from his driving seat to amble over.

"Morning, scumbags. Have ya got a good haul today?"

He helped himself to a metal plate and grabbed some large portions of the dripping food.

"It ain't none o' yer business, ya old cesspit, but if ya really wanner know we've got a fine catch," replied Festergum.

The sharing of food among these three was a common occurrence and aroused no comment from the two who had lit the fire and cooked it. They ate in silence for some time until Scabbage, always eager to get "one-up-gnome-ship", could no longer contain himself and blurted out, "We've got ourselves a fairy prince."

Festergum kicked his shin.

"Ya WOT!" exclaimed Pustular, dropping a sausage

which had been halfway to his mouth.

"Yev been meddlin' with the fairy folk?" Pustular exploded. "Ya must be round the bend and on the way to loony land! That type of foolery will come back to bite yer bum as fast as ya can say Jack Robinson!"

"Well 'e was that annoying!" Scabbage protested.

"'E was such a stuck up son of a battery hen!" Festergum complained.

"Tried to tell us our business," Scabbage moaned.

"Couldn't 'ave 'im bossin' us about, could we?" Festergum whined.

"BUFFOONS!" Pustular yelled as he stamped back to his wagon, taking the rest of his breakfast with him. He gobbled it down, wiped his hands on his breeches, tossed the plate back to them and hauled himself back up into the driver's seat. He just stayed long enough to light his foul pipe.

"I just hope them up there under the mountain will see it as a joke," he added as he whipped his team of rats into motion, "I doubt it!"

"Mark my words, nuthin' good'll come of it!" This was his parting shot as he rumbled off down the hill.

"Miserable old geezer's always jealous of us," Scabbage muttered.

"'E's bound to be put out 'cos he ain't caught one himself," Festergum snivelled.

They finished breakfast in glum silence and as soon as the rats had cleaned up by eating the scraps, the pair of gnomes continued their journey uphill, taking it in turns to drive for a few hours and then sleep for a few hours on a plank under the seat.

They crossed the Windy Heath blown along by a fair breeze, traversed the Moaning Moor by teatime, with heavy duty earplugs rammed in their ears so that the depressing ululations would not drive them completely insane and by midnight they found themselves perched on Cut Throat Crag. They gained admittance to the mountain using their password which was 'Festeranscab'. They were very proud of having invented this password by putting parts of their names together. Such intellectual feats are rare in the life of a gnome.

Hornbeam had not slept all night. When Tansy, Flum and Hootsmon had left him he climbed the spiral staircase to stretch out on a couch in his observatory and stare at the night sky. He pondered the concerns that had been brought to him at teatime and he tried to work out who could be behind a dastardly plan to rob Nature of such essential creatures.

When morning broke it was mild and fine and he was to be found sitting on his doorstep weaving willow wands to finish a large basket that he had been making. He expected Tansy and Flum to return at any moment and from time to time he glanced behind him at a sleeping form snuggled under a blanket in his biggest armchair. He persuaded a woodpecker to hammer on a tree that was further away so that the noise would not wake his slumbering guest.

It was not long before Tansy and Flum skipped into the clearing in front of his door. Tansy had been up since dawn, looking for clues and questioning other butterfly and moth fairies. Flum had just consumed a hearty breakfast and felt ready for anything. They were chattering to each other and calling out 'Good morning' to every creature that they met.

"Sssh!" whispered Hornbeam. "You'll wake my visitor and she needs her rest. She had a very unfortunate adventure in the night."

"What visitor?" Tansy whispered. "When did she arrive? She wasn't here at teatime, was she?"

"No, Hootsmon brought her in at about 3 o'clock in the morning," Hornbeam told her. "He found her when he was out on night patrol on the north side of the wood. He was lucky to spot her lying in the long grass in the Rolling Meadows because her fairy luminescence was down to a very feeble glow. She was in deep shock, bruised, dazed and very scared. Hootsmon grabbed a passing flittermouse, and got him to help lift her onto his back. That's how he carried her back here."

(Flittermouse is a fairy word for bat. You can imagine what a dog's breakfast Flum might make of it).

Hornbeam scratched his head and looked a bit puzzled.

"She was very nervous of the bat, for some reason, we can't work out why. Anyway she managed to cling onto Hootsmon so that he could bring her here. When she'd warmed up a bit and had drunk some camomile tea she told us a garbled story about black rats, nasty gnomes and a fairy caught in a net. It was difficult to understand her so we decided to let her sleep."

"Can we see her?" Tansy asked.

"Yes, take a look. You may know who she is."

Tansy tiptoed into the parlour and peeped over the back of the old armchair to examine the sleeping face. She beckoned to Flum and when he looked over the chair back he silently mouthed "Humming bleck, it's Sylfia."

Turning around to tiptoe back out of the room he caught the tip of his toe in a rug and tripped. He catapulted towards the door and collided with a milk churn, making a sound like dustbin lids clashing together. He continued his flight out of the door and bowled head first into Hornbeam's basket. A flock of chaffinches, three wood pigeons, two magpies and one jay all flew down to add to the commotion by tittering loudly at his misfortune.

"Thank goodness the milk hasn't been delivered yet," Hornbeam observed, dryly.

Sylfia opened her eyes, sat up and flung her arms out of the blanket to give Tansy a hug.

"Oh, how glad I am to see you," she said. "Such a terrible thing has happened."

"So sorry!" Flum exclaimed as he extricated himself

from the basket and looked around for his glasses which had also gone flying. He put them back on his nose and checked to see if they needed another straightening spell. They were fine. He shooed the birds away, picked up the milk churn, straightened the rug and turned to Hornbeam who was waiting with an expectant look on his face.

Flum explained that they had met Sylfia in the company of Plimlimmon and that she had a wonderful singing voice and that last night she should have been at Mulberry Wood Fairy Choir Practice, not getting lost in the Rolling Meadows.

"I think it's time to listen to her story again," Hornbeam said. "This time we'll listen more carefully, especially to the part where a fairy gets caught in a net."

All four of them gathered in the parlour and drank mint tea while Sylfia, slowly and carefully, recounted the events of the previous evening. She started with how Pim had wanted to show her a shortcut and she finished with how she had encountered the flittermouse.

When her story was done everyone sat for a while with their own thoughts and feelings, wondering if the characters in Sylfia's story could be connected with the problems discussed yesterday.

Their new friend sat wide eyed and trembling to think how close she had been to capture and she quaked to imagine where Pim might be at this moment and what sort of trouble he might be in.

Tansy felt sorry for Sylfia because it was not an ordeal

that she would have cared to face on her own. She was also worried about Pim because it did not matter to her that he was a snobbish fool. No-one deserved to be taken away in captivity.

Flum simply felt extremely guilty because of all the unpleasant things he had said about Pim. He still thought of him as an annoying bully, a supercilious know-all, but now he felt guilty for saying that stuff about how Pim should go away and never come back.

They were interrupted in their thoughts by a humming in the doorway where a large bumble bee was waiting on the threshold.

Hornbeam went over to the door and ushered her in.

"Mrs Bumblehum! I'm so glad that you managed to escape the other day. Come in please. Come this way."

Her humming intensified when she caught sight of Flum because she recognised him as the fairy who had collided with her and Hornbeam had to reassure her that he was a very good chap, just a bit clumsy, that's all.

Flum caught a look from Tansy which meant, "Don't you dare get her name wrong!"

He just smiled and nodded his apologies, keeping his mouth tightly closed.

Hornbeam explained that he had invited Mrs Bumblehum to the house for a very special purpose and now Sylfia would also be able to help him in the same way.

"I would like you all to follow me to my library upstairs," he said.

The company, puzzled and intrigued, did as he requested.

When they were assembled in the library Hornbeam climbed on a step ladder and selected two large volumes from a high shelf. He passed these down one at a time and Tansy and Flum put them on the round polished oak table in the centre of the room.

Each tome was bound with black leather.

On the front of one the title slowly appeared in glittering green letters. The letters began to flash on and off. A faraway bell tinkled and a mellifluous voice murmured the title.

Rogues, Villains, Thieves and Undesirables
Report any Sightings to the Court of
Magical Management

On the front of the other the title appeared very suddenly. It was displayed in red letters which glowed all the time and made a buzzing noise. There was another secretive voice to tell the title but this one sounded impatient and more than a little cross.

More Rogues, Villains, Thieves and Undesirables
I Can't Believe There Are So Many
It's an Absolute Disgrace

In each book the names were arranged alphabetically. Hornbeam invited Mrs Bumblehum and Sylfia to make themselves comfortable on cushioned stools at the table. He explained that they were going to look at the illustrations in the books to see if they recognised any of the creatures there.

There was one character to each page and, as well as a moving picture of their face, there was a brief description.

Here is one example of the type of information given.

BLUNDERBUG ~ IMP ~ formerly known as Bloomsbury when she was a fairy. Wanted in connection with several robberies, especially the theft of the second best silver ball-gown belonging to Her Royal Highness Princess Celestia and the Very Best Gold Wand belonging to the Royal Chamberlain His Hugely Honourable Hugonopolis. She has not been seen since the theft.

Hornbeam helped Mrs Bumblehum to turn the pages while Tansy and Flum looked on with fascinated horror to see images of miscreants making faces at them from the pages.

It was not long before Sylfia gave a little shriek and stopped at a page in the "F" section.

"That looks like one of them," she cried.

Beneath the image the entry read as follows:

FESTERGUM ~ GNOME ~ forger, gambler, swindler, charlatan, con-gnome, cheat. Wanted for obtaining money and valuables using a false idetity. Works with an accomplice. Served six years for circulating forged bank notes. Escaped. Has a scar down his face. Lost his false teeth. Dribbles.

'Well done, Sylfia,' said Hornbeam and he marked the place with a piece of paper so that she could continue to the end of the book.

He went back to helping Mrs Bumblehum until both she and Sylphia had looked at every page in their respective books. Then a swap was made.

This time it wasn't long before a terrifically loud buzzing from the bee indicated that she had found a face that she recognised. She had stopped under the letter "P".

PUSTULAR ~ GNOME ~ bandit, smuggler, embezzler, looter, blackguard, scoundrel. Wanted in connection with The Great Drain Robbery when priceless works of art were smuggled out in barrels through the sewers underneath the National Elf Gallery. Usually works alone, smokes a disgusting pipe and, what's more, doesn't smell so good himself.

"Thank you, Mrs Bumblehum. That's marvellous," said Hornbeam. No sooner had he congratulated the bee when Sylfia cried out again. "I'm sure that's the other one."

This was under "S" for Scabbage, as you might have guessed. The image was amazingly life-like and everyone shrank back a little from the page thinking that his scrofulous rash might be infectious.

SCABBAGE ~ GNOME ~ burglar, picpocket, pilferer, shoplifter, rapscallion. Jailed for the theft of valuable jewels from the house of the Royal Chancellor. Escaped. Thought to be leading the life of a vagabond. Easily led into trouble by other villains. Wears battered old hat. Poor complexion.

Hornbeam put a marker in each of these other two pages and then waited for the searchers to finish their books.

"Now we know who we're looking for. Thank you Mrs Bumblehum. You've been a great help. We'll try to find your would-be captor as soon as possible. Can I get you anything before you go?"

A low buzz, trailing off to a faint hum indicated that the bee was pleased with her detective work but would like to get back into the open air.

Hornbeam showed her out without any further delay and as she passed Flum he stepped back and touched his forehead in salute.

"Goobye Mrs Humble ......" A sharp kick to his ankle from Tansy made him start again. "Goodbye Mrs Bumblehum."

The bee gave him one sharp 'zzz' as she went by.

"Thank you again, Mrs B. Watch out for gnomes with nets!" Hornbeam called after her.

Back upstairs in the library the fairies were still sitting around the table.

"Now we know the sort of creature that we're after," the elf said as he rejoined them.

"It seems that we need to speak to some pretty nasty gnomes."

"We need a plan," Tansy said, thoughtfully.

"Tell me what to do," Flum cried, enthusiastically.

"I'll help if I can," Sylfia murmured, swallowing hard.

"Thank goodness for all of you," Hornbeam said, giving each a smile of encouragement.

"Now this is what I think we should do ......"

Chapter 5

Festergum and Scabbage had been admitted to the mountain through the first portal to the left. They had told the questioner at the door that they were carrying butterflies and moths. They had not mentioned the fact that a fairy was present among their cargo. Festergum had told Scabbage that such a prize should be kept as a "sur-prize". Scabbage had not got the joke because he could not spell and it was not much of a joke anyway. He just looked puzzled and gave a grunt.

The rock face had opened to reveal a tunnel going down into the heart of the mountain. It was lit by beeswax candles held in sconces at regular intervals along the walls. The pleasant smell of beeswax was unfortunately masked by the more unpleasant odours that drifted up from the labyrinthine depths.

The stench of rat droppings and sewage was mixed with the rancid smell of stale cooking. Less easily identifiable odours also contributed to the fetid atmosphere and it got worse as the tunnel went deeper into the mountain.

At last the tunnel ended in an open space which resembled a courtyard in a medieval castle except that it was not open to the sky. It was deep inside the mountain and so its high roof was made of rock. As in the corridor, beeswax candles provided the light.

The gnomes drove in under an archway while other arches around the roughly rectangular area framed thick wooden doors. Each of the doors was firmly locked. The floor was made of crazy paving in red, grey, pink and brown slabs and it was more or less even and fairly smooth.

The two gnomes waited. They knew it would not be long before keys would be turned in the locks and the scraping of wooden doors would be heard on the paved floor. Sure enough, within a couple of minutes two doors opposite the entrance arch creaked open just a fraction.

The creatures behind the doors revealed themselves slowly. First, each stuck out a head and studied the newcomers with pallid watery eyes. Arms and shoulders followed, then a waist with a pair of limpid wings attached. Finally, pairs of spindly legs emerged. The complete body of each creature seemed at first to be that of an undernourished fairy. The illusion was short lived. An observer would not lose time in noticing that these beings were completely without colour or fairy glow. They resembled the shadows of fairies. They were dressed in black, dirty white and dusty grey and their wings resembled cob webs. Their colourless eyes were dull and their facial expressions ranged from vacant to mean and from mischievous to downright nasty.

On further acquaintance you would learn that they do not laugh with merriment, only with sarcasm or scorn. They never smile with kindness, only with self-satisfaction or greed and they do not sing beautiful, well modulated songs about love, eternity and longing. They only titter and giggle and sing rude rhymes or hurtful ditties.

They had all been fairies once upon a time, it is true, but their love of mischief and their sense of self-importance got out of control. They hurt and destroyed too much of the good in their lives and they valued the bad things too highly. They turned into imps.

During this process they destroyed much of themselves, so much so that, as well as their bodies becoming shadowy, their thought processes became limited. Finally they lost their ability to think for themselves and with that went their self respect. They became distrustful, jealous, angry and stupid. Many of them can no longer talk sense, spell easy words, solve simple puzzles or even remember their own names.

Now, you might say 'I'm not very good at spelling. Am I turning into an imp?' and the answer is 'No!' Lots of people have trouble with spelling. It is a very common difficulty. The point is that imps used to be able to do everything very well but they lost their capabilities and it was nobody's fault but their own. They chose to follow the wrong path and that is a completely different state of affairs.

They once had beautiful fairy names like Zanethli, Effemera or Sophronia, but those names have been forgotten. Now they form gangs of three, four or five and call themselves silly names like Giggle, Niggle, Wiggle and Riggle or Tangle, Spangle, Jangle and Mangle.

When about twenty of them had slunk into the hall they surrounded Festergum and Scabbage and started to fly around the wagon laughing, pointing their long pale fingers and chanting their silly songs. Two of the chants sounded something like this.

"Festergum, Festergum
He's the one who smells like dung
Sits all day on his bum
If a bee comes he'll get stung"

"Scabbage is a gnome
With very little brain
Pack him up in rat pooh
And put him down the drain
Flush him
Crush him
Slush him
So he can't crawl up again"

The imps believed that their songs were uproariously funny and when they had finished singing they rolled on the floor, giggling hysterically, holding their sides and waving their legs in the air.

Festergum and Scabbage had heard it all before and took very little notice. Just occasionally one of them would throw a punch at an imp who strayed too close but this just made the tormentors laugh even more.

The two gnomes kept themselves busy unlocking the doors along the sides of the wagon and taking out each metal cage which contained a live moth or butterfly.

The captive insects fluttered in desperation bruising their wings on the sides of their cages. They were terrified by the noise and confused by the sudden change from pitch black darkness inside the wagon to the dim light in the hall.

Only one door was kept locked and the gnomes stationed themselves in front of it with Festergum holding the key.

When the imps had laughed their fill and were reduced to smirks and occasional giggles they began to fetch hand carts. These were stored along the walls on either side of the entrance to the tunnel. They loaded the cages onto the carts and when they were full they lined them up on the opposite side of the hall.

The rats were unhitched and led away through a door labelled "Rat Runs" while the two stag beetles were untied and taken away through another door labelled "Pets' Corner". When all this had been completed the imps gathered around the gnomes and waited for the last door on the wagon to be opened.

"This one's special. We'll be taking it ourselves to

Their Majesties. Just lend us a cart will ya?" growled Festergum.

Pim was lying in his metal cage inside the wagon and through open doors in the sides of the wagon he made out the faces of imps in the dim light. He would have called out in furious indignation but something told him that his usual reactions to situations were not going to help him anymore.

During the journey he had drifted in and out of consciousness stirring when there was a commotion or when the wagon bumped over rough ground. The chemicals in the spray had made his head ache horribly.

He had heard the roar of the waterfall, the raised voices of the gnomes at breakfast, the wind blowing on the heath and the gale howling on the moor. He had heard the gnomes demanding to be admitted to the mountain and he had heard the rumbling and banging as the side of the mountain opened and closed.

He had decided early on not to call out in case he was given another dose of anaesthetic and he was trying desperately to remain calm and dignified but it was becoming increasingly difficult. It was especially difficult to maintain his composure now that he seemed to be inside a mountain.

There was a tight knot of panic in his chest and a painful stab of fear in his stomach.

"We take the goods in. You collectors eat, get paid and then leave," an imp sneered as he brought his emaciated face close up to Festergum's. He drew a little dagger that was as sharp as a razor and the rest of the impish company followed suit stabbing at the gnomes, playfully at first, but with increasing menace. It became very uncomfortable and Festergum was glad that he was wearing his tough goatskin waistcoat and Scabbage congratulated himself for deciding not to cast off his thickest underwear, despite the warm sunshine that morning.

Suddenly, with great speed and accuracy, Festergum rammed the key into Scabbage's open mouth and, using both of his hands, clamped his companion's jaws tight shut around it.

"Take us to your leaders, or he swallows the key," he hissed.

This stand-off lasted for only a few seconds. A door banged open at one end of the hall and a chilly wind blew in. There was a loud clang as a heavy staff struck the stone floor three times. It made a tremendous ringing sound which induced the imps to drop their daggers and cover their ears. Some imps moaned, dropped to their knees and crawled under the wagon.

Twenty armed guards marched into the hall. They were clad from head to foot in shimmering armour made out of silvery-blue iridium steel. Their faces were obscured by helmets but, even in candlelight, the glint of their mischievous eyes could be seen through the slits in their visors. Each had a short sword hanging in a scabbard from a belt at his waist and each carried a long spear.

Only the strongest, tallest and most malicious imps were considered for this Imperial Guard.

They marched into the hall in two columns which divided so that when they came to a halt there were ten guards standing to attention on each side of the room.

They were accompanied by a very unusual personage, for one who lived under a mountain. In this rocky domain you might expect to meet a dwarf who would be broad with thick muscular arms and legs. He or she would have strong work- hardened hands and long grizzly hair sticking out in wild disarray. If he was a male dwarf his beard would be thick and matted or, if combed, it would be braided and tied with ribbons to keep it in order.

This creature however was not broad or thickset and, although his hair was long, it was straight, jet black, well oiled and parted very neatly down the middle. Curls lay flat against his skin all along his forehead but they were not natural. They had been plastered with oil and shaped by hand. His moustache and beard, also well oiled, were long and drooping and had been twirled at the ends to make them pointy.

His skin was alabaster white and his glittering black eyes looked out from under heavy hooded lids. This gave him a look that was both ghostly and menacing. He had used kohl, like an ancient Egyptian, to draw black lines under his eyes and along his eyelids. Any living creature who tried to return his stare would soon look away, shuddering, because his eyes glittered with icy malevolence. They were the eyes of a viciously cruel wizard.

His thin lips were painted red and curled into a very slight smile. It was a cruel smile that could, in a flash, turn into a sneer.

His teeth were pearly white and very even, like tiny piano keys. He had extraordinarily long fingers which ended in disturbingly sharp nails, more like talons.

He wore a pair of tailored grey pinstripe trousers and a black velvet jacket with a crimson carnation in the button hole. Over this he wore a long black cape that had a red silk lining. His shirt was made of finest linen and was snow white with a stiffly starched collar and immaculate cuffs. His waistcoat was made of purple satin and on his feet he had glossy black shoes with pointed toes.

In one of his long thin hands he carried a rod of ebony which had a silver crown on the top and in his other hand he carried a top hat that was large enough to accommodate a whole family of magician's rabbits.

The sight of this character was unexpected and arresting but nothing prepared the gnomes for the sound of his voice. It was captivating. Their jaws dropped open and the key fell from Scabbage's mouth into Festergum's outstretched hand. For once in their lives they felt that they did not want to speak. They actually wanted to listen. The voice was low, silky smooth and entirely persuasive.

"Good evening. I wonder if I can be of any assistance. My boys and I were just strolling by and we couldn't help sensing a modicum of tension, or I might even say a degree of conflict, in this hall."

The imps remained motionless and some still covered their ears. The gnomes simply gazed at the newcomer, entranced. He spoke again.

"Oh, forgive me. How rude. I have not introduced myself. I am Macciovolio Malovericci, Chamberlain to Their Majesties The Imperor and The Impress. If you would like to meet them, please follow me."

He turned to go and the gnomes started as if they had just woken from sleep. Hastily, Festergum used the key to open the last door and pulled out the cage containing Pim. He hurried towards the chamberlain with the front end of the cage balanced on his right shoulder. Scabbage caught hold of the other end of the cage, hoisted it onto his left shoulder and stumbled after his partner.

They left the hall with an escort of six guards on each side of them and the other eight following closely behind.

The door slammed shut and the imps breathed a sigh of relief. Quickly they pushed the wagon into a corner where it would remain until needed again and they took the loaded carts out through the doors by which they had entered. Each was slammed shut and locked from within.

It was late afternoon when Pustular approached Mulberry Wood on his return journey. While he was crossing the Rolling Meadows he caught sight of his destination and knew that it was time to put out his smelly pipe. He stowed it away under the driver's seat. He did not want to alert the wild life to his arrival.

Other eyes had seen him coming though and, as he approached the wood, he became aware of someone singing. It was a beautiful, haunting melody which touched his withered old soul.

The rats, too, had pricked up their ears to listen and they slowed their pace.

"What's the matter with you lot?" said Pustular, speaking very slowly and dreamily. "It's just a soppy song. Get a ......"

He was going to say 'move on' but his voice trailed away as he fell into a trance.

His head lolled and his arms fell useless to his sides. His eyelids felt heavy and his lips parted as he began to smile a vacant smile.

The rats stopped and, lying down in the grass, fell fast asleep.

Pustular felt his wrists being grasped firmly by small hands, but he was powerless to resist and, what is more, he did not want to resist. He knew that he was being lifted from his seat and he waited for his feet to be placed on the ground but to his surprise and delight this did not happen. He wondered for a moment if it could be true and then, yes, he knew that it was. He was flying!

Over the rest of the meadow and into the wood he glided. Through the trees he flew, between oak and ash, holly and chestnut, willow and yew, on and on. Then, quite suddenly, he found himself in a clearing in front of a tree with a door in the trunk and he was being lowered gently to the ground.

The old elf, Hornbeam, came out to meet the three fairies and the gnome. He was dressed in his oldest clothes and he had besmirched his face with dirt and grime.

"Here he is," Tansy gasped. "Sylfia entranced him so deeply with her singing that we found him as light as a feather to carry."

"Well done everyone! Bring him in, will you? Put him in that chair."

Then Hornbeam began his interrogation.

"Who are you?" he asked, raising his voice and speaking rather slowly,

Pustular grinned and appeared to stare into empty space. He answered in a monotone, like a human who has been hypnotised.

"Pustular. Collector, in the service of the mountain folk."

"What do you collect?"

"Bees, or anything to do with butterflies and moths."

"Who are the mountain folk?"

"Imps."

There was a sharp intake of breath from each of the three fairies.

"Which mountain do the imps belong to?"

"Bulzaban. North of here."

"How do you get there?"

Pustular described the journey in a very precise, mechanical way and at the end he drifted off again, into an even deeper sleep than before. Only the arm of the chair prevented him from rolling onto the floor.

Hornbeam called out, "Hootsmon, he's all yours now!" and the owl appeared in the doorway.

"The spell will last for a few more hours," said the elf. "When he comes round set him to work in the wood. Any job you like, the harder the better. He won't get far without transport and if he tries to run away your sharp-eyed birds will soon bring him back. They'll enjoy the fun. He can sleep in the parlour. I've locked all the inside doors so he can't steal anything of value. He can live on acorns and mushrooms although he deserves a far greater punishment than that. We'll be off now, old friend."

"Och aye. Don't you worry. I'll see to everything here. Now, you wee folk take care o' yourselves. Good luck and hurry back."

Chapter 6

Macciovolio and his guards marched very quickly along the tunnel. The two gnomes had to jog to keep up. If they flagged then they would feel the points of spears digging into their shoulder, backs, arms and legs. Each gnome began to regret the decision to bring the fairy to Their Majesties. This was not what they had expected at all and they began to distrust the chamberlain, now that his persuasive voice was silent. They would have dropped their burden and run for it, if it had not been for the spears.

The journey was a long one and as the tunnel took them up through the mountain the gradient was steep. After some time, they started to pass holes in the rock walls where they could feel fresh air blowing in on their faces. The air in the tunnel was becoming much more pleasant, almost fresh, but the march was relentless. The gnomes felt that their legs were turning to jelly and they began to gasp for breath.

Pim, who was having a very uncomfortable ride, shaking to and fro against the bars of his cage, complained constantly in Festergum's ear.

"If ever I get out of this I will see to it that you two are thrown into the deepest, darkest, smelliest dungeon with only gnawing rats and biting insects for company."

"When His Majesty the Fairy King hears about this you two will be locked up in a fortress in the middle of nowhere, forever, and they'll throw the key into a bottomless pit guarded by fire breathing dragons."

"You'll be made to suffer a million times as many tortures as I'm suffering now and they'll never stop. It'll serve you right."

The gnomes did not have any breath to answer him but then, just when they were beginning to feel that being stabbed in the back and run through by spears would be preferable to going on with the pain in their legs and the monotony of Pim's complaining voice in their ears, the procession came to a halt.

They were standing in front of a pair of huge double doors. The doors were decorated with gaudy scenes of imps dressed up for a carnival. The colours were rich and intense; flame red, glittering gold, vivid violet, turquoise blue, gaudy yellow and shimmering green. The handles on the doors were made of gold and fashioned like bees. Near the top of each door there was an emblem in the shape of a crown and these were also made of gold.

Macciovolio banged his staff, the doors swung open and the procession marched into the Imperial

Throne Room. It was an enormous chamber, hexagonal in shape, and it had been made by chiselling away the rock inside the mountain. The walls had been plastered over to make them smooth and then painted with the same vivid colours that had been used on the doors. The insides of the doors were also covered with paintings so that the scenes told a continuous story all around the room. Like the pictures on the outside of the doors they too portrayed imps having a marvellous time; hunting lions and unicorns in a forest, feasting and carousing in a festive hall, performing dare devil feats in a circus ring, fighting a battle to repel invading goblins, sailing the ocean in a storm to bring home heaps of plundered treasure.

In all of the stories told in the pictures there were two main characters with crowns on their heads, one male and one female, and both were painted larger than life.

The two walls which were on the right of the gnomes as they entered, and the two which were on their left, also had double doors in the middle, but the sixth wall, directly opposite to them, had a marble dais in the centre and on the dais were two marble thrones. On each side of the dais there was a large marble fireplace and logs burnt merrily in each grate.

Looking up the gnomes saw that a huge dome of glass formed the roof. Through it the moon and stars were visible in the night sky. Around the walls brackets held flaming torches, the light from which combined with the firelight to illuminate the room.

Looking down the gnomes thought that they were gazing into a perfectly circular pool of black water. Deep in the pool there seemed to be thousands, if not millions, of small creatures moving about. Some of these tiny creatures reflected the light from the torches and that made them appear to be on fire. It was like staring down into a vast, dimly illuminated, cave full of fireflies. To their amazement Macciovolio walked straight over the pool towards the opposite side of the room. Gingerly the gnomes followed him and found that they were not walking on water but on glass!

The thrones were empty because the Impress was seated in front of the fire on the right and the Imperor was standing by a table in front of the fire on the left.

The thrones were upholstered in red velvet and the cushions were embroidered with gold thread. On the back of one throne the embroidery spelt out HIS and on the other it said HERS.

HIS was short for His Imperial Supremacy and HERS stood for Her Excellent Regal Self.

The Imperor was playing with his toy soldiers and the Impress was painting by numbers. The scene on her canvas was "Storm over the Mountains" and only required four paints which were black, blue, purple and white. You could tell that the Impress had to concentrate hard because her tongue was sticking out of the corner of her mouth.

Their costumes were brightly coloured garments, like those shown in the wall and door paintings. They both wore thick make-up to cover their pale faces and on their heads they wore large frizzy wigs. A bright blue powdered wig balanced on the Imperor's head and a luminous pink coiffure adorned the Impress. Golden crowns were balanced precariously on top of their wigs and various other items of jewellery hung about their persons so that they glittered and jangled as they moved.

"Hi there, Mac!" the Imperor called. "What you got there, mate?"

"Your majesty, these two gnomes are usually employed as collectors but today they have taken it upon themselves to bring into the mountain a personal gift for you and the Impress."

Macciovolio smiled a mischievous smile.

The Imperor stepped up to the cage to take a look and immediately backed away in fear.

"Oi, Doris. Come and have a look at this!"

"Yeah, coming! Oh, damn. I've done that bit purple and it should've been white."

The Impress flung her paintbrush away, cursing to herself, and flounced over.

"What have you got there then? Oh, my giddy aunt, a fairy in a cage! I've never seen that before."

She stood by her husband and they stared at Pim. Pim stared back at them.

"Are you thinking what I'm thinking, Burt?" she asked. 'He's one of those Purple Peacock pillocks isn't he?"

"Them that had us thrown out of court, ya mean?" her spouse mused, scratching his ear. He bent down to peer more closely and straightened up with the light of recognition dawning in his eyes.

"You're damn right he is! Let's hang that cage outside and let the crows peck him to the bone!"

It was indeed Pim's family that had brought about the downfall of these two regal imps.

They had been engaged in fraudulent activities while in the service of the Fairy King. Until their downfall they had been very important fairies with great power and influence at court and both had been glamorous and influential friends of the King and Queen. Their expulsion from the palace and subsequent disgrace had driven them into hiding in a shadowy underworld where they had lost their beautiful appearances and their fairy glow had faded.

They had lived for some time in a gloomy old cinema, hiding from the authorities and wiling away the time by watching old movies. This is where they had chosen their new names. Doris had taken her name after watching Doris Day in 'Move Over Darling' and Burt had called himself after his hero Burt Lancaster in 'From Here to Eternity'. Then the developers moved in and the old cinema was bulldozed to make way for a supermarket and they had to flee to the mountains.

Their rise to power as rulers of the imps was due to The Sorceress, who we will meet later, and her faithful servant Macciovolio. Burt and Doris were very impressionable and at the same time very, very vain. It was an easy matter for any magician worth his salt to use them as magnets to attract most of the imps of the earth into one place under this mountain.

Macciovolio interrupted their plans in his most persuasive tone.

"May I be so bold as to suggest that there is an alternative punishment, your majesties?"

"What ya thinking, Mac?"

"It seems to me that it would delight and entertain you more if I could turn this proud and aristocratic young fairy into an imp. An imp who could be trained to use his inborn sense of importance to help me – I mean you – to run this business. You would have revenge on his family and a useful prince to do your bidding."

Doris gave the matter some thought while Burt kicked the cage petulantly.

"Ya know, that sounds quite interesting." The Impress said thoughtfully, for her. "What d'you think, Burt?"

"Only if he gives me no lip and I can kick him about if he does."

"I'll set things in motion immediately, your majesties." Macciovolio simpered, bowing low in false respect. Then he remembered the gnomes.

"Have you any instructions concerning the two gift givers, my Imperial Master and Mistress?"

"Hell, yeah! What do they think they're doing, bringing an enemy into our palace?" Burt drawled in his cowboy voice. "They can feed the crows instead, eh Doris?"

His wife was miles away, gazing at Pim and remembering former glories. She gave a little start.

"Just as you like, Burt."

Macciovolio turned away and grimaced.

When Hornbeam and his three fairy friends reached the meadow the wagon was still there and the rats were still sleeping peacefully in the grass. Hornbeam patted them gently and spoke quiet, encouraging words to bring them out of their trance.

They had brought food for the animals as well as provisions for themselves and, while the rats fed on the best meal they had had since being taken into captivity, the fairy folk searched the wagon.

In the storage box at the back they found a net and a spray gun just like those that had been used to trap Pim. They even found Pustular's old pipe under the driver's seat. Tansy wanted to hurl it into the bushes to get rid of the lingering smell but Hornbeam insisted that they keep it.

"I could use it as part of my disguise," he said. It was true that, dressed in his old clothes with dirt on his face and viewed from a distance, he did look remarkably like an old gnome.

Then they loaded their supplies.

"Why do we need bags of brimstone and charcoal, Hornbeam?" Tansy asked.

"It may come in handy," he replied.

"Why do we need a bag of dog biscuits?" Sylfia inquired.

"Oh, you never know," he answered.

"And why do we need a dozen spools of invisible elfish thread?" Tansy wondered.

"It might be useful."

"Why do we need four packets of gubblebum?" Flum asked.

Looking over his shoulder Tansy corrected that to 'bubblegum'.

"Just in case. It has many uses, you know."

Hornbeam's last reply was muffled, coming as it did from deep inside the wagon.

"Why is he loading such a lot of stuff? Apart from the food I can't see why we would need more than half of it," Sylfia said.

"It's a mystery," Tansy replied. "We just have to wait and see. Hornbeam is full of mysteries."

Soon they were on their way. Hornbeam was the driver and the fairies flew along beside the wagon, singing, dancing and playing games. When it grew dark Hornbeam produced an elfish lantern which he hung on the front of the wagon. The fairies had their own luminosity and could fly through the night without any other light but Flum was the only one who was used to doing this for long distances. Tansy and Sylfia found it more pleasant to snuggle up beside Hornbeam on the driver's seat, and doze off as he told them ancient stories of fairy folk and forest lore.

When they reached the other side of the Rolling Meadows they made camp, lit a fire and cooked their supper. The rats thought they were in seventh heaven when they were given yet more food before being allowed to sleep again.

The fairies did not like to be inside the wagon for any length of time. This is because it was made of iron and iron is the most magically inert of all elements. It is the one least susceptible to enchantment and, in fact, it can render a wide range of magical powers completely useless. That is why Pim was so helpless in his iron cage and why, when they stopped for the night, these fairies much preferred to sleep underneath the wagon.

During the blackest hour of the night Tansy stirred in her sleep. She thought that she could hear a roaring sound as if a strong wind was rushing by and when she peeped out from her woolly blanket she thought that she could see a strange red light in the sky. It lasted for only a few moments and then it was gone. The night returned to silent blackness. Shivering, she turned over and went back to sleep.

As soon as it was light enough to see the ancient road across the marsh the party roused themselves and set off, making for the south bank of the Great Rumbling River and the waterfall where they would be able to cross.

Chapter 7

At daybreak Lummock was sitting on the North West side of Bulzaban Mountain. He was dressed from head to foot in his winter clothes. His hat, jacket, trousers and boots were all fashioned from goatskin. The warm breezes of spring may now be blowing softly in the south, through places like Dingle Dell, but up here on the north side of the mountain it was a different story. The chill of winter could still be felt in the wind blowing down from the north and the sun's rays were not strong enough to warm up the rocks until afternoon.

He was chipping flint to make a new axe and he hummed to himself as he worked. When trolls have a party they 'sing' very loudly and clash stones, rocks and heads together to make a babbling riot of noise.

The tune Lummock hummed to himself was not like that. It was more like a proper song. It had no words because he had learnt it from a little bird that had been blown off course the previous autumn. It had lost its way in a storm and, while it waited for a break in the weather, the troll had sheltered it and given it food. It had sung to him and when the time came for it to resume its journey Lummock found that he could remember the melody. It was a simple, repetitive tune but it cheered him up as he worked.

To his annoyance sheets of black crows started to fly up the mountain side and some landed on the ledge that he had chosen to occupy. In a short while there were more than fifty perched around him, above him and below him.

It was clear, however that they had not come to see Lummock. They were avidly watching a grate in the cliff face above his head.

"Go away," he growled. "Lummock's working. He's not got food for nasty crows."

They took no notice and more flew in to join what was already a large flock crowded together on Lummock's ledge and the surrounding rocks. The troll tried to shoo them away but without success. Those nearest to him fluttered away but settled back again almost immediately.

Eventually a grate in the cliff face above his head was pushed open on its hinges and it clanged against the mountain side. A huge mound of scrap food and other rubbish was tossed out and much of it landed on the head of the troll.

"What the ......? Arrrgh! Lummock is getting very cross now," he shouted, waving his arms about to bat the rubbish away.

He had inadvertently chosen to start the day by sitting

on a crows' feeding station.

No sooner had this realisation dawned than more rubbish rained down on him and yet more was to follow. In the last load to be tossed out there were two objects that were much heavier than the rest. They careered out of the hole in the mountain side and landed – thump – thump – on the troll's refuse-decorated head.

"Ow! Lummock's hurting now! Lummock's not just cross. Lummock's crosserest!"

He stood up and shook his fists at the hole in the mountainside. An imp reached out to close the grate and noticed him looking like a mound of goatskin with rotting vegetables attached.

The imp roared with laughter and after he had banged the grate shut other imps took it in turns to peer through the bars and cackle with laughter, each one louder than the one before.

The more Lummock spluttered and raged the more the imps laughed. Eventually they were called back to work deep inside the mountain but their peels of laughter could be heard echoing down the tunnel as they went.

When they had all gone the troll sat down among the feeding crows and proceeded to peel off the stinking debris.

"Lummock hates nasty imps," he muttered to himself. "Lummock hates nasty cackly impy things."

After a time it became apparent that he was not the only one complaining. Two other smaller voices were groaning quietly beneath the detritus. The owner of each voice was gradually regaining consciousness after being knocked out in the fall.

Crows also started to investigate the sources of these small voices. Lummock was a big troll and no crow, whatever his size, would dare to attack him but two smaller creatures that were barely alive beneath the rubbish! That was another matter.

Lummock found the creatures easily enough because crows had started to peck at them and the faint moaning sounds turned into high pitched self-pitying screeches.

The troll quickly tossed the rubbish and crows aside to unearth or, more precisely, unrubbish two gnomes. Each one was bound from head to foot in strong impish rope and they looked like a pair of sausages with faces.

"Little nomies!" cried Lummock. "Lummock's got little nomies! Nice is that. Lovely surprise for old Lummock."

These two gnomes, as you may have guessed were Scabbage and Festergum and they were both in a bad way. They were dizzy from being knocked unconscious in the fall. Every muscle and bone was aching from being trussed up like joints for the oven. They were also scared stiff and the latest fright, worse than the prospect of being pecked to death by crows, was the imminent danger of having their bones crunched by an angry troll.

"P-p-please Mr. Troll, don't eat us," Scabbage begged.

"P-p-please yer honour. B-b-best troll in the whole world, you are," Festergum whined and for once in his life his flattery was without sarcasm.

By this time a great many crows had crowded around

the two tasty morsels. Lummock batted them away and, picking up both gnomes, he tucked one under each arm and jumped down from the ledge. He loped off up the mountain track and onto Rippling Ridge, a rocky path that ran along the top of an undulating ridge and led eventually to the summit of the mountain.

Some of the biggest and fiercest crows pursued him for a while pecking at the pieces of gnome that stuck out from under Lummock's substantial arms. They realised, however, that they would not be able to wrestle the gnomes from his muscular grip and soon they gave up the chase and returned to scavenging on the ledge.

Lummock sat astride Rippling Ridge and set down the two trembling bodies on the ground in front of him.

'Poor nomies. Let Lummock have a look at 'em,' he crooned.

If, instead of crossing the Rumbling River to get to the northern bank, you were to turn right at the stinking Slushy Swamp you could follow this great river eastwards to the sea. As it meets the coast it widens into an estuary and on the banks of this estuary stands the fine old port of Mistanmurk.

Sailing eastward from this port you would cross the Sea of Forgotten Dreams, which is part of the Great

Eastern Ocean, and after three days and three nights, with a fair wind behind you, the enchanted island of Isolagloria should hove into view. On this magnificent island you would find the glorious palace of one of the most powerful magicians that ever lived.

She is an enchantress, a shape-shifter and a witch and she has a number of names but the Fairy Folk simply call her The Sorceress.

They see her in the wind, rain, hail, frost and snow and in the thunder and lightning of a storm. Whenever they feel fear or discomfort they blame it on her irritability and malice.

Over thousands of years she has accumulated a vast amount of wealth and some of this fortune she has acquired by joining in the big business of humans. They know her in the form of a clever business woman in a smart suit and high heels with a briefcase under her arm from which she will withdraw a copy of The Financial Times and burn holes in the share prices with her fierce and penetrating gaze.

In olden days dragons used to guard hidden hoards of treasure. They slept on mounds of gold and silver, never spending any of it, knowing exactly how much should be there and turning into a fierce fighting machine if the least little bit of it should be stolen.

Needless to say, dragons have become redundant in modern times due to the invention of toughened steel safes, combination locks and internet banking.

The Sorceress, however, still takes great pleasure in

turning into a huge red-fire breathing dragon with polished scales as tough as any armoured tank.

She spends Wednesday afternoons in this form inspecting her treasure in the deep vaults beneath her palace on Isolagloria.

On other days of the week she may adopt the dragon form so that she can soar up into the sky and fly off in whichever direction takes her fancy. On these journeys she drops in, unannounced, on her various business concerns around the world.

This dragon is known as Grimlick and The Sorceress finds it is the best form in which to terrorize her workers.

When Lummock was breaking rocks on the northern side of the mountain Macciovolio was standing like a statue on the eastern side, watching the dawn, waiting expectantly. He was confident that Grimlick would fly in towards him from Isolagloria over the Sea of Forgotten Dreams.

He was besotted by his mistress and waited in breathless anticipation. He adored The Sorceress more than anything else in the universe. She was the only thing that he had ever loved. Everything and everyone else he thoroughly despised or simply hated.

His heart raced as he drew his cloak tightly around him against the biting wind.

She was horribly cruel, true, and completely uncompromising, yes, but she was stunningly beautiful, gloriously magical, utterly magnificent in every way and she was coming to see *him*.

She would want to hear his monthly report, give him instructions and perhaps (joy of all joys) seek his advice. He could hardly wait.

Lost in his own thoughts and wicked schemes he did not notice the air behind him warming up and it was not until he heard the rattling of metal scales that he spun around to find himself gazing up into the lustrous bewitching eyes of his beloved mistress.

He fell to his knees.

"Forgive me, My Queen. I expected you to fly in from the east."

The dragon shuddered and the shape of the beast began to change. Her mouth gave one last spurt of flame before belching a cloud of dense black smoke. The scales began to tremble and ripple before finally melting away.

Macciovolio coughed and his eyes watered, but he had seen this before and he found time to dodge behind a rock. There he remained until the transformation was complete.

Shimmering and tinkling, the scales fell away and melted into thin air. Underneath was revealed the body of a beautiful woman.

She wore a figure-hugging gown of golden silk that glistened in the morning light and her hair tumbled in gorgeous dark brown ringlets right down to her waist. Around her head she wore a gold band studded with diamonds that flashed with all the brilliant colours of the rainbow.

"I flew over here during the night," she informed her

grovelling servant. Her voice boomed like a church bell. "I had business with the Wizard of the West. What is your news, Apprentice?"

Macciovolio still hoped that one day she would call him by his proper name.

"All goes well here, Illustrious Majesty. 'Imps and Insects Inc.' is a booming business in Bulbazan Mountain. Twenty shipments have been sent down to the port of Mistanmurk this month. Everything is as normal except ......"

"Except what?" his mistress boomed.

"A fairy prince was brought into the mountain, Your Magnificence."

"Why?" With just this one word she made the ground shudder.

"It was a gift for the Imperor and Impress, Most Powerful One. Two gnomes smuggled him in."

"The Imperor and Impress," she scoffed. "Never mind that pair of fools. What is your course of action?" The ground rose and fell as if a minor earthquake was moving through the mountain.

"I intend to turn him into a prince of imps, My Queen, or, failing that, to exterminate him."

"And the gnomes?"

"Crow food, Your Majesty."

"I hope so. I don't want any runaways, turncoats or informers. See to it!" she boomed and with that the ground trembled as though it was being struck by a hundred sledge hammers.

The Sorceress stretched out her arms and her body metamorphosed back into a gleaming dragon. She swished her tail, unfurled her wings and rose into the sky. For a few seconds she gazed down without pity on the cowering, obsequious wizard that was Macciovolio and then, with one powerful movement of her mighty wings she swept up into the air. She soared up to the highest peak of the mountain, wheeled twice around the summit and finally, with one magnificently deafening roar, flew off over the sea.

Macciovolio gasped while tears of joy and wonder stung his eyes. Slowly he made his way down the mountain track until he reached a concealed entrance beneath an over hanging rock. He struck the rock with his staff and a door appeared. He muttered a magic spell and the door swung open to admit him. He stepped inside, the door closed silently behind him and in the blink of an eye its outline disappeared leaving no trace in the landscape.

Chapter 8

When Hornbeam and the fairies reached the waterfall it was decided that not all of them had to go underneath it. The rats trusted Hornbeam now and it was obvious that he should continue to drive. Flum volunteered to sit beside him and hold up the umbrella that they had found underneath the driver's seat. The other two fairies avoided the risk of a soaking by flying over the river to wait on the opposite side. Tansy and Sylphia sat down at the top of the high bank on the other side of the river and waved their encouragement.

Hornbeam took a deep breath and clicked his tongue to make the rats go forward. After the initial shock, which was a bit like walking under a cold shower with your clothes on, both he and Flum began to enjoy the novelty. It was like being in a weird damp tunnel with its moss covered rock wall on one side and a curtain of water on the other.

The noise of the cascade was deafening and there was

no point in talking but when they looked at each other they could not help laughing out loud. It was amazing, invigorating and exciting.

However, when they emerged on the other side of the river, Hornbeam looked up and the smile immediately left his face. The other two fairies were no longer waiting at the top of the bank and this made him feel very uneasy. Something told him that they should proceed very cautiously and when he said this much to his companion, Flum peered ahead anxiously, hoping that his friends would reappear, but they did not.

The pair got down from the wagon and led the rats up the path, slowly and quietly. Near the top Hornbeam whispered the command for the animals to lie down and, to his relief, they obeyed. It was wonderful to see how these persecuted animals responded to his kind voice and gentle treatment.

He and Flum crept up to the top of the path and looked over. What they saw made them gasp with horror. Tansy and Sylfia were completely surrounded by imps and all of those imps were slowly advancing towards their captives, daggers drawn.

Hornbeam ducked down out of sight again and pulled Flum down beside him. He had to restrain poor Flum by wrapping one of his arms around the fairy's neck and by clamping a hand over his mouth otherwise it was clear that he would have cried out and run to the rescue. Instead of helping his friends he would have been captured or killed himself.

Gradually Hornbeam, let go of Flum and they crouched side by side and out of sight in the grass to one side of the path. Flum was incandescent with rage, his fists and teeth were clenched, but he waited to hear what the old elf wanted him to do.

Hornbeam thought for a few minutes then crept back down to the wagon. He rummaged in the storage box and pulled out the net and spray gun. He gave one corner of the net to Flum.

"Follow me and do as I do," he whispered.

Flum nodded, his eye wide with fear and his heart pounding.

They climbed up to the top of the bank and stood up. Their arms were down by their sides and the net was on the ground between them.

"Stop that threatening behaviour at once," Hornbeam called out in a strong, clear voice.

"Yeah! You custardly cowards!" shouted Flum. "Pack it in!"

The imps turned to stare at them and then, with a howl of indignation, almost the whole pack launched themselves in the direction of Hornbeam and Flum.

Only two imps were left behind and they continued to guard Tansy and Sylfia.

Hornbeam waited until the tip of the dagger of the leading imp was about an arm's length away from his throat and then he shouted, "Up!"

Both he and Flum lifted the net high above their heads. At the same time they moved apart and Flum fluttered up into the air so that he could hold the top of the net on the same level as Hornbeam.

The imps ran as one body into the net wall and quickly became entangled in the mesh.

Hornbeam and Flum ran right around them to meet on the other side and the whole gang was trapped. The chord was pulled tight, turning the net into a bag, and the imps were yanked off their feet and turned into a writhing bundle on the ground.

The captives yelled and kicked and those on the outside of the bundle tried to cut through the net, using their daggers. Those on the inside of the heap also struck out with their weapons but only succeeded in stabbing each other. Some of the howls of indignation turned to screams of pain.

"I think it's time you all calmed down," Hornbeam said as he sprayed them with a mist from the spray gun. The noise gradually abated and the writhing bundle became still. One by one they relaxed, falling down onto the grass or on top of each other, fast asleep.

Hornbeam strode over to the other two imps and looked them up and down.

"Don't you think that it would be extremely silly to continue with this antisocial behaviour?" he said. "Judging by what has happened to your partners in crime, you can see that we're not prepared to put up with it."

One of the imps stared back insolently.

"We're imps. This is how we're supposed to behave," she said. "What are you? An old gnome? We're supposed to give *you* the orders, not the other way round. You're just a slave."

"I may be old," Hornbeam snorted, "but I'm not a gnome and I have never in my long life been anyone's slave."

"You look like a gnome," she replied, sulkily.

Hornbeam ignored this and turned to the other imp, studying him thoughtfully.

"I think I recognise you from when you were a young fairy. Isn't your name Pimpernel? And, if I'm not mistaken, you and Tansy have the same great-grandfather. What do you think you are doing with your dagger pointed at your second cousin's throat? You should be very, very ashamed?"

To everyone's astonishment, the imp, who indeed used to be a young fairy called Pimpernel, dropped his dagger and burst into tears.

"Pickle," he wailed. "That's my name now, Pickle. I hate it," he sniffed.

He turned up his tear-stained face and stared back at Hornbeam.

"I remember you now. You're the elf they call Hornbeam, you live in Mulberry Wood and every fairy knows who you are. Yes, I am ashamed but when I got into bad trouble I didn't know how to put it right and I couldn't see how to go back."

He put his face in his hands and sobbed again.

Tansy stopped being afraid and patted his shoulder. Sylfia started fumbling in her pocket, looking for a clean handkerchief.

"And you," Hornbeam said, turning to the more belligerent imp. "Should we know you?"

"Doubt it." She was as sullen as ever and still pointed her dagger at Sylfia's throat. She looked with disdain at the other imp who continued to snivel.

"When I was a fairy I was lady-in-waiting to Her Royal Highness the Princess Celestia. Didn't fit in, really. They called me Bloomsbury then. Now I'm known as Blunderbug. Quite a come down, eh? I got bored, you see. Wanted adventure and freedom but didn't go about it the right way. Got branded as a thief, and so I was. The Sorceress picked me up and here I am. There's not much you can do about it now."

"Put down that knife and we'll talk about it," Hornbeam ordered. They gazed at each other for a few moments then, silently shrugging her shoulders, Blunderbug handed him her dagger. Hornbeam put a hand on her shoulder and took the other snivelling imp by the elbow. He steered them both away to sit with them under a tree further up the road.

As soon as they had gone Tansy, Sylfia and Flum started hugging each other, laughing and crying with relief.

Flum scrambled back down the bank and brought up the rats and the wagon onto level ground. They made camp in about the same spot as Festergum and Scabbage had done.

The sleeping imps could no longer cause any trouble, so

they tipped the inert bodies out onto the grass and each one curled into a more comfortable position for sleeping. They deprived each one of his or her dagger and they stowed the weapons away with the net and the spray gun in the box at the back of the wagon.

Then it was time to prepare a delicious and well earned brunch.

They looked over to where Hornbeam sat with the imps and watched his stern face as he spoke to them. He was obviously administering very, very serious counselling. Pickle had dried his tears but his head was still bowed and Blunderbug looked straight at Hornbeam but with less arrogance now. Occasionally she would nod and say 'yes' or shake her head and say 'no'.

"I'm glad that I'm not being ticked off by Hornbeam," Flum said. "He's scary enough when he's being nice."

"Nonsense," Tansy told him. "He's always a sweety."

"As far as I'm concerned, you're all wonderful," Sylfia gushed. "If I have to have an adventure then I'm glad it's with the three of you."

Flum blushed with pleasure and grinned from ear to ear. Sylfia smiled back at him and Tansy had to clear her throat and cough to remind them that they were supposed to be helping her to prepare the food.

Hornbeam and the two imps came to join the fairies at the campfire for the meal which should be called breakfast even though the sun was now high in the sky and it was nearly midday. Hornbeam's two interviewees looked brighter, more hopeful, less like imps.

They sounded more intelligent and they had fresh plans.

"We want to become fairies again," Pickle told them. "Hornbeam says it's possible if we work at it but we have to join the Pixies of the Western Mountains and do three months of Outward Bound and three months of Community Service. After that we can go back to our fairy families and try to persuade our communities that we've reformed. Then we'll have to wait while they decide whether we can rejoin them. Hornbeam says that he'll put in a good word for us if we do well in the mountains."

The fairies groaned at this plan and looked at each other knowingly.

"You're marking bad," spluttered Flum.

"He means you're barking mad," said Tansy, "but I don't see that you have many options."

"We haven't," said Blunderbug. "This is the only one there is if we want to return home. It's a chance we have to take."

The fairies nodded sympathetically and said no more on the subject.

Mountain Pixies are notoriously tough and austere. They believe that unremitting hard work and constant exercise are good for the soul. Their diet is plain and simple. Their main food consists of porridge made from dried heather and goats' milk. Their regime includes jumping into icy cold mountain streams at five o' clock in the morning and wrestling each other in the winter snow to see who will have the honour of staying up all night to tend the campfire and guard the goats. They race barefoot through the mountains, up and down the screes that are slowly moving rivers of sharp slate and finish the race by skipping and sliding over slippery boulders that lie at the bottom of deep moss-lined gullies. They make precipitous jumps off cliffs into fast running white water and scramble up ghylls only to dive down again, over waterfalls and into deep dark pools.

They are foolhardy risk-takers who have to be tough, resilient and courageous to survive what they refer to as 'the good life'!

"What about your companions?" Sylfia asked.

"When they wake up we'll tell them what we plan and they can make up their own minds," Blunderbug answered with a shrug.

"They can come with us, or take their chances elsewhere. Some may follow the river down to Mistanmurk and go to sea and others might want to come with us. They'll have to if they want to go home one day. One thing's for sure, they won't want to go back into Bulzaban Mountain. We've failed in our task. We were told to guard the mountain against intruders and we've lost our daggers. There's nothing but severe punishment awaiting us there."

"Now, tell us all you know about what goes on inside that mountain," Hornbeam said. "We know that gnomes have been employed to catch bees and Lepidoptera and they take them there in iron wagons like the one over there. We captured that one in the Rolling Meadows."

"Some gnomes come from a lot further away than that," Blunderbug told them. "They collect from far and wide, in fact any place where pollinating insects are plentiful. We could collect on the heath and on the moor but it's only worthwhile in summer time."

"The wagons are driven down tunnels which go deep inside the mountain," Pickle went on. "Imps meet the gnomes in reception halls and if the cargo is made up of bees it's taken to the middle of the mountain. The bees are put into a huge hive which runs up through the centre of the mountain and they stay there making wax and honey for the rest of their lives. Periodically, the hive is cleared of dead bees and they are taken down a refuse tunnel to be thrown out of the mountain, on the northern side. It's a dangerous task.
I had to do it for a number of weeks when I first arrived. We had to wear protective clothing but, all the same, some imps were stung to death."

He paused, remembering the horror of it. The others waited patiently and Tansy, as a sympathetic relative, patted his shoulder.

"All the way up the hive there are platforms and doors where imps can go in but bees can't get out. Gangs of imps go in to collect wax and honey all day, every day. An imp has to collect a quota of honey or wax before he or she is allowed to stop."

"There's something else to collect," Blunderbug reminded him.

"Yes, royal jelly. It's very valuable and the guards

take that away themselves."

Hornbeam would have liked to hear more about the guards and who they worked for but Tansy asked another type of question.

"But, what do the bees feed on? You say that they are trapped inside the mountain. How can they collect pollen and nectar?"

There was an uncomfortable silence and the imps looked at the ground.

"Speak up you two," Hornbeam said, gruffly. "We might as well know the full horror. Don't stop now."

Blunderbug took a deep breath and went on, speaking rapidly.

"That's where the butterflies and moths come in. They are taken to a factory in another part of the mountain. Pollen is brushed off their bodies and they are squeezed for nectar. This kills them and the pollen and nectar are used for food. Their bodies are also made into cakes of food but first the wings are taken away."

"Why?"

"The scales of the wings are used to make beautiful material for clothing. The fabric is absolutely gorgeous and it is turned into very expensive high fashion clothes."

"What happens to the eggs and caterpillars and pupae?"

"They are looked after until they change into adults. They have no nectar or pollen but their bodies and wings are used in the same way. Nothing is wasted."

"What happens to the wax and honey?" Hornbeam asked.

"The honey is used in making confectionery and medicines and the wax and royal jelly are made into cosmetics and toiletries. Humans love all of those things. Sweets, cosmetics, beautiful clothes are all things that make them happy but nor for long. They soon want more so there is a constant demand," Blunderbug sighed.

"That constant demand means that The Mistress gets richer and richer."

"The Mistress?" asked Hornbeam.

"Just another name for The Sorceress."

"I feel sick," said Tansy. She hung her head and spoke into her arms which were folded across her knees.

Flum left the group and went to sit by himself under a tree. For the first time in his carefree life he looked sullen and genuinely angry.

Sylfia was distraught and crept closer to Hornbeam. The old elf laid a reassuring hand on her shoulder.

"Those poor creatures!" she wailed.

"This is a wicked crime against nature," Hornbeam hissed through clenched teeth. "We must put a stop to it. The earth is in even more danger than I thought."

Whether he was speaking to those around him, or just to himself, or to the whole world it was not clear.

All this time, Pim was suffering the attentions of the persuasive Macciovolio. He had been tipped out of his cage into a cell that had three stone walls and a fourth side composed of iron bars that ran from floor to ceiling.

The cell was at the end of Macciovolio's office where the wizard sat from time to time during the course of the day, at a huge wooden desk that was old and polished with beeswax until it shone like glass. When present in the room he would sometimes shuffle papers or give orders to the captain of the Imperial Guard but most of the time he spoke to Pim about the benefits of entering his service.

Pim did not speak much but lowered his eyes and slowly ate and drank the meagre rations that were passed to him through the bars.

At last, when it was evening, Macciovolio approached Pim's cell. His silky cloak rustled and his black eyes glittered with flinty malevolence.

"After all, my young friend, what choice do you have? You can become my loyal assistant or you can become food for the crows, as Burt and Doris have suggested."

Pim shrugged his shoulders. He knew that he was already losing his fairy powers. His face had become grey and gaunt and his luminescence was fading. His beautiful shimmering purple wings were losing their lustre and he was beginning not to care very much about himself or his fate.

His tormentor gripped the bars of his prison with both of his long elegant hands and his astonishingly sharp nails scraped on the metal. He spoke with mock concern but his lips curled in a sneer.

"You'd better hurry up and decide, young fellow. If I completely lose my patience with you, it will be most unfortunate. I could dream up a far worse fate than being pecked to death by crows, one that would make that sound like a holiday. You have until the morning when I will need your answer at dawn. That's my last word on the subject."

Macciovolio flounced out of the chamber on other unpleasant business.

Pim buried his face in his hands. It was quite clear to him that he should not give in and he must die as a fairy because that would be the noble thing to do. His family would expect it. He could never, ever become an imp.

Chapter 9

Hornbeam and the fairies did not finish their discussions with the imps until late in the afternoon and then they started out for the Howling Heath. As they jolted along the rough grassy track between the purple heather and the yellow broom they spoke little. Each of them was thinking about the dreadful activities going on under the mountain to the North. As they approached the foothills of The Blackscarp Mountains with Bulzaban's gloomy peak in the distance, their nerves jangled and their courage might have failed if each one had been alone.

It was dusk when the track led them up onto the Moaning Moor. The sun had set in a blaze of spectral colours and the sky glowed a deep purple. They felt the darkness beginning to envelop them as if they themselves were hands slipping into black velvet gloves. The horizon disappeared and the way ahead turned black and mysterious.

The wind changed its sound. On the Windy Heath it

had wailed and sighed, roared and growled and worn out the poor travellers with its gusting and buffeting.

Now on the Moaning Moor it came to them as a deep, sonorous, aching groan. It was as if the earth itself was belching up its ghostly dead and the restless spirits were rising up to smother any poor creature that strayed near them. Misery clutched at their hearts and every last speck of joy was wrenched out of their souls. They were gripped by a fearful dread and a strange longing for death. Sylfia sang some soothing songs in faltering tones in an attempt to combat their despair.

At last, when they had almost abandoned all hope of surviving, the wind dropped and they came to the final stage of their journey. If it had been daylight they would have seen a steep rocky road ahead which led up the side of the mountain and out of sight, as it snaked around boulders and through gullies, climbing steadily upwards towards Cut-throat Crag. They could not see this because it was a black night and their way was lit only by Hornbeam's lantern and the fairies' glow. Our travellers could, however, feel the start of their ascent up the mountain side. The vegetation of the moor was left behind and the way was no longer springy with gorse or spongy with moss. The way was hard and littered with stones and rocks.

The rats picked their way gingerly around boulders and the noises made by the wagon changed. As well as the regular clanking and creaking, new sounds were added to the vehicle's orchestra. There were unexpected grinding, scraping and hammering sounds. The wheels would sometimes be jammed by immovable obstacles and when this happened the travellers were jerked and thrown around. All three fairies took to the air but none of them strayed far from the wagon. Sylfia, especially, remained close to Hornbeam, clinging to the corner of the wagon that was nearest to his head.

Tansy stared into the blackness all the time, trying to make out what lay ahead and suddenly she gave a little cry.

"Stop a moment, Hornbeam. I think I saw the flicker of a light. Look up there."

The old elf brought the wagon to a halt and all four of them peered into the blackness ahead.

"I see it. Up on that ridge," he said. "Who or what can it be, I wonder?"

"We can see their light so they may have seen our glow," said Tansy.

"I'll fly ahead and take a look," said Flum.

"Fly low," Hornbeam told him. "Use the rocks for cover and take one of those impish daggers."

"I'll come too," said Tansy.

"You'd better let Flum go alone, Tansy," Hornbeam said. "He's used to flying on his own at night. Remember what happened to Sylfia in the Rolling Meadows?"

This made Sylfia shudder as she recollected that evening.

Tansy saw the sense in this but disappointment showed on her face.

"Don't worry, Tansy," Hornbeam said. "There'll be plenty of other adventures for all of us before this is finished."

The party proceeded more slowly, giving Flum a chance to reconnoitre, but not so slowly that anyone watching would notice a change.

Flum returned in a rush, dodging from rock to rock.

"Two sleepers at a campfire, snoring," he panted "Big enough for notty gromes but too big for easly wimps."

The other three took a second to translate.

"If they are too big for weasly imps and are indeed grotty gnomes shouldn't they have a wagon like this one?" said Tansy.

"If we drive past them they'll wake up," Sylfia pointed out. "Is there another way?"

"Not that I could see," said Flum.

"I think it's our turn to spring an ambush," Hornbeam chuckled.

Scabbage and Festergum had had an exhausting twenty four hours. It had been one gruelling event after another. Imperial Guards had frog marched them through a long steep tunnel right up through the mountain and almost to the top. The Imperor and Impress had not been thrilled with their gift and had been impolite enough to condemn them to a very unpleasant death. After being trussed up and thrown out of the mountain as food for crows they had been extracted from the rubbish by a huge hungry-looking troll.

They had been unceremoniously bundled down the mountainside, each one tucked under an arm of the aforementioned lumbering troll.

He had stowed them away in his hovel all day and they had been frightened out of their wits by his wide grinning mouth with its huge teeth and tendency to drool saliva.

As trolls go he was amazingly kind and gentle, feeding them tit bits of food, and telling them he was their friend. Gradually they recovered enough from their bumps, bruises and stiff limbs to feel a little better but friendship was never going to be on the cards because of the aforementioned mouth and teeth.

It soon became clear to them that this was an extremely lonely troll and, as the day wore on, they also realised that it would be very difficult to escape his company.

He pressed them for stories about themselves, their upbringing, their work, their journeys, why they came to the mountain, what had happened to their wagon, why they had been tied up and thrown out of the mountain.

Trolls have a reputation for eating anything and anyone so the gnomes did not like to refuse his requests.

By the end of the day Lummock had learned all there was to know about Scabbage and Festergum and a lot more about what happened under the mountain.

As he listened to them, hour after hour, his slow brain sifted through the information. He formed the impression that he was right to dislike the nasty mocking imps and that what they were doing under the mountain was actually bad as well as secret.

Eventually the sun went down and Lummock became very sleepy. He had never concentrated so hard in his life and his brain was seriously over-worked. The gnomes began to speak very softly and slowly and, before long, Lummock was stretched out across the doorway snoring like a foghorn. The gnomes took their chance to squeeze past him and slip away. They scrambled off Cut-throat Crag and ran as fast as they could down the rocky road towards The Moaning Moor. When they were satisfied that they were far enough away to be out of the grasp of a troll-sized fist on the end of a troll-sized arm they fell down beside the road, desperate for sleep.

Before leaving the hovel they had each grabbed a long piece of wood from the troll's firewood store. They had set them alight in his fire and used them as torches to light their way down the mountain. When they stopped they propped them up between boulders and found the light comforting as they stretched out on the ground to sleep. It was the glow from these that Tansy had spotted from further down the mountain.

Imagine their feelings when they woke to find that they were captives for the third time in twenty four hours and this time they were neatly enveloped in a net. Struggling to get free made them even more entangled until finally they were unable to move and all they had to fall back on was some choice verbal abuse directed at each other.

"Get yer foot out of me mouth, ya big smelly oaf," Scabbage growled.

"Get ya knee out of me eye, ya fat lardy fool," Festergum snarled.

At last they managed to sit up, tangled together and looking like a strange multi-limbed creature with two heads. When this much had been achieved they could start to direct their abuse at their captors. They began by calling Hornbeam a highwayman, murderer and thief. There was a chorus of indignation from Flum and Tansy but then everyone was silenced by an unexpected command which was delivered in a high and piercing voice.

"Be quiet you villains! How dare you!"

All heads turned to where Sylfia was standing. Her fists were clenched and her voice was icy with rage.

"What have you done with Pim?"

"Oo the 'eck is Pim?" said Festergum.

"The fairy I saw you stealing in Mulberry Wood," Sylfia snapped.

"Oh 'im. We – er – we lost 'im somewhere," Scabbage stammered.

"Come to that," said Festergum, changing the subject, "what 'ave you done with our ole mate Pustular? That's 'is wagon you've got over there. I'd know it anywhere. It's got mucky stains on it from 'is pipe smoke."

"It seems that Pim is not the only thing that you've lost," said Hornbeam, ignoring the question. "What has happened to *your* wagon?"

Scabbage and Festergum could see that they were in a similar sort of fix for the second time in one day but this time it was not a slow-minded troll asking the daft questions. This was a wise old elf with three sparkling young fairy companions and they all seemed to know a lot already. The question was, what lies could the wily gnomes tell to get out of this fix and minimise the punishments that were sure to be coming their way?

Just then the ground began to shake and a thumping noise could be heard further up the mountainside. The vibrations were quite gentle at first but then their amplitude grew bigger and bigger until the ground shook in an alarming fashion. The vibrations signalled the approach of a very large creature running on very large feet with very heavy footsteps.

Scabbage and Festergum looked at each other in a knowing way and whispered "Oh, no, not 'im again!"

The fairies looked at each other and drew together while Flum handed out daggers. They steeled themselves for whoever, or whatever, was approaching.

Before long Lummock the troll rounded a bend in the road, stopped abruptly, caught his breath and looked down on them all with surprise and pleasure.

"Here you are little nomies," he puffed. "Lummock's been looking for you. You in a fix again?" he panted.

Catching sight of Hornbeam his eyebrows went up

in surprise and then he grinned with delight.

"Mr Elf, sir. On Lummock's mountain? What an honour, sir. Can Lummock help you? What have Lummock's nomies been doing?"

"Good evening, Lummock. I'd forgotten that you live here," Hornbeam answered, beaming up at the ragged giant. "We know some of the things that they've been up to. Can you tell us more?"

"Is it you, Mr Hornbeam? What a surprise! Yes, Lummock knows everything about these two nomies!"

Scabbage and Festergum groaned.

The fairies looked at Lummock with interest. They had never been this close to a troll before. They knew that none of them are very brainy but that some of them can be gentle and kind. Too many, however, can be fierce and cruel. They assumed that, because Hornbeam had greeted this one in a friendly manner, he must belong to the first category.

"Just a minute, Lummock," Hornbeam said. "You're giving me a crick in the neck. How about sitting down over here? Make yourself comfortable. Would you like some tea and biscuits?"

"I'll make some rosehip tea, Hornbeam, but I don't think we have any biscuits," Tansy said.

"We have Lummock's favourite biscuits!" Hornbeam smiled. "Don't you remember packing them?"

Tansy looked puzzled but Flum sprang up.

"I'll get them! I know what trolls like best. Bog discuits!"

"I remember now," Tansy exclaimed. "You said they might come in handy!"

The two gnomes had been fooled by the sheer size and muscular strength of the troll. They groaned again when they realised that he was a friend of wise old elves and very partial to tea and dog biscuits.

While the tea was being made Hornbeam introduced his fairy companions and Lummock beamed with admiration and pride. He had never been so close to such magical, shining creatures. For a long time he was unable to speak. He just smiled a loony smile and stared a dreamy stare.

He came back to reality when a pail of tea was placed in one of his huge hands and twenty biscuits were poured into his other. He was told to help himself when he had finished those. He slurped and munched happily for a while until Hornbeam judged that it was time to ask him some simple questions.

"Listen, Lummock, those two villains captured a fairy in Mulberry Wood and they took him away in a wagon like that one over there."

"Ugh! Lummock knows those wagons. Nomies knock on the mountain near Lummock's house and nasty imps let them in."

"Do they?" said the elf. "That's very interesting. If you can tell us more about how they get in, that will be useful. Now then, the gnomes, I mean nomies, say that they lost the fairy. Did they tell you where?"

"Nomies didn't tell Lummock that."

Hornbeam's face fell and it was the turn of the fairies to groan.

The captives in the net smirked and winked at each other.

"But," Lummock went on, his face creased up with concentration, "nomies took a present into the mountain for the nasty imps. Impress and Imperor didn't like it. They hated it. They hated it to bits. They threw the nomies out for crows to eat. Lummock rescued 'em. That's what they told old Lummock."

He looked so proud of this that Flum flew up and patted him on the head and Tansy flew up to give him a kiss on the cheek.

Festergum and Scabbage nudged each other and looked tense again.

"Thank you, Lummock," Hornbeam said. "Eat up, now. Have another cup of tea."

Hornbeam turned his attention to the gnomes in the net and stared at them for a considerable length of time. The gnomes wriggled and shrugged and tried to look nonchalant.

"That must have been very disappointing for you," he said.

"What ya' mean?" Festergum growled.

"You must have thought you had something very precious if you took it to the chief imps."

"Well, ya' win some, ya' lose some," the gnome shrugged.

"How did you gain an audience with their Majesties?"

"We asked and we wuz took up."

"Up where?"

"To the throne room."

"Who took you?"

"Some smarmy geezer. Said 'e was the Lord Chamberlain or summit."

"How did you find him?"

"We didn't. 'E found us. 'E just appeared."

"Did you have to go far?"

"Yeah, blimey, it was miles. Up and up we went through a long tunnel and guards poking us with spears and making us run and carrying that cage as well. It was murder."

"Carrying that what?"

Festergum was silent.

"Would that be a cage from your wagon?"

More silence while Festergum chewed his bottom lip and Scabbage glared at him.

"Was the fairy called Pim in that cage?"

There was still no reply.

"Now here's the deal," Hornbeam said, very solemnly. "I believe that you took Pim to their Majesties, hoping for a reward. You thought they would like to have a valuable fairy prisoner. They did not. We want to know what they did with him.

"If you tell us we will make sure that you have safe conduct back to Mulberry Wood. You will stand trial there for all your crimes against nature but it will be a fair trial. We expect that you will be found guilty and that you could serve a prison sentence. On the other hand, you could earn the chance to reform and be accepted back into honest society. It will mean working hard to make up for the harm that you have done."

The gnomes scowled and made dismissive noises with their tongues and teeth.

"Most importantly as far as you two are concerned," Hornbeam paused here before continuing in a menacing voice, "if you don't tell us what we want to know we'll take you back up the mountain and hand you over to the imps. This time, when they turn you into crow's food, Lummock won't be there to save you."

The gnomes stiffened in horror and made little whimpering noises that turned out to be gnome versions of pleas for mercy. Hornbeam remained silent and stern while the gnomes squirmed,

"Looks like the game's up, Scab. 'E really means it. Can ya see a way out?"

"Nah, ah bloomin' well can't," his partner in crime sniffed. "Ah suppose we'll 'ave to tell 'em what happened. That way we'll stay alive."

"We captured the fairy and took 'im into the mountain. It's true," Festergum began.

"What then?" Hornbeam snapped.

"We told the imps that we wanted to see the Imperor and Impress but, before they could answer, this Chamberlain bloke came in with guards and marched us up to the throne room."

"Who is he?" the elf asked.

"Called himself Mucky Molio or summat."

"Is he in charge?"

"Reckon so. 'E sure 'as powers and all the imps did what 'e sez, no bother. When 'e speaks you 'ave to listen. 'E's spooky. They wuz really scared of 'im."

"What sort of powers?"

"Magical, ah reckon."

"OK, what happened when you got to see their Majesties?"

"They didn't like the present, as we mentioned to the troll before, and we wuz taken away and tied up with the rubbish. Those two are the stupidest rulers you've ever met, no kiddin'. The Chamberlain pretends that they are important but you can tell that he thinks they're brainless."

"Is that so? That's very interesting." Hornbeam mused. "Now, think carefully, before you were taken away, did you hear what they said about Pim, the fairy you had captured?"

"Yeah, we've got memories. We ain't trolls y'know. That fuzzy 'aired pair of painted eejits were scared stiff. They 'ad summat against 'im big time. They said 'e should be turned into crow food an' all."

The fairies, who had been staring at the gnomes with eyes wide and mouths open, now gasped and Sylfia started to cry.

The gnomes stared at her as if they had never heard a noise like that before.

"That bloke, Mucky Molio, said he had a better

idea, though," Festergum continued at last.

Hornbeam and the fairies looked up hopefully.

"Yeah, he said he would take him away and see if he could turn him into an imp instead."

The gnomes thought that this news would cheer up their captors but, to their surprise, the effect was similar to the one created by the prospect of being eaten by crows. They were exceedingly puzzled because at least the fairies' friend would still be alive. They could not comprehend that, for a fairy, the business of turning into an imp was a fate as bad as death.

"We can't say 'nuthin to suit this lot, Scab. I give up. Let's just wait and see wot 'appens next."

Hornbeam turned to the troll and said "Will you help us, Lummock? We want you to tell us where your house is and how to get into the mountain. We also need someone to escort these two prisoners back to Mulberry Wood. Will you take them and turn them over to my friend Hootsmon? He will look after them until we return. The fairy world will be very grateful to you and you will be a great hero to the three you have met here. To bring these villains to justice would be a great act of kindness."

Lummock gazed at Hornbeam and his jaw dropped open in astonishment. Finally he managed to stammer out some jumbled words.

"Lummock – me – on fairy business? No! Too daft is Lummock! Too slow he is! Hornbeam – can't think – me – fairy hero? Magic stuff! Lummock? No!!!"

Sylfia dried her tears and flew back to settle on his shoulder. His eyes widened with wonder as she crept close to his huge head. She looked up at him with tears in her eyes and he gazed back at her, adoringly.

"Please Lummock. You are so strong and kind. We know you can do it. We can't take them with us because we've got to go into the mountain to find Pim. He's our friend, you see, and we must rescue him, if we can. We can't leave those two alone to wriggle free and cause more trouble. They'll say and do anything. Please help us."

Lummock's face creased up in a million wrinkles as his broad face broke into a soppy smile.

"Lummock'll do it, pretty fairy. Yes indeed! Lummock'll do it for his beautiful magical friends. New fairy friends! Much nicer than nomies! Best thing ever for poor old Lummock!"

There were thanks all around accompanied by much hand-slapping and patting of backs.

He embraced all four of his new friends and each had to shout out very loudly to avoid being squeezed to death. One huge hand sent Flum reeling down the mountain path but he managed to roll off the edge and fly up into the air instead of plunging down into a ravine.

Lummock had already slept and eaten so he lost no time in getting ready. He told them how to get to his house and how the gnomes gained entry to the mountain. While doing so he secured each gnome in a single bundle, using ropes instead of the net. He made a pack to carry on his back which contained a flask to collect water from the streams on the way and the rest of the dog biscuits that he liked so much.

What the two gnomes would make of the dog biscuits was not considered but, after all, you will eat almost anything if you are really hungry.

He listened carefully and nodded solemnly as Hornbeam gave him detailed instructions but he was not hopeful that he would remember it all. He knew where to find Mulberry Wood and anyone living there would be able to direct him to the great magical tree.

He knew that when he got to the wood all he had to say was, "Hornbeam sent these. Will you look after them, please?" or something like that.

Very soon, with his new friends calling out their thanks and best wishes, he loped off down the mountainside full of pride and determination.

The party decided that it was a good opportunity to slink under the wagon and grab a few hours rest before daybreak.

It was still a very black night and when the fires were put out the silence was profound but sleep did not come easily to them and when they did doze off they were disturbed by nightmares in which they were pursued along dark tunnels inside the mountain by cruel imps and voracious crows snapping at their heels.

Chapter 10

Inside the mountain Pim was hunched in his cell, dreading the coming of dawn. He had been left alone in the dark and since his fairy glow was almost gone he could make out very little of his surroundings inside or outside the cell. There was a clock on the wall of Macciovolio's office but it was so gloomy that the hands were barely visible. He could, of course, *hear* the time as the clock ticked steadily and the chimes told the hours. To him it was the sound of his young life ebbing away.

Then something made Pim look up. He had sensed a presence in his cell and a shiver ran down his spine.

He stood up and peered into the shadows, looking for a shape and he strained his other senses too, trying to detect the faintest of sounds or the odour of a creature nearby.

At length he sat down on the bench again and leaned his back against the wall.

"It must have been a spider," he said to himself.

Almost immediately his blood ran cold and his heart skipped a beat when a cold, bony hand was placed on his shoulder and a thin rasping voice whispered in his ear.

"Not a spider, my lad."

Pim shot up like a fire cracker and leapt to the other end of his cell.

He shrieked. "Who, or what, in fairydom are you?"

It had been a long scary night and he would have liked to disguise his fear but unfortunately he was coming to the end of his tether. His voice trembled and he had to blink hard to stop tears of desperation from rolling down his cheeks.

"Keep calm, young 'un. I won't harm you. I'm not the enemy. On the other hand, I'm not a friend either, am I? Not yet anyway and maybe not ever but we'll have to see what develops won't we?

"I would very much like to say that I'm your fairy godmother. That would be nice wouldn't it?

"I would be able to wave a wand and grant you three wishes at least one of which would be a way out of this pickle you're in. Unfortunately, I'm not anything to do with fairies. Add to that the fact that I'm not even female and that hope goes straight out of the window."

As Pim stared in the direction of the voice an outline of the newcomer became visible. A lambent glow started to illuminate the figure but it was very different from a fairy glow. It did not come from within and suffuse the whole body with magical beauty. This was more like an artificial light, like switching on a torch inside your coat pocket and letting the light glow through the holes in the fabric. It was a dull, red light and it was matched by the light from the creature's eyes because they also were glowing red in the dark.

The creature was sitting sideways on the bench with one spindly leg dangling over the side. The other long, thin leg was bent at the knee and its foot was resting on the seat. He had wrapped his extremely long thin arms, which had very bony elbows, around this knee and he looked completely relaxed, as if he were at home.

He was just like a very tiny, skinny man, dressed all in green. He wore a doublet and hose and on his head was a pointy hat which flopped down over one shoulder. His face was coarse and brown, neither very wrinkled nor very smooth. It was difficult to tell whether he was old or young. He didn't look cruel, like an imp, but on the other hand he didn't look very kind, like a fairy. For the ten-millionth time a huge wave of nostalgia washed over Pim and he longed for home. He thought for the millionth time of the beautiful Sylfia and wondered why on earth, sea or sky he had not listened to her.

"You have intimated that you are not here to harm me, sir, and you claim that you are not able to help me, either," Pim said. "Would you therefore do me the honour of explaining what *does* bring you here and, if possible, what, or who, you are?"

Pim realised that, if he was a diplomat at a palace garden party, such a string of questions would not be polite, not the right thing at all. However, he was a prisoner, kept under a mountain, sentenced to death in the morning and absolutely scared stiff. In such a situation he found it very easy to excuse himself for any lack of etiquette.

"I warn you that I am in no mood to entertain you and I am too concerned about my own safety to engage in small talk," he added.

"I didn't say that I couldn't help you," replied the little man. "I only said that I don't have the talent or correct gender to be an FGM."

"FGM?"

"Fairy God Mother! Keep up, lad!

"I'm here because I live here, you see. This mountain has been my family home for thousands of years. I'm on my own now and those lousy imps wouldn't have lasted a second if the rest of my clan had still been here, I can tell you. We who live in dark places have a way of not showing ourselves, unless we choose to be seen. I make it my business to watch them and I don't like what I see, that's a fact. Now then, have you heard of Rumpelstiltskin?"

"Er – no, I don't think so," Pim hesitated, taken by surprise.

"No, I suppose it's not a story for baby fairies. It concerns one of my ancestors and some humans. Humans used to tell it to their children, and may still do so, as far as I know.

"Why it should ever have been popular among them I can't imagine because it puts their kind in a very bad light. They even refer to my honourable ancestor as a *manikin*. Can you believe that? As if any of my kind would ever pretend to be a human, even a small version. Humans are a despicable race."

"I don't mean to be rude or inhospitable," said Pim, "but I fail to see how any of this can be of use to me right now. My plight is too serious to be remedied by children's stories."

"Patience, my lad! That's the trouble with your generation. You want everything done yesterday. We *boggles*, and our close relations the *troggles*, tell our own stories in our own way, at a slow and steady pace.

"When RSS was alive his land was ruled over by a greedy young king."

The boggle stopped when he saw another puzzled look on Pim's face.

"RSS is my abbreviation for Rumpelstiltskin, OK?"

Pim nodded. "Thank you, please go on," he said.

"Well, also living in this country ruled over by the greedy young king was a very foolish miller who made up all kinds of tall stories just to sound clever and important. Don't both of those characters sound typically human?"

"I don't know," Pim said, diplomatically. "I don't know any humans."

"You're lucky, my lad. Anyway, one day a courtier heard the miller bragging ten to the dozen in the village pub. His tall story for the day was that his beautiful daughter could spin straw into gold. I ask you. What a fool!

"The next thing he knew he had been taken into custody and was grovelling in the presence of the king, promising to bring his daughter to court so that she could demonstrate her skill."

"What a cowardly parent! Why didn't he just own up and let himself be kicked out into the street?" Pim asked.

"Precisely! My point entirely! That's humans for you! But no, that very night the poor young woman found herself locked in a room of the castle with a whole heap of straw. They brought in a spinning wheel and told her that the king expected her to spin all of the straw into gold by the morning.

"When she said she couldn't do it and it had all been a dreadful mistake the palace guards advised her to try her best because when the king didn't get his own way he had a habit of lopping off your head."

"So he was not just greedy, he was a tyrant as well," Pim observed.

"Yes, indeed. She was busy crying herself sick when RSS heard the commotion and made an appearance, just as I did for you. He kindly volunteered to do the job for a very small payment. He just took a cheap glass necklace in exchange.

"In the morning he thought that he'd done a good job. The room was full of glistening gold and there wasn't a bit of straw in sight so he went back to his usual activities around the castle, lurking, sneaking, spying and that sort of boggly thing.

"Then, to his surprise, he heard her sobbing the next night but in a bigger room of the castle. There was even more straw to spin this time but he set about it, feeling very sorry for the poor exploited girl. This time she only had one of those cheap rings that you can win at the fair but he took it as payment. If he hadn't she would have felt bad about him working all night for nothing wouldn't she? They were getting to be quite friendly, you see and I think he may have been falling in love with her.

"The third night he heard her wailing again and this time she was locked in an absolutely huge room which was tightly packed with straw and had the same dinky little spinning wheel standing in the middle. They hadn't even given her better equipment for this mammoth job!

"RSS said that he was absolutely fed up with this stupid king and his greedy ways and that she should run away with him to a life of freedom. She replied that she couldn't do that because her father would lose his head and it would be disrespectful to let that happen, even if he was an old fool. She told RSS that the king was going to marry her, if she could spin this third batch into gold, and she would live in comfort for the rest of her life. She said that RSS could share in her good fortune, if he helped her one more time.

"My honourable ancestor said that he understood about her father but he felt that she would be making a dreadful mistake if she married a man like the king but the miller's daughter said that she would turn the king into a kinder person. All she had to do was show him some love and affection which was probably what he had lacked in his childhood.

"RSS said he would believe that when he saw it and he

didn't expect the king to be a good husband or a good father so she had better hand over her first child to him so that he could bring up the little one as a decent human being. Then, when the king pegged out, the country would have a simple, well brought up individual to be its king or queen.

"The miller's daughter had nothing else to offer and she was sure that her boggle friend could be persuaded to take something else later on, so she agreed and the deal went ahead.

"A vast amount of straw got spun into gold that night and the next day the king married the miller's daughter. Of course his majesty did that because he wanted this golden girl to make more money for him in the future when his current stash ran out. It was a bonus that the miller's daughter was beautiful, kind and loving and the king had the chance of gaining something far more precious than gold – a reasonably happy marriage.

"His new wife did soften him up quite a bit. He was still extremely grumpy in the mornings and he still thought that he should have his own way in everything but she did stop him from lopping peoples' heads off on the merest whim and his subjects were much happier for that.

"He and his wife had a number of children, five I think, and I believe that they all turned out quite well, some kinder than others."

"Did RSS take her first child?" Pim asked.

"No he didn't get any of them, not even the first.

He was too kind hearted and gave the queen three chances to guess his name instead. She sent out servants to spy on him and one came back with his name just in time. I think RSS had changed his mind about looking after a baby and he deliberately let his name slip one evening while he was dancing about in the woods. That's not something a boggle usually does for fun, dance around in the wood I mean.

"After all, children can be a great deal of bother and human children are probably the worst of all. He made a show of being absolutely furious and did that old magician's trick where he pretended to tear himself in half and fall through the floor but secretly he was greatly relieved to get out of the deal."

There was a pause before the boggle grinned and said, "There you are, young fella. That's the way to go. I must have shown you a way out."

"Thank you for telling me such a fascinating story," Pim said slowly. "Your powers of narrative are excellent and your companionship has helped the time to pass. I was able to forget my own problems for awhile. However, the fact remains that I'm still here and I, or you, or we have not solved the little problem of my impending doom. Should I offer to spin straw into gold to buy my freedom?"

"Could you? No, don't answer that! No, what I think is that you're missing the point," the boggle sighed.

"I am?" Pim sounded puzzled again. "What point is that, sir?"

"In the story, lad, it's in the story."

"Oh, I see. Do I have to guess your name? Let me see. Dougal? Brian? Zebedee? Florence? Is it any of those? How about Parsley? Sage? Thyme? No, too girly. What about Arthur? Merlin? Galahad? Lancelot? Ivanhoe? Darcy? Willoughby?"

"Stop, stop, you don't have to do that," the boggle cried. "If you really want to know I'll tell you my name."

"Yes, please," Pim said.

The boggle sighed and looked at his feet.

"O.K. You might as well know. My name is Cudlip."

"Cudlip?"

"Yes."

"Honestly?"

"Yes."

"I'm so sorry."

"Thank you."

There was a long pause.

"Now, back to the story," the boggle resumed. "Think about how each behaves. The miller is a braggart and always makes things up. The king married the girl and he might have pretended to love her but we know that he just wanted to own a moneymaking machine. The girl says that she is going to give RSS her child but she would never have done that in a month of Sundays. RSS is honest right up to the end but then he pretends to be a very angry person because he has lost a guessing game. In actual fact he is relieved not to have the responsibility of bringing up a human baby. What are they all doing?"

"They're all pretending something," Pim exclaimed.

"Exactly!" cried Cudlip, triumphantly. "Pretending can get you into scrapes, it's true, but it can also get you out of them, my friend. Think about that carefully.
Now I must get back to my poking and prying I have quite a bit of that to do before the night is out. Good luck in the morning!"

With that the boggle started to fade.

"Just a moment", Pim whispered and reached out to shake hands with his new friend but before he could do that Cudlip had disappeared and all was black once more.

Pim sank down on the bench and stared into the darkness. All he could do now was to wait for the tramp of feet at dawn and in the meantime he would consider the benefits of pretending.

Chapter 11

On the mountain side the rescue party had slept fitfully and all were awake before dawn. While Hornbeam lit a fire and Tansy stood guard, Sylfia brewed tea and Flum sorted through the provisions, choosing some items of food for breakfast.

When the rats had been fed and watered, they all sat down by the fire to eat. They kept their backs to the sheer cliff face which was on one side of the mountain path. That way they could look out in all other directions and spot the approach of any unwanted visitors.

"We know how to get into the mountain now," Hornbeam said. "It seems that there is a control room where imps work a mechanism to open the door. I hope that they'll believe that I'm Pustular and let me in."

"When we get inside won't there be more imps waiting to unload the wagon?" Sylfia said. "Those in the control room will pass the message along won't they? When they find that you have no cargo they'll know that you're an intruder, even if the rest of us stay hidden."

Her eyes were wide with fear. She looked just as worried as when she and Tansy had been held at knife point on the high ground above the Rumbling River.

"That's true," Hornbeam said.

"Can we use magic to open the door for ourselves?" Tansy wondered.

"We could, but the imps will be able to detect the door opening and the result will be the same – they'll capture us almost straight away."

"Could we find another way in?" Sylfia asked, "one that isn't guarded?"

"It would be very unlikely that such an entrance exists and if it does it would take us far too long to find it," Hornbeam replied.

"We'll have to use dull-skuggery," Flum said firmly.

They all turned to look at him. Hornbeam smiled and gave him a wink.

"You're absolutely right, Flum. We may even need some 'piggery-jokery' as well! We have to make sure that the imps who let us in don't remember doing it."

Tansy looked at the other two fairies. "We used the magic of music on Pustular. He went into a dream and did as we asked. Can we use that again?"

"It could work," Sylfia said.

"Of course it will." Hornbeam said brightly, grinning with pleasure. "We'll add a little spell as well, just for good measure."

"I love Sylfia's singing," Flum said, dreamily. "Even the

Sorceress would be enchanted by it."

"Thank you for your confidence in me Flum," Syflia murmured, beaming at him.

She looked at him so lovingly with the reflected light from the fire dancing in her smiling eyes that Flum's heart flipped over and nearly burst with pride.

"Break it up, you two," Tansy said briskly, making them both blush and look away in confusion. "We haven't got time for lovey-dovey stuff at the moment. We've got to free Pim and all of those poor insects first. Then you can spoon your lives away."

"Go easy on them, Tansy," Hornbeam insisted. "There's nothing wrong with a bit of mutual confidence-building. We need to support each other if we are going to be brave enough for whatever lies ahead."

Tansy was immediately contrite. "Yes, sorry. You're right, Hornbeam. Sorry, sorry, you two. It's just that I'm so worried and I want to get everything back to the way it should be as soon as possible. The situation's making me so miserable that I easily get cross."

Hornbeam spoke kindly to her in a very quiet voice. "We understand, Tansy, but if we rush into this without thinking we could fail in our task and make even more trouble for ourselves.

"I think it would be best if you fairies fly high up the mountainside above Cut-throat Crag so that, when I arrive, you will be stationed above the door of the control room. When the imps hear me knocking and open up their little hatch they will see me, pretending to be Pustular sitting on his wagon. I'll pull my old hat well down to obscure most of my face and I'll have his smelly pipe, as well. I think I can remember how his voice sounds. While I'm talking to them Sylfia can start to sing and you other two can chant the words of a special elf spell I'm going to give you. The imps will drift into a dream state, just as Pustular did, and, while under the influence of the magic, they'll do as I ask. When they have set the mechanism working to open the door you can fly down to join me. The enchantment will last until we are inside the mountain then they'll 'wake up' and wonder why they've opened the doors. If I know anything about imps they'll probably blame each other and start to fight. That's what imps usually do when something has gone wrong."

"I'd better practise the spell now," Flum said. "I don't want to get it mixed up."

"It doesn't matter, Flum. When you use elf magic it's not so much what you say but how you say it," Hornbeam told him. "Mixing up the words can be a good thing. The more confused they get the better. If anyone tries to jog their memories later whatever they remember won't make much sense."

The words of the spell were simple. It went like this.

I may be kith or I may be kin, open the door and let me in
I may be a friend with gifts to bring, fling wide the gate
and let me in.

Hornbeam taught them how to say the spell in a very persuasive manner, using an old dialect of woodland elves. It made the instructions sound very important and it was impossible to ignore them.

Tansy and Flum found themselves itching to open the doors of the wagon, even though they usually hated to go into the vehicle.

Sylfia hummed some tunes to herself until she had the one that would be best suited to the task. It was a cheerful dance tune that got the feet moving in a purposeful manner. She sang it in such a way that it was sure to have a hypnotic effect so that anyone listening would fall into a trance, tapping their feet, nodding their heads and moving in time to the rhythm. She looked around and that was exactly what the others were all doing so they had to move apart to rehearse their performances. Hornbeam practised speaking in the same way as Pustular and when he tried it out on the others later they all applauded and said he was a born actor.

Sylfia sang them her song. Everyone was entranced again and when she finished she had to shake them all awake.

Then it was the turn of Tansy and Flum to repeat the elfish spell, using the intonation and old words in exactly the same way as Hornbeam had done. At first they still sounded like young fairies trying very hard to be old elves. Hornbeam had to take them through it again, word by word, to get the right enunciation and degree of persuasion. Fortunately, both of them were quick at learning spells and in a short while Hornbeam said that they sounded like genuine elves.

"With more work on the dialect you'll probably be able to persuade me to wear my trousers on my head," he said.

Tansy laughed and then she pressed her hands to her temples and said, "Oh no, you old tease! I'm not going to be able to get that image out of my head for the rest of the day!"

Hornbeam and Tansy laughed heartily at this piece of banter. Sylfia and Flum, felt slightly embarrassed but they nudged each other and tittered.

Before long they were all ready to go and Hornbeam spoke softly to the rats, reassuring and encouraging them. He promised that, if he and his companions succeeded in their mission, he would free all of them to live their normal lives again. The team nodded their heads appreciatively and sniffed the morning air. They seemed to be savouring the prospect, sometime in the future, when they might be able to run free above or below ground, whichever they chose, and without any chains.

Hornbeam climbed up on the wagon, wearing his disguise and the fairies flew high above, looking ahead towards the end of their journey. The party moved off cautiously and each one of them felt extremely nervous as the weight of such a huge responsibility bore down upon them.

Pim sat in his cell, waiting for dawn and the tramp of feet in the corridor.

Daylight could not penetrate into his prison but he knew by the chiming of the clock that the time was approaching. Any moment now, Macciovolio would stride into the office and demand his answer.

When the door did fly open Pim jumped to his feet and stood to attention, his heart pounding. It hammered so strongly that he thought it would burst out of his chest.

Macciovolio swept in and four Imperial Guards followed, clinking in their glistening armour. Each guard carried a flaming torch and the sudden intensity of the light made Pim close his eyes tightly for a few moments. When he tentatively opened them again he saw that Macciovolio was standing very still, studying him intently through the bars of his cage, and his wizard's eyes were shining with a dark, sinister glow. The guards were positioning the torches in sconces around the room. When they had completed this task they lined up behind their master and, like him, stood motionless. Pim could see their evil little eyes, glinting inside their helmets, and they stared at him with a malevolent curiosity.

"Well?" Macciovolio boomed. His deep voice resonated around the room and it had the same effect as the regular beat of a distant war drum, heralding the approach of enemy troops.

Under the gaze of the Lord Chamberlain, Pim felt that his mind was being scoured and that every tiny capsule of his brain was being poked and prodded for signs of deceit or duplicity. He shuddered and steeled himself. With gritty determination he drove away good thoughts about Mulberry Wood on a warm summer evening; about his friends and family singing and dancing from soft dusk to rosy dawn; about the feelings of fellowship and belonging. He stifled all the good emotions that kept welling up inside him.

"Tell me what you have decided, young fellow, and make it snappy!"

Pim gulped in air and heaved a profound sigh as the words struggled in his throat and threatened to strangle him. When finally they flew from his mouth there was no clawing them back.

"I shall become an imp, sir."

There was a long pause before Macciovolio spoke. He opened his eyes wider than usual and tilted his head slightly to one side.

"Really?" he said, very slowly and quizzically. He raised his eyebrows an inch or so then, as he continued to scrutinise Pim, his eyes narrowed once more and he frowned.

Pim thought, "He doesn't believe me," and black despair began to engulf him again. All he could do was continue to stare straight ahead and close down all good thoughts of home.

As Macciovolio continued to stare, Pim felt that it was not just his brain that was being scrutinised now. He felt that a cold clammy hand had been placed around his heart and every one of his emotions was being weighed and evaluated.

All at once, Macciovolio stopped looking at Pim. He turned on his heel and strode over to his desk. He flung out his cape behind him and settled himself into his huge leather armchair.

"Very well, we will complete your transformation as soon as possible," he said.

He pointed at two of the guards.

"Grim and Glum will accompany you to the Bath House where you will get cleaned up, fitted with the finest clothes and groomed to Imperial Imp perfection."

He sniffed the air and wrinkled his nose.

"When you return here looking and *smelling* more like a Prince of Imps I will outline your programme of training. We will also discuss how you will fit into this illustrious company known as 'Imps and Insects Inc.'"

He pointed one of his dagger-like fingers at the lock of Pim's prison door and casually muttered a spell.

"Em-as-es-ne-po!"

The cell door flew open and Grim and Glum strode forward without delay to stand right beside Pim, one on each side. It was clear to Pim that all three of them were going to be close companions for some time.

As Pim was marched away shoulder to shoulder with his new companions, Macciovolio remained at his desk and his disturbing gaze followed the trio out through the door. When they were out of sight a grimace of deep distrust settled on the wizard's normally inscrutable face.

Hornbeam halted at the top of the track. Directly in front of him was the sheer cliff face of the mountain that towered over Cut-throat Crag. Curious crows wheeled about in the sky and he studied them anxiously, hoping that they had not noticed the three fairies perched on a high ledge above his head.

He had pulled his old hat down over the bridge of his nose and stuck Pustular's evil smelling pipe in his mouth. It tasted even worse than it smelt but the good thing was that it made him cough and that had the effect of making the words 'NOCK HEER FOR ASSISTUNS' appear on the cliff face.

Hornbeam groaned, shook his head at the atrocious spelling and conquered the urge to correct it. Instead, he knocked hard using the bowl of the pipe.

A few seconds later the slate door of a peephole high above his head slid to one side and a disembodied crackly voice called "Password?"

Hornbeam was taken by surprise. Nobody had mentioned anything about passwords but he thought about Pustular and guessed that he would probably be belligerent in this situation.

"What d'ya mean? Ya know who I am ya silly fools. It's Pustular. Ya can see that it's me!" he yelled.

"Yeah, now we come to sniff hard we're getting the

same old smell but not as strong as usual. Are ya trying to give up that old pipe? So what ya got there then?"

"I've got something for ya to hear. Listen very carefully."

With that, Sylfia began to sing her song and the other two fairies flew down from their perch, put their heads very close to the peephole and started to chant the spell.

Suddenly, one of the imps on guard stuck his head out of the hole. His eyes were wide with wonder and his arms were waving about furiously in time to the music.

Then he caught sight of Tansy and with a whooping sound he leapt out of the guard room, grabbed her hand, flung his other arm around her waist and began to dance with her.

Before she could react to this they had waltzed round and round five times and then soared upwards, higher and higher, towards the mountain top, twirling and jiving as they went.

"Keep singing, Sylfia! Keep up the chant, Flum," Hornbeam called. "Don't stop whatever you do. Persuade the other guard to flick the switch and open the door."

The other guard was leaning out of the hole, gazing upwards, and following the gyrations of his fleet-footed friend."

"I'll give it 7 out of 10. You need to work on your turns," he called out dreamily. He had a soporific smile on his face and was waving his hand in time to the music while pointing his index finger at Sylfia as though he was her conductor. Then he called out "You'd better hurry up, Rinkle, I've got a very strong urge to open the door and let Pustular in. I can't stop myself. I'm going to do it now so you'd better hurry up. You'll get locked out if you stay up there!"

So saying he ducked back inside and there was a grating noise as he started to pull a lever. His companion saw what was happening and, with Tansy still in his arms, he dived downwards with the speed of a kestrel after a mouse and straight in through the hole.

A second later, there was the metallic noise of machinery in operation and the entrance to the mountain opened to admit Hornbeam. Unfortunately, at the same time, the sliding door to the peephole of the guard room moved across and clanged shut.

Hornbeam, Sylfia and Flum were stunned by the speed of what had happened and for a time they were frozen in suspended animation unable to believe it. They had lost Tansy. She was inside the mountain with the imps and they were still outside.

The door to the mountain still stood open for them but it would not be so for long. Very soon there was the whirring of unseen cogs and the rattling of hidden chains as the machinery started up once more and the door began to close.

Hornbeam had to make a decision and he did so in the blink of an eye.

"We have to go in," he called up to the fairies.

"There's a timed mechanism on this entrance. We must get inside before we're locked out. Quick, let's go!"

Hornbeam was right. He just had time to drive the rats through at top speed. The two fairies flashed in after him, with just a wing scale to spare, before the giant door clanged behind them and the early morning light on the mountainside was shut out.

"Phew! That was a squarrow neak!" Flum panted, trying to catch his breath. "I think I've had my shadow cut off! I hope Tansy's alright. Can I go and find her?"

"No, not yet, Flum. We've got to get our bearings," Hornbeam said, looking around him.

"I don't like to think of her with those dreadful imps," Sylfia said, shivering and blinking away the tears that were once more welling up. She moved closer to Flum and he placed a comforting arm around her shoulders.

Hornbeam tried to reassure them both.

"Don't worry, either of you. She's clever and quick. I bet she'll find somewhere to hide before they come to their senses. We must hope that there aren't any other imps watching her but I expect we would have seen them at the window."

Despite these reassuring words they were all desperately worried and it showed on their faces.

"First things first," Hornbeam said. "We've got to hide this wagon. It's not supposed to be here, remember."

They saw that they were in a tunnel lit only by torch-light and that it led downwards into the mountain.

"What's that smell?" Sylfia asked, wiping her face and trying to look brave.

"Detritus, decay, evil," Hornbeam answered causing the fairies to shudder. "Let's go. Keep a look out for a place to hide."

"What sort of place, Hornbeam?" Flum asked.

"We're looking for a tunnel that runs off to the side of this main one, or a hidden cave perhaps. It has to be off the beaten track, dark and uninhabited, of course. When we find the right place we'll know it and we can hide the wagon, free the rats and explore on our own."

"And find Tansy," Flum added.

"Of course. Don't worry you two. She'll be fine, I'm sure."

Hornbeam placed a gentle hand on the head of each fairy and gave them an avuncular smile but, secretly, he was horribly shocked to have lost contact with Tansy. He was mortified that he had lost control of the plot and until he could find Tansy and be safely reunited with her he would remain horribly worried and deeply ashamed.

Chapter 12

"Let me go now, Rinkle," Tansy crooned. "The music has stopped."

Rinkle was still starry eyed but he let her go without any fuss. He looked around in confusion, not quite sure where he was, and then he sank to the floor, looking dazed. There he sat, gazing up at her, as if she were the most adorable thing on the planet. His companion was just as confused and sat in the corner with a dreamy smile on his face drumming the floor with his feet and whistling quietly to himself.

Tansy flew to the door that had slid across the hatch and felt around for a latch or a handle but there was nothing.

"It must have been opened using a password spell," she murmured to herself. Then she turned back to the room, flew past the dreamy looking imps and followed the walls around looking for an alternative exit.

"If I can't get *out* of the mountain, I'll have to go *in*," she reasoned.

Sure enough, there was a wooden door which was bound to lead out into a corridor or another room. She turned the brass handle round and round but it had no effect and the door remained tightly shut.

Tansy was desperate now for when she turned back to look at the two guards she could see that they would soon be regaining their senses. Their smiles were beginning to waver and faint shadows of their disgruntled scowls flickered on and off their faces instead. Their eyes were beginning to re-focus and mischief would soon be shining out of Rinkle's eyes.

In desperation, Tansy looked around for somewhere to hide and noticed that along one wall there was a bank of levers very like those you would see in a railway junction box. Apart from a table, two chairs and the remains of the imps' breakfast there seemed to be nothing else in the room.

She tried an invisibility spell but she knew that it was unlikely to work inside a mountain. Fairies need fresh air and sunlight, or moonlight, for their magic to be really effective. Underneath the earth, surrounded by dense rocky material, the reliability of her spellwork was greatly reduced.

For a while her form became a dull shadow and she disappeared for a few seconds but she could not maintain the illusion and quickly ran out of power, returning quite naturally to her normal scintillating self.

Only one course of action remained. She went along

the row of levers and pulled each one in turn. There was a great deal of noise as various unseen doors opened and to her great relief one of them was the door between this room and the rest of the mountain. She flew out at the speed of light.

"What was that?" Rinkle asked his companion, shaking himself and rubbing his eyes.

"I don't know. It was like lightning," the other imp replied, yawning. Then, looking over Rinkle's shoulder, he saw the open door. He grabbed Rinkle by the upper arm and shook him.

He shrieked. "What did ya do that for, ya silly fool?"

"I dunno what you're talkin' about. Let go of me," Rinkle shrieked back.

"What've ya opened all these doors for? We'll get hung out as crow's food, ya eejit!"

"I didn't do it, ya liar. It must've been you!"

"Watchit! Don't you blame me, ya lying toad!"

Just as Hornbeam had predicted the two imps started to fight, punching, scratching, gouging and wrestling on the floor.

Meanwhile, Tansy flew through a long tunnel of rock and did not stop until it branched at the end. She had no idea whether she should turn left or right.

Looking back, she could see that doors had opened all along the walls of the tunnel on either side of the passageway and right up to the control room. Each of those levers must have opened at least one door, probably several at a time. Sounds of surprise and indignation emanated from the little rooms which turned out to be sleeping compartments for imps. Many of the occupants had been wakened by the unexpected opening of their doors and were soon to be seen standing in the doorways, rubbing their eyes and scratching their heads. They wanted to know 'what the 'eck' was going on.

Others were caught in the act of dressing and one or two were jumping around with one leg in their trousers and one leg still out. Some had got tangled in their bedclothes, so great was their haste to get out of bed and see what was going on. Some were searching under their beds for weapons. All thought it was a surprise attack and pandemonium was breaking out.

Tansy hid behind the last open door on the left of the corridor and peeped over the top, looking back at the way she had come. Back in the control room, she could see that Rinkle and his companion were still going at it hammer and tongs while some imps had emerged from their rooms and were urging on the two wrestling imps, shouting for one or the other and laying bets. The situation could have developed into a full scale riot if it had not been for the tramp of metal-soled boots advancing along one of the branching tunnels.

Fortunately the door that Tansy was hiding behind had swung right back, almost against the wall. She was able to duck down behind it and squeeze into the very small space between door and wall.

Four members of the Imperial Guard turned the corner and halted beside Tansy's door. They spread out across the corridor, with their spears bristling, and in this way they formed an impenetrable barrier. They gazed around with magnificently supercilious expressions trying to gauge the extent of the disturbance and its possible causes.

"Att – en – shun!" one of them bellowed.

The whole corridor fell silent and imps were frozen like statues into a variety of poses. The only sounds that could be heard now were the gasps, grunts and yelps of the two imps who were still fighting in the room at the end.

The gleaming, imperious, frightening warrior imps advanced very slowly down the corridor. As they swaggered along they pushed stray imps back into their rooms and slammed the doors shut.

Tansy had to move with the speed of light once more and just managed to disappear around the corner of the tunnel before her door was slammed shut.

In the act of closing this door the guard thought he saw a flash behind him but when he turned to look there was nothing there.

When they reached the last room before the end, the guards hauled two of the imps out into the corridor before slamming the door shut on the others inside. The two imps isolated in the tunnel were marched in front of the guards into the control room.

Rinkle and his companion were first hauled to their feet by the collars of their coats and were then shaken hard until their teeth rattled.

"We'll see what the Lord Chamberlain has to say

about this," one of the guards barked.

"You two, take their places."

So it was that two imps, who had neglected their duty and were suddenly aghast at what they had done, were dragged off down the corridor to wait outside Macciovolio's office and two other imps, who smirked with pleasure at the disgrace of others, were installed in their place.

Tansy gambled on the guards taking the same tunnel to go back as the one down which they had come. For this reason she flew some distance along the other tunnel and crouched in the shadows. Here she waited for the guards to turn the corner and march off with the disgraced imps in their midst.

She decided that, if the imps were being taken off to jail, then she should follow because that would be the place to find Pim. After all, he would be a prisoner somewhere under the mountain, and those guards would very likely deliver their miscreants to the same place.

If the guards led her to Pim then she would go and find the others and they could concoct a plan to set him free. There was one small difficulty, of course. How would she ever find the others in this rocky maze of rooms and passages?

"One problem at a time," she thought. "Just follow the guards for now."

She set off after the marching soldiers, keeping her distance and staying in the darkest shadows, low down, near the bottom of the wall. Wherever there was a torch burning she flashed by, like a stray spark, and immediately dropped down again into the darkness.

She was surprised to find that they were not going down into the mountain which was where she expected cells and dungeons to be. The imps marched along on level ground and, as they turned this way and that through the maze of passages, Tansy realised that the tunnels were becoming wider and more carefully constructed. After turning several corners she noticed that the floors became paved with slabs and brightly coloured paintings started to appear on the walls.

Where doors had been left open Tansy could look into spacious apartments. They were brightly lit and, fortunately for her, sparsely populated. The imps who were visible through the open doors to these rooms were all busily employed at their tasks and they glanced up only briefly as the military party marched past. Tansy had to be careful not to flash past before their heads were bent back to their tasks.

Before long they came to the end of their journey where the final corridor opened out onto a large paved courtyard. There was enough space for it to serve as a drill hall and that was indeed its primary function. On each side of the entrance was a large statue of an Imperial Guard and Tansy hid behind one of these. There was a gap between the feet through which she could see most of the hall.

She saw that heavy wooden doors were set in the walls at intervals all the way around the hall and she noticed that outside each door there was another pair of stone figures. One statue stood on each side of every door and they were all the same as the one Tansy was hiding behind.

She noticed, too, that each door had a polished brass handle, brass hinges and a brass lock. Hanging on the wall to one side of each door there was a bell to pull in order to gain admittance and on each door there was a sign telling who or what might be found inside.

The party had stopped outside the largest and most imposing door which was directly opposite the entrance to the hall. The sign on this door was very ornate and the brass was polished to such a high degree of brightness that it shone magnificently in the torchlight. The name on the door read 'The Lord Chamberlain Macciovolio' and, even if Tansy had not heard of a powerful wizard being involved in this enterprise, she would have recognised by the magnificence of his name plate that just such a personage must be found inside. The other doors were not so grand and they had quite ordinary sounding labels such as 'Bath House', 'Guard Room', 'Armoury', 'Mess Hall' and 'Gym'.

This was obviously the heart of military operations under Bulzaban Mountain and Tansy judged from the trembling limbs and terrified faces of the captives that it was a centre of cruelty and powerful control.

She was beginning to think that it would be a good idea to flee. She could go back up the corridor and look for a tunnel leading down into the mountain. Hornbeam,

Sylfia and Flum would be down there somewhere because their way in had been much lower down than hers.

She was about to do just that when the door to the Bath House was suddenly thrown open and three figures marched out. The threesome proceeded to cross the hall and join the group already assembled outside Macciovolio's door.

Her eyes were drawn to the figure in the middle of this new group because his posture and bearing were so very familiar to her. He turned to look across the hall in her direction as though he had sensed her presence. For a few moments she thought that the look in his eyes was that of a troubled friend, reaching out for comfort and reassurance, but then that fleeting impression was gone and in the next instant she looked again into the same eyes and encountered only cold and haughty disdain.

She clamped her hand over her mouth to prevent a gasp of dismay from escaping.

"Oh, Pim," she thought. "What is happening to you? Don't look like that. It's only me."

Tansy just knew that she would have to stay here now, now that she had found Pim. She could not leave until she had found out what was happening to him.

Whatever happened fairy intuition told her in the strongest terms that her future would be bound up with his.

Chapter 13

When they had got their breath back Hornbeam led the team of rats and the two fairies down the only available tunnel into the mountain until they came to a place where a number of smaller tunnels ran off in different directions. They stopped at this point and examined their options.

The main tunnel continued on down into the depths of the mountain and would surely end in a place where imps would be waiting to unload incoming wagons. The smaller tunnels must provide alternative routes into the mountain and, although their destinations were unknown, they did not appear to be so well used and might therefore be judged safer. Some of these smaller passages seemed to climb upwards, others appeared to disappear downwards and the rest, at least at the start, remained on a level course. It was difficult to judge where any of them might end up because they were all unlit, unsigned and soon disappeared around corners.

Hornbeam decided that they should allow the team of rats to choose a tunnel and lead them through the darkness.

"After all, they know the mountain and we don't," he reasoned. So the animals were encouraged to sniff each alternative pathway and make a choice.

When they had made their choice they set off as a team with no further hesitation. They used their well developed senses of touch and smell to navigate through the narrow, pitch black passage that they had chosen. On either side of the wagon there was just a tiny gap between the wheels of the vehicle and the rocky wall of the tunnel.

Hornbeam and the two fairies knew that they were still going down into the mountain but the passageway was not so steep. The air got warmer and smellier so that breathing the stuffy atmosphere became an unpleasant experience and one which they would normally have avoided at all costs. They began to feel rather light headed and unsteady as they rumbled along placing their trust in the special underground knowledge of the rats. They did not speak much and each of them entertained their own private fears as to what might lie in store at the end of the tunnel.

At last they emerged from the tunnel and found themselves in a good sized cave which was dry, with a high ceiling, and a flow of fresh air blowing in through a crevice somewhere. The atmosphere was sweeter and cooler but, even more importantly, the cave was empty.

They fumbled in the wagon and found three elfish lanterns. When these were lit, they could examine their surroundings in more detail and it pleased them to see that there were a number of small fissures in the walls that were just big enough for an elf or a fairy to squeeze through. Peering through these cracks they sometimes saw smaller caves on the other side and sometimes they saw tiny passages stretching away into the darkness which could serve as hiding places, or a means of escape, if necessary.

"This is excellent," Hornbeam said. "I wouldn't be at all surprised if these rats hadn't led us here on purpose. Well done, my friends. You've earned your freedom. Let's slip off those chains and let you go!"

The rats were freed from their harnesses but before running off they took it in turns to snuffle up to Hornbeam touch his hand by way of salute. They wanted to show their gratitude for his kind treatment of them.

The old elf smiled and thanked them for their good service. He wished each one a happy retirement and told them to make their way out of the mountain as soon as possible, to avoid being captured again.

Flum and Sylfia patted the rats as each one passed by and wished them "Good luck!"

The two of them went to the mouth of the cave and waved until the last one had disappeared.

When all of the animals had gone they both felt over-whelmed by loneliness. It was as though old friends had left them and gone to live far away, forever. They turned back towards Hornbeam hoping that he would have a plan of action to raise their spirits and make them feel closer to finding Tansy and Pim.

To their surprise the old elf was nowhere to be seen. They called out his name and looked for him in the wagon and underneath it. They searched around the cave and looked through all the cracks and crannies thinking that he might have been investigating one of these. They even flew up to the ceiling to see if he had found a way out up there.

"Hornbeam, where are you? Don't go off without us!" they shouted.

At last they heard a faint, muffled cry drifting up to them from somewhere deep in the rock beneath their feet.

"Down here," it called.

The two fairies crawled around the cave floor, feeling for gaps large enough for an elf to fall through.

"Where are you?" Sylfia called. "What happened? Did you fall? Are you hurt?"

There was a pause and then another voice answered. "No he's not hurt. I took him in to find out why you're banging around on my roof. Would you like to come and join him?"

The two fairies sprang to their feet and stared down at the floor.

"We don't know," Sylfia replied nervously. She looked up at Flum and then back down at the floor.

"Who are you? What do you want with us? Are you

going to let Hornbeam go?"

"It could be a micked wagician!" Flum whispered anxiously. "Or even a weddling mitch!"

They could not discuss the matter any further, however, because the rock between their feet split apart and their legs were whipped away from under them. Before they knew it they were sliding down a polished ramp at high speed. The ramp turned into a helter-skelter and, after making five corkscrew turns, they were deposited onto a large lumpy mat at the bottom of the slide.

"Over here," the voice called. "Come and join us. You're very welcome."

The fairies found themselves in another cave but this one looked like someone's sitting room. It was lit by a dull red glow. They had no idea where the light was coming from for there were no lanterns hanging from the ceiling nor were there any torches around the walls. There was not even a fire burning in a hearth because there was no fireplace to be seen anywhere. Even though there was no fuel burning in the cave, it did feel very cosy and well ventilated.

There was enough light to see every detail of its contents. It was well furnished with comfortable armchairs and they were arranged around a low table in the middle of the room.

Around the walls stood cupboards and bookshelves interspersed with some special items of furniture. There was a large grandfather clock, a hat stand, an umbrella stand, a tall desk and a sideboard. Beside the tall desk there was a stool and on top of the desk, next to the green leather writing surface, there was a silver inkstand carrying a white feathered quill. On top of the sideboard there were two candlesticks made of white polished marble and a fine porcelain bowl with a pretty flower pattern on all sides. The candlesticks carried red candles which had not yet been set alight and hanging on the wall above them there was a mirror in a gilt frame.

There were also half a dozen ornate picture frames hanging on the walls. These picture frames looked like the ones that can be seen in mansions and palaces and would usually contain portraits of ancestors. Closer inspection, however, revealed that five of the frames were empty and the sixth picture seemed not to be finished. Only one face appeared in this picture taking up only a small area of the canvas and even though there was room for a large family group the rest of the sitters were absent.

Sylfia and Flum dusted themselves down and Flum adjusted his glasses, placing them carefully back on his nose, so that he could make his way over to where Hornbeam was sitting. As he and Sylfia approached the elf rose stiffly to greet them. He winced as he stood up and the two fairies noticed that he was rubbing his elbow.

"I'm sorry to have disappeared like that," he said. "That helter-skelter ride was a bit of a shock wasn't it? I've not done anything like that for many years. It shook me up a bit."

"It would have been fun if we had known where we were going and who we were going to meet," Sylfia commented, looking in the direction of their host who had remained seated and silent.

"We thought some strong magic had whisked you away," Flum said, staring at the seated figure. "This is not some trummoxing flick of The Sorceress is it?"

"No, Flum. We're just being investigated by a boggle or a troggle. He hasn't told me which, yet."

"I'm a boggle, Mr Elf," his host told him. "You're the first elf to come into my house in a very long time. I couldn't help wondering what was going on. We boggles are top of the tree when it comes to minding other peoples' business and, if we can help or hinder in any way, it is our boggle duty to do so."

"Can we trust you?" Sylfia asked. "You said this is your house but if you live under this mountain surely you must work for the imps."

"There's no logic in that, little miss," the boggle replied. "If you live by the sea, do you have to be a sailor or a fisherman? If you live in a forest do you have to chop wood? If you live in a stable do you *have* to muck out the horses? I watch imps. I annoy imps. I *hate* imps. I would drive them all away if I could but I wouldn't *work* for them not even if you promised me a fortune in gold and pearls. No, I certainly wouldn't."

"Why do you live here, then?" Flum asked.

"This is my home, that's why I live here, young fellow. The imps drove all the other boggles away but not me. They can't get rid of me as easily as that, no indeed. I keep the old place tidy. I mop and clean, dust and polish so it's all ready for their return."

"Why do you have empty picture frames?" Sylfia asked, looking around her and taking in the contents of the room.

"Boggles take their images with them when they go. My face is the only one left. See it over there?" He pointed to the frame that had only one face on the canvas even though there was room for a lot more.

"I left the family picture frames there for when my lot return. They'll waltz in here one day as if they've never been away expecting everything to be spick and span, food on the table, beer in the barrel, frames on the wall. That's the boggle way."

"What if you had gone too?" Flum asked.

"Oh, in that case they'd never return. I'm the caretaker, you see. Cudlip the Caretaker, that's me."

"Is that your name? Cudlip?" Sylfia asked.

"I'm afraid so."

"It's a lovely name."

"No it isn't, but thanks all the same. You're the loveliest liar I've ever met."

They smiled at one another.

Hornbeam had been listening with interest as the fairies interrogated the boggle. Now it was his turn to ask a question.

"Have you seen any other fairies in recent days? We're looking for two, both are our friends and both are probably inside this mountain."

"Yes as a matter of fact only last night I was having a

chat with a young fellow who had been locked up by that dandy of a magician Macciovolio."

"Macciovolio you say? I think we've heard of that character, although we weren't given his proper name. The fairy may be Sylfia's friend Plimlimmon. Did he seem rather haughty, in the manner of a young aristocrat?"

"Yes, that could be him. It was like we were meeting at a palace garden party and not in a rotten dungeon."

"That sounds like him, doesn't it Sylfia?" Hornbeam said.

Sylfia nodded. "Did he seem to be – um – alright, all things considered?" She asked this rather nervously, not sure whether she would like to hear the answer.

"I snuck into his cell in the usual boggle way. Boggle behaviour makes a lot of folk jumpy and nervous, you know, and it was the same with him. He got used to me very quickly though and it helped that I told him one of my stories. He seemed very interested and I was able to offer him some sound advice. He seemed to have a lot to think about."

"Well that's something. He's alive and entertaining visitors," Hornbeam said, looking at Sylfia. She gave him a wan smile.

It seemed as though Cudlip would have said more on the subject of Pim but Hornbeam went on quickly to ask about Tansy.

"You haven't seen a young female fairy have you? She's vivacious, colourful, daring, a good dancer?"

Cudlip shook his head. "Sorry, I can't help you there.

Do you know what's going on in this mountain?" he asked them.

"We have a good idea," Hornbeam replied. "It's horrific and we'd like to put an end to it, if we can."

"If only you could. If we could get rid of those evil imps my folks would come back home."

Flum had been fidgeting all the way through this conversation and, although for Sylfia's sake he was glad that Pim had been seen alive, there was only one fairy whose fate he was really interested in. He wanted to know what had become of Tansy.

"Can you tell me where the control room is?" he asked abruptly, as soon as the boggle had finished speaking. "I must go and find Tansy."

"That's your other friend is it?" Cudlip guessed. "Well you'd better come and have a look at this."

He walked over to one of the bookcases and gave it a push. The complete set of shelves, with the books still in place, swivelled smoothly around on an unseen pivot. As it turned, another room was revealed on the other side of the wall. Cudlip beckoned to them and they all slipped through the gap. They stepped out into a space which was even more clean and tidy than the one they had just been sitting in. The table top was made of polished granite as were all the worktops around the room. The cupboard doors gleamed with bright new paint and above their heads shiny copper pans hung in rows. There was a double oven with glass doors. Green, red, yellow and blue lights in a panel above the doors displayed the time, temperature, pressure and humidity.

"This is the kitchen but recently I have used it as my operations room as well," Cudlip told them proudly.

Sylfia was full of admiration for the gleaming room but she was also puzzled.

"It's beautiful but where is the fireplace? How can it be a kitchen without a source of heat?"

"It must be the modern magic!" Hornbeam exclaimed excitedly. "The energy comes along copper wires and you connect your oven and your other equipment to it," he told her. "It makes things hot when you switch it on. I learnt about it when I was watching humans. They use it all the time. It's called lektrissity. Where does yours come from, Cudlip?"

"There's a powerful waterfall on the north side of the mountain. The Sorceress had a giant wheel installed and that is connected to huge slabs of lodestone. They turn constantly and always will, as long as the water keeps flowing. That produces the energy. Boggles understand about the magic of materials, you know, so I just tapped in to it. Now then, this is what I wanted to show you."

He walked over to one of the long walls in the room and pulled on two cords that were dangling there. As he pulled on each cord a large map unfurled and the two of them hung side by side, covering the wall from top to bottom and from side to side.

"One is a map of everything inside the mountain that is above me and the other shows everything that is below me. I've lurked and sneaked and spied on those pesky imps every day since they arrived. Drawing these maps has kept me busy and I did it believing that one day they would come in handy. This might be the day," the boggle said, looking around at them quizzically, before heaving a deep sigh.

"I did think, though, that I'd be showing them to my own people."

Cudlip sighed again and gazed at his handy work with a mixture of pride and sadness.

Sylfia moved close to him and placed a hand on his arm.

"Thank you, Cudlip. We really appreciate it. I'm sorry your people aren't here yet, but I'm sure we can make use of these until they arrive."

"Yes, of course you can," he said, brightening and grinning at her. He patted the hand that she had rested on his arm.

"If those idiot relatives of mine choose to run away they can't blame me when they miss all the fun. Let's get on with teaching those pestiferous imps a lesson!"

Chapter 14

After Tansy had looked into Pim's eyes he had abruptly
turned his head away and had jumped back into step
with his companions, Grim and Glum. The three of
them marched up to the door of Macciovolio's office
and Grim held a brief conversation with the guards
who were waiting with the two trembling imps from the
control room. Tansy could see from her hiding place that
they agreed to take the miscreants into Macciovolio's
office first. They rang the bell, a voice called out the
command to enter and the captives wriggled in the
clutches of the armoured guards as they were bundled
in through the door. It closed behind them with a bang.

Pim and his two companions were left outside and
Grim and Glum relaxed a little turning towards each
other to exchange theories about what might have been
going on.

Pim was not included in their conversation so he
strolled a little way away from the office door, keeping his

back to them, so they would not see him staring hard at the place where he thought he had seen Tansy. He moved into a better position so that he could look along the wall and behind the statue. She wasn't there.

He breathed a sigh of relief. It was far too dangerous for one lone fairy to be here. He was amazed that she had appeared under the mountain at all and he wondered how she had got in and, having got in, how she had found her way to this hall. He could not help wondering if there were other fairies with her and if he could dare to hope that a rescue was possible.

Then he wondered how he should behave if she was discovered. It would blow his cover to acknowledge her, but how would he be able to stand by and do nothing if she was going to be hurt?

Presently the door to Macciovolio's office flew open and the prisoners' escort marched out. They were now carrying two bundles.

Pim looked around in vain for the two imps that had been taken in as prisoners but they were nowhere to be seen. Shockingly, he realised that *they* were the bundles. He took a closer look and was astonished to see that the prisoner imps had been transformed into carcasses, sucked dry of all bodily fluids and trussed up like the dry remnants of a spider's meal.

This was the magician's instantaneous punishment for inappropriate behaviour. It was not only cruel but sickeningly carnivorous.

In the short moments before Grim and Glum sprang

to attention Pim took the opportunity to shudder and close his eyes against the horror that was passing by. Then he took up his position once more and marched with his companions back into the tyrant's den where he had spent the night in a cell.

Once inside they found Macciovolio sitting in his leather armchair, with his feet on the desk, wiping his mouth and chin with a huge silk handkerchief.

He turned his flinty gaze on Pim and looked the newly-prinked fairy up and down.

"Yes, much better. You look more like a Prince. As you might have noticed I have just had to punish some insubordination because the culprits couldn't even remember what had made them behave in such an unseemly manner. Indeed, they couldn't even remember pulling certain levers that put the whole of Imps and Insects Inc. at risk. Sometimes I shudder to think how much of this top quality enterprise has been placed in the hands of a race of incompetent fools. Tscha!"

He rose from his seat and walked round to the front of the desk. He fingered Pim's new clothes which were well cut and of very good quality. He looked into the eyes of his new employee for some moments and then, quite suddenly, his face broke into an evil, lopsided grin.

"You know, this gives me an idea for your first assignment. I'm going to send you to find out what happened over there and while you're at it make sure that it never happens again. Off you go then, all three of you. Chop, chop!"

Pim saluted and, turning on his newly booted heel, strode out with his metal clad companions.

Once outside, Grim and Glum relaxed again.

"Not without breakfast first," Glum growled.

They marched Pim towards the mess hall and stood outside as Grim rang the bell but when the door opened Pim did not follow them inside.

"I'm just going back to ask the Lord Chamberlain what my new name should be," he told them. "You need to know that too, don't you? I'll join you in a minute."

The other two looked at him suspiciously and stared after him as he walked back across the hall to ring the office bell. In fact, Pim did not ring the bell. He was tall enough to hide the bell when he stood directly in front of it and so he could mime the action of ringing it. The other two went into the mess hall, leaving the door open for him to follow. As soon as they had gone, Pim ducked out of sight behind one of the statues that stood outside Macciovolio's door.

Tansy was hiding there and he whispered to her very rapidly.

"I sensed that you were here again. I'm pretending to be one of them. There was no other way. Whatever happens you have to trust me. If I was really one of them I would have given you up to them, wouldn't I?"

Tansy looked into his eyes and was relieved to see that the old Pim was back, arrogant and conceited but totally trustworthy.

"Of course I'll trust you. You need to know that I'm

not the only one here. Hornbeam, Sylfia and Flum came too but I got separated."

"Hornbeam? That's good to know. He's the wisest creature in the wood," Pim said, feigning cheerfulness. "Now I must go. Remember this though, I'd rather die than become an imp!"

He emerged from behind the statue just in time. A split second later Glum looked around the door frame of the mess hall and said, "There you are. What did he say?"

"He hasn't decided yet," Pim replied. "Just call me Pie for now."

"Pie? Why should we do that?"

"Because it's short for 'Prince Imp Elect'."

"Phew! You really do fancy yourself, don't you?"

"Do you two want anything to eat or not?" Grim called out.

"Yeah, we're both coming!" Glum sneered. "Both of us will join you now, me and His Lord High Everything Else."

He gave a sarcastic laugh and pushed Pim through the doorway into the mess hall.

They ate their breakfast sitting at one of the trestle tables that were arranged in rows up and down the mess hall. While chewing and munching, Glum grumbled and Grim snarled at the staff of catering imps who flew up and down and round and round to serve them. Pim was too excited to eat and he was glad when the meal was over. His mind was in turmoil and he wanted very much to talk to Tansy again but he had no idea how that might be achieved.

Soon they were marching out of the drill hall and up the corridors that turned into the tunnels leading to the control room.

Pim looked with interest into the chambers and halls as they passed by and he tried to distract his sullen companions by asking questions about what was going on in each. He could sense that Tansy was following them and he did not want his two companions to notice. She was darting from one shadow to the next and, when necessary, she disappeared from view in the twinkling of an eye.

They turned into the tunnel that led up to the control room door and, in a loud voice, Grim called out every imp who slept and worked in that area. On his orders they lined up on parade.

They were told by Grim in a bellowing voice that they were all in disgrace. When one imp wailed that what happened earlier was Rinkle's fault and nothing to do with anybody else Glum summarily ran him though with his spear. After that there was no further complaint.

Grim announced that nothing like this was going to happen again and, since no adequate explanation had been given ten imps would be taken from the section each week to work in the hive. They would work there for the rest of their lives, and that meant a short life, until stung to death by bees.

The ten taken to the hive from this area each week would be replaced by more reliable workers from elsewhere in the mountain. This would go on until all of those assembled here had been replaced. The punishment would stop if a proper explanation was given for the incident that morning or when the names of Rinkle's co-conspirators had been supplied.

Immediately, the imps clamoured to give the names of some of their fellow workers, especially those that they did not like, but Grim would not tolerate this for long. He ran a selection of them through with his spear until the noise stopped and the rest stood in sullen silence again.

"Not just random names, you fools, I need a 'Proper Explanation of Events!'"

His voice boomed along the tunnel and the workers quailed. Then a small but clear voice rang out. It tinkled in a way that only a fairy voice will do, especially when its owner is feeling great emotion.

"This is not fair. I know they're imps and I should dislike them beyond measure, but they don't deserve this. It was me. I opened the doors and caused all this fuss."

In horror Pim turned to look at Tansy. She was standing in the middle of the corridor at the place where it branched into two with her hands on her hips and a determined look on her face.

Grim, Glum and all of the assembled imps, turned to stare at her.

Pim wanted to shout "Run Tansy! Fly away! Don't do this!" but it was too late, Grim and Glum were advancing towards her and Tansy was standing her ground. This gave

Pim no choice. He stepped in front of the two guards and grasped her by both wrists.

"Grim and Glum, see to those imps. Put them back to work. I'll escort this interfering busybody to Macciovolio. He'll be fascinated by her story!"

He managed to whisper to Tansy. "Stay close and when we get to the end of that tunnel ......"

There was no time to whisper anything else because at that moment he felt a restraining hand on his shoulder.

"Not so fast, Princey. I'll be coming with you!"

To his dismay, Grim placed himself firmly on the other side of Tansy and took her arm in an iron grip.

"Glum can look after a few stupid imps. This is much more interesting. Off we go."

As they marched back down the tunnels and corridors, Tansy stole glances at her two captors. Pim, on her right, was staring straight ahead so that Grim would not see the panic that he felt must be visible on his face. He did not want to be suspected of having sympathy for their prisoner.

Grim, however, would catch her eye from time to time and, when he did, he sneered most unpleasantly while gripping her arm even more tightly and making her wince with pain. He was feeling very pleased with himself because to have solved the mystery of the opening doors would be a huge feather in his cap and Macciovolio was bound to be very pleased with him. Grim was determined to claim the credit and reap any reward that might be forthcoming.

He was hoping to rise higher in the organisation and saw no reason why he might not one day become Macciovolio's apprentice. He could see that, under no circumstances, should he allow the new imp, impostor prince that he was, to become the sole favourite. Grim would need to block any action that could lead to a rise in Pim's power and influence.

The three of them marched along together, two in great misery and trepidation, and one elated by the prospect of earning a little praise from his cruel and powerful master.

None of them noticed a small, rotund figure lurking in the shadows, even though this creature was so full of rage and indignation that he had to clap his hand firmly over his mouth and nose to prevent the escape of angry snorts and insulting expletives.

He wanted to cry out "Let her go, you bastardly dullies! You're no better than bowardly cullies. You're a traitor, Pim and that's the worst creature of all! Just you wait!"

Flum was here because he had made a small copy of the section of Cudlip's map that showed him the way to the control room and he had arrived there in time to see Tansy step out of hiding and declare herself to be responsible for the opening of the doors. He had wisely remained hidden while she was taken into custody because there was nothing he could do against the spears and the armour. One thing he could do, however, was employ moth camouflage to blend in with his rocky surroundings and by doing so he avoided capture himself.

Now, as he followed Tansy and her escort at a safe distance, he seethed with rage. Never in his life had he felt such hatred and it was all directed towards Pim.

The imps were detestable and that went without saying. He had always known that they caused chaos and unpleasantness wherever they went and, before they had begun to endanger his little world and threaten his friends, he might have almost feel sorry for them. But now it was not just the bad behaviour of silly imps making him mad, it was the behaviour of a treacherous fairy that made his blood boil.

No matter what he had been through, Pim would never be able to justify joining the enemy and treating Tansy in this way.

Flum had to rescue Tansy, he told himself and, at the same time, teach that big headed traitor a lesson, one that he would never forget. He would do that or die in the attempt.

The only thing was though, Flum was not at all clear on the particulars of the rescue or even what his next move should be. In fact 'totally clueless' was the phrase that sprang to mind or, as he might say, he was 'plummoxed and fuzzled.'

When he had thought some more it became clear that he would have to leave Tansy for now and use the map to return to the others. He needed to tell Hornbeam who would be able to use Cudlip's maps and insider knowledge to hatch a plan.

He also wanted to see Sylfia at this moment because

it was she who always made him feel like a hero. She just had to smile and he would feel courage and hope welling up inside.

"I'll just see where they take Tansy first," he told himself.

So it was that Tansy and her escort were tracked by Flum all the way back to Macciovolio's office.

Chapter 15

"Look down there," said Cudlip.

Hornbeam looked and gasped with astonishment.

They had been crawling on hands and knees, and
sometimes bellies and elbows, through very narrow air
ducts and now they had reached the end of one of those.
The opening was covered by a grill and the two of them
were lying side by side in a very cramped space in order to
peer out through the mesh.

Hornbeam had asked his host to take him to a place
where he could see the hive for himself. Sylfia had not
wanted to see millions of bees in captivity and so she
had stayed behind to sort through the wagon and unload
some essential supplies that could be stored more safely in
Cudlip's house.

Hornbeam was stiff after crawling for ages through
narrow spaces and he was now glad to have a rest.
Cudlip the spy had been leading him unerringly
through a maze of slim passages which formed part

of the mountain's ventilation system.

The old elf stared out of their hiding place in amazement. He could see part of a vast cavern which was so tall that from their position it was like being half way down a gigantic well.

Rising up through the centre of this cavern was a huge cylindrical construction made of glass and the nearest part of its wall was about twenty imp strides away from them. The glass tower rose up above their heads until it was lost to sight and disappeared into the dark upper reaches of the cavern.

Similarly, when Cudlip looked down to see if he could see what the building was standing on, he could not because it went down, down into the mountain until it too was lost in the darkness.

Wooden platforms encircled the outside of the central glass cylinder and stairs ran between the levels. Creatures were moving about on the platforms, ascending and descending the stairs and entering and leaving the glasshouse by way of revolving glass doors. Cudlip whispered that they were imps.

The imps were unrecognisable because they were dressed from head to foot in white suits with helmets on their heads. The suits were made of a heavily padded material and their faces were hidden behind masks so that their eyes looked out through goggles with thick lenses. Some of these creatures carried shiny metal buckets. Those going into the glass construction carried empty buckets and those coming out carried buckets brimful with golden honey. Other workers carried small hatchets and canvas bags. When they emerged from the hive their bags were full of lumps of white wax.

The cavern was lit by flaming torches which were housed in sconces set at intervals around the circular cavern walls. As well as providing light the flames of these torches served to help ventilate the cavern because the rising hot air drew fresh air up from below. The reflected light from the flames made it difficult to see through the glass walls and into the hive which meant that Hornbeam could only just make out insect shapes moving about behind the glass. There were fixed platforms inside the hive as well which were continuations of the floor outside. These platforms inside supported the bodies of innumerable insects that crawled unceasingly over and between the platforms. Hornbeam managed to identify them from their colour, shape and noise as bees. He was looking into a gigantic, industrial-sized beehive.

The outlines of imps wearing their peculiar clothing could also be seen moving about among the honeycombs. They were draining honey from some of the combs and hacking at others with their hatchets to break up the wax. The continuous droning sound of so many bees made the watchers feel as though they were inside an enormous, smoothly running engine except that the smell in the air was overpoweringly that of the sweet scent of honey.

"I'm not sure what magic they use, but the bees can't get out through the revolving doors and can't escape," Cudlip whispered.

"Those imps are wearing special clothing to protect them from the bees. The clothing only lasts for a certain time and then it gets worn out. Each imp has to make sure that he or she works hard enough to collect the right amount of honey or wax on each visit. In that way he or she will achieve the desired quota on time and then be released from duty before the protection wears out."

Hornbeam looked more closely and saw that the imps leaving the hive with buckets of honey were going up to a level above and the imps that left with bags of wax were going downstairs to a level below.

He asked, "where are the imps going when they leave the hive?"

"Those with honey are going to a collection vat two floors up and those with wax have to take it to a wax milling machine on the next stage down. From there the products are taken to other rooms for processing and packaging. Everything ends up in a warehouse at the bottom of the hive deep down in the mountain."

"What happens then?" Hornbeam asked.

"Tunnels connect the warehouse to the north side of the mountain where there is an underground railway station. All the goods that are manufactured by Imps and Insects Inc. are taken down by rail, at night, to the port of Mistanmurk. They're hidden in the holds of ships before dawn and leave on the next tide."

"What about the top of the hive? Where is it?"

"The hive goes all the way up through the middle of the mountain and ends up at the throne room of the

Imperor and Impress," Cudlip replied. "The top of the hive is the middle part of the throne room floor. It's made of glass, too."

"A glass floor? My, oh my," Hornbeam gasped.

"The roof of the throne room is also made of glass and, since it's at the top of the mountain, it lets in sunlight. At night, as well as having the light from the torches, they switch on hundreds of little magic lights. They're set in the walls all the way up the cavern. See those little round things studding the walls at regular intervals? They use the human magic that we were talking about. I 'borrowed' a few spare ones that were lying about and I use them in my house."

"Very ingenious!" It was not clear here whether Hornbeam was referring to the use of electricity by the imps or whether he was alluding to Cudlip's talent for making good use of anything that was going spare.

Just then Cudlip felt a disturbance as heavy feet began to clatter on the stairs above their heads.

"Sssh!" he murmured and shrank back from the grill pulling Hornbeam away with him.

He backed them both up the ventilation duct to a place where they could talk quietly without being heard.

"Those were the boots of Imperial Guards on the stairs. It's best not to risk being seen by that lot."

"Imperial Guards? They sound as though they might be in charge," Hornbeam commented.

"In a way you're right. They're the creatures of that psychotic wizard and, if anyone can be said to be in charge, it's him."

"Macciovolio?"

"That's him. "Mad, bad and dangerous to know" and, come to think of it, dangerous even if you don't know him."

"What do his guards do down here?" Hornbeam wondered. "Surely the imps will be working hard enough. Their lives depend on it."

"Royal jelly. They'll be checking to see if any has been collected. It's too valuable to go through normal channels. It is taken by them to specially trained imps for processing."

Hornbeam knew all about bees, some of his best friends were bees, and so he knew about the jelly. He knew it was a very special food for bees but he did not know why it was particularly valuable elsewhere. He asked Cudlip if he could explain.

"Not really," he said in reply. "Maybe humans think that it gives them special powers or that it even helps them to live longer. Who knows? What I do know is that this sorry affair is all to do with vanity and greed. Let's go. There's more for you to see."

It was some time later that the two of them trailed back into Cudlip's house. Hornbeam was worn out and visibly shaken by the sights he had seen in the later stages of his tour.

He had seen hundreds of dead bees being shovelled out at the bottom of the hive and thrown into a chute that emptied them onto a giant slag heap of rotting bodies.

He had seen processing rooms full of butterfly and moth bodies where the first of three frightful machines plucked off their glorious wings and stacked them in neat piles.

Then a second machine squashed what was left of the insect to extract any nectar stored in the body or any pollen grains sticking to the outside of it.

Finally, what was left of each carcass was tossed into a vat where a mangling machine mixed them together with coarse brown sugar and shredded them to pulp. The minced up shreds were then squashed together to make cakes of food and these cakes were another source of nourishment for the hungry bees at work in the hive.

Worst of all were the nurseries. Here eggs hatched into caterpillars which were then fattened up on mounds of vegetation that had been dragged into the mountain by agricultural imps.

When the caterpillars changed into pupae they were hung up on hooks, row on row, in a long wooden shed. The temperature was carefully controlled and imps stood by, armed with nets and spray guns. Whenever a butterfly or moth hatched out, and before its wings were dry, it was caught in a net, sedated in exactly the same way as Pim had been, and then sent to the processing room where it was immediately deprived of its wings. These poor new creatures had never flown in a wood or field, never fed on nectar or gathered pollen on their soft furry bodies. What was left of them, after their extremely short lives, was immediately mangled in the vat.

Sylfia was waiting for them and, as soon as they landed at the bottom of the helter-skelter, she ran out of the kitchen to give them her news. She was weeping and wiping her face on a dishcloth.

"Thank goodness you're back! Flum was here. It's bad, really bad! What shall we do? What *can* we do? Everything just gets worse and worse." She buried her face in the dishcloth and sobbed.

"Calm down, Sylfia! What are you saying?" Cudlip asked.

"What is it, my dear? Take your time and explain." Hornbeam guided her gently to a seat and offered her a clean white handkerchief to replace the dishcloth. "Things are never as bad as they seem, you know." He tried to sound as consoling as possible but his hand shook a little for he had seen so many bad things that day and he dreaded to think what this might be.

"But you don't know it all yet," Sylfia continued, between sobs. "Flum said that he saw Tansy being arrested by Pim! Pim, a fairy! Pim a friend! I can't believe it. He and one of the Imperial Guards marched her from the tunnel outside the control room to the guards' headquarters. They all went into a room that had 'The Lord Chamberlain, Macciovolio' written on the door. It's awful! What does it mean, Hornbeam? Why should Pim behave like one of them? I don't understand!"

Hornbeam slumped down beside her. He looked very pale and tired.

He asked her, "Where is Flum now?" His voice was

very quiet but the muscles of his face were clenched betraying the strong emotion that he was feeling.

"He was very keen to get back." Sylfia told him, wringing the hankie into a soggy rope as she spoke.

"I said he should wait for you to return but he said that he had to get back. I begged and begged but he insisted on going. He just waited long enough for me to make up a pack of food and water. He's gone to keep watch."

Here Sylfia's voice cracked and she started to sob.

"And – and – rescue Tansy – or – or – murder Pim – if he gets the chance. I'm so – worried about them – all of them – all three you know." Her voice trailed off and she wept again but softly this time, more to herself.

"Yes, so am I. There's no point in hiding it," Hornbeam whispered. "What I need now is thinking time. Why don't we all have a nice cup of peppermint tea. That's good for shocks. Come on, I'll need your help to make it. Keep busy in a crisis, that's the thing. Let's go with Cudlip to the kitchen. Three heads are even better than two."

They looked at Cudlip who was smiling at them, not in a mocking, insensitive way but with sympathetic curiosity.

"I never say no to a cup of tea and I think I might be able to help you. I think I know what's going on with that young fellow – er – Pim is it? It may be that he's taken some of my advice."

Without a word, Sylfia and Hornbeam followed Cudlip into his kitchen and, while he put the kettle on, they quietly set the table for tea.

Chapter 16

Tansy stood before the wizard, Macciovolio, and felt the force of his evil malevolence.

"Another fairy? What a pleasant surprise. You're just like buses," he hissed sarcastically. "It's becoming quite the thing these days for fairies to visit me. Would I be right in assuming that you followed this other one here?"

"Yes. That's right," Tansy said. She looked at Pim and felt like winking but instead she changed her expression to a puppy dog look of adoration.

"I was in the wood on the night that the gnomes seized him and I just had to follow and see where he was being taken. I love him so much and I can't live without him."

"That's clever," Pim thought to himself. "If only it were true! She's a wonderfully brave and lovely fairy."

"Did you come alone?" Macciovolio asked.

"Yes, all alone." she fibbed.

"Mmmm – that remains to be seen. We have ways of finding out whether intruders are speaking the truth."

The wizard's words sent shivers down Tansy's spine and Pim looked desperate but before either of them could speak, Grim stepped forward and caught his master's attention.

"I don't trust either of 'em, sir. He didn't tell me that he knew her. He said he would escort her here on his own. I bet they were going to leg it. He's only *pretending* to be an imp, I'm sure."

"No, that's not true," Pim butted in. "I'm as committed as any of you but, when I saw her standing there, it was a shock. I didn't expect to bump into a fairy so soon, especially one who knows me so well. I was taken aback and I needed time alone with her. I wanted to persuade her that this is the best way and that she should join us for her own good. I didn't want to be interrupted by a bully like him."

He frowned at Grim and Grim snarled back but ignoring this display of bad feeling Pim turned back to Macciovolio.

"I'll prove myself, sir, just give me time."

This was a good performance from Pim. His best so far, and very convincing, but it was not possible to see whether the wizard believed him or not. Macciovolio was being as inscrutable and cunning as ever. There was no way of really knowing what he believed and he could be playing games for his own amusement. At any time, without warning, an invisible magic axe might fall or a concealed spell might go off like a bomb.

Ignoring Pim for the moment Macciovolio turned to

Tansy and brought his face unnervingly close to hers so that she felt his glittering black-eyed stare almost boring a hole in her forehead. She backed away a little.

He hissed at her, "how did you get in, Miss Lovey Dovey?"

"I danced in," Tansy said defiantly, refusing to be cowed and staring straight back into the wizard's malevolent eyes.

"You danced in? What rubbish is this? Where are the imps who opened the door? Let me see if they agree with that."

Grim cleared his throat.

"Er – you – um – we – I mean – they were exterminated, Your Magnificence, because they said that they couldn't remember anything."

Macciovolio raised his fist to strike Grim but stopped in mid air when he heard Tansy speaking.

"I enchanted them," she said. "They were under my spell. I knocked on the mountain side where it said 'knock here' and when they opened the hatch I danced them into a stupor. While they were in a trance I pulled all the levers and escaped into the corridor before they woke up. That's what happened, truthfully. I wouldn't tell a lie."

Tansy's fingers were firmly crossed behind her back.

"No, sir, she wouldn't lie. She is always very truthful," Pim added.

"Silence, you," he snapped at Pim while continuing to glare at Tansy.

Then the wizard fell silent, thinking.

"A Dancing Enchantress," he mused. "I may have a use for you but while I'm thinking about what to do with you, Miss Dancing Queen, let me invite you to make use of my guest room."

In the blink of an eye his expression changed again and his lips, which had been curled in a false smile, reformed into a sneer of contempt.

"Throw her in!" he ordered, indicating the cell and snapping his fingers at Grim.

Grim grabbed Tansy around the neck and waist and threw her into the same cell that Pim had once occupied.

Macciovolio turned the key in the lock and, for extra security, muttered some magic words under his breath.

He dismissed Pim with a jerk of his thumb but when Grim started to make for the door he found that Macciovolio had barred his way.

"You're looking for some praise, I suppose, you grovelling toady," he hissed.

Grim gulped and shook his head.

"No, sir! Just doing my duty, sir!"

"You may have done well today. I won't deny that, but ......" and here he jerked his thumb in the direction of Pim who was standing by the door, "...... just make sure that this other one lives up to his promise otherwise you'll be back to shovelling bee carcasses before you can say 'impostor'!"

"As for you," he added, turning to Pim. "That one in the cage is no longer your friend. Got that? You're my creature now and that means that you must be her enemy. Is that perfectly clear?"

Pim stared straight ahead, blinked and nodded. He dared not look at Tansy.

"Now, get out of my sight, both of you!"

The wizard strode to the door, threw it open and pushed them out. When they had both passed through he slammed it hard behind them so hard that the frame shook and the brass fittings jangled.

There were many ways out of Cudlip's house because it was not like a normal house, or at least a normal house that you would find above ground. Above ground most houses have a front door and a back door and that's about it. Some houses might have side doors or patio doors and lots of houses have garage doors but you usually only need the fingers on one hand to count the ways in or out.

Cudlip's house, however, was more like a rabbit warren or a badger set with many ways in. Not any of his doors were visible to a passer by, as the three friends had discovered when they first arrived outside his home. As well as special additions such as helter-skelters or slippery slides to get in, he had installed spiral staircases and one-way revolving doors to get out.

Flum thought he had found the same door as when he left Sylfia the first time and when he stepped through it he thought he was in the same tunnel as before. He was still very upset and angry and, in his haste to get back to Tansy, he had forgotten that one tunnel under the earth is very like another especially if it has been constructed by the same group of builders or engineers. Cudlip's people had discovered the best materials to use under this mountain and the best size and shape for their tunnels with the result that they all looked identical.

Believing that he was starting from the same point as the first time, Flum used his map again in exactly the same way as before. He found that he was rising higher in the mountain just as he had before. He found that the tunnels became smoother and more lived in, as before. He began to come across doors to rooms and inside the rooms there were imps going about their business, as before. Everything convinced him that he was making the same journey as before. Unfortunately he was not travelling east, as before, but he was moving in a westerly direction.

Flum began to wonder why his journey was taking so much longer this time.

It could be that he was flying more slowly but, on the other hand, it was not safe to travel very fast. He still needed to be very careful. He had to be ready to dodge into the shadows if he saw imps ahead. Sometimes he had to camouflage himself to blend in with the rock wall until they had gone past. At other times he would hide behind an open door, or squeeze into some other dark space, until they had turned off the corridor and disappeared into one of the many rooms.

As time passed he became more anxious. He stopped to examine his surroundings in detail. It was then he noticed that the paintings on the walls were different. There were no depictions of war here. There were no paintings of mad magicians with staring eyes who rode fire breathing dragons and caused lightning to spring out of black clouds in a blood-red sky in order to strike down hundreds of terrified foes. Here there were no muddy fields full of open mouthed victims grimacing and gasping for their last breath as the Imperial Guard charge down on them, their eyes just visible as glittering specks of malice through the slits in their helmets.

In these corridors Flum found himself looking at scenes of rural bliss. He adjusted his glasses on his nose and stopped to stare.

There were pictures of sun kissed meadows with bees collecting pollen from a myriad of brilliantly coloured flowers. Others showed rolling hills where delicately patterned butterflies flitted over blossom laden purple heather. Other butterflies swayed on golden gorse, sucking nectar, as the stems seemed to wave gently in the summer breeze. The pictures showed bright blue sky which was flecked with cotton wool clouds and even the floor beneath Flum's feet felt different. It was soft and spongy and felt warm to the touch, so different from the cold hard flagstones that he was expecting.

It smelt different, too. The air around Macciovolio's headquarters did not smell sweet and welcoming like it did here. The wizard and his followers exuded pungent, acrid, sulphurous odours that warned of death and inspired only fear and despair.

Flum was interested to know where he was but, at the same time, because he was lost he knew that he should go back to the beginning. Indeed, he was just about to do so when he was stopped in his tracks. The most amazing odours came drifting down the passageway. They steamed up his glasses, assailed his nostrils and very quickly wrapped his brain in a warm fuzz of sheer delight.

He began to tremble in anticipation of deliciously succulent food. He had not realised just how hungry he was feeling. He would have walked through fire or flood to get to the source of this olfactory delight. He felt that his whole life had been lived up to this moment so that he could experience the taste of whatever was producing that seductive mixture of smells.

Then a sweet, grandmotherly voice called out gently.

"Come in, my dear and see what I have been making, especially for you!"

Flum thought how strange it was that she knew he was coming. All that delicious food would have taken hours to prepare and it would be very rude to walk away now.

"I wonder where she is," he murmured to himself.

As he said those words a door swung open at the end

of the corridor and light spilled out showing him the way. The light gave a soft rosy glow that stretched towards him through the otherwise dimly lit corridor.

He was drawn towards it like a moth to a flame and he could not, for the life of him, have resisted.

He felt as though he was going home and would find a place where all his appetites would be satisfied. He would be able to curl up, safe and warm, without a care in the world and all of his problems would be solved. There would be no need to worry any more about the treacherous Pim, the danger that Tansy was in or what the weird, evil wizard had in store for them all. Here there would be someone to care for him, just as his own dear mother would have done at home.

As if in a dream he trod the comfy floor up to the open door, swallowing hard to empty his drooling mouth of the saliva that filled it to overflowing, and looked inside.

The room was like the kitchen of a Victorian mansion. In the middle there was a huge deal table, scrubbed to make it squeaky clean. The table was loaded with all types of delicious food. There were cakes and pies, both sweet and savoury. There was steaming gravy lathered over sweet and tender cuts of meat that had been roasted to perfection and draped with aromatic herbs. There was steaming hot Yorkshire pudding, crispy potatoes and every sort of firm, fresh vegetable, steamed or roasted. There was a jug of hot vanilla custard and a bowl of strawberry jelly. There was jam roly-poly pudding, treacle tart and chocolate sponge. There was ice cream, in all flavours, not just vanilla, strawberry and chocolate but other, more unusual, varieties like butter fudge and chocolate nut parfait.

Behind the table was a fat, elderly lady with a jolly face. She had twinkling blue eyes, which, at first, resembled Flum's own eyes. Her hair was frizzy and grey and had hairpins sticking out of it at all angles in an attempt to keep the hairdo tightly in place. The hairpins were not really a great success because many curls and wispy ends had escaped to give her coiffure a wild and unkempt look. She was dressed in a pink and white striped gown which had a voluminous skirt and was covered at the front by a large apron of starched and gleaming white cotton.

"Ah, there you are," she said. "Come in, dear boy, and refresh yourself. Look at what I've made for you. It's all for you, you know, dearest boy. You've had such a hard time lately, haven't you? You poor thing, but all will be better now. Tuck in, eat up and leave nothing untouched. There's more if you want it. It's no bother."

"It all looks shcrumptious and mells sabsolutely wonderful," Flum slurred dreamily. He had truly never seen such an excellent array of food in all his life.

"Ah well, you see my darling," the smiling cook told him. "This is not just *food*, this is *Magic Super Food*!"

Flum's mouth rounded into an O shape as he slowly walked towards the table in a trance and gazed into the face of his benefactress. He noticed that her eyes were not just sparkling blue but now they were twinkling with many other colours. Each of her orbs was a kaleidoscope of jewelled patterns that were forever shifting and changing. In fascinated delight he moved closer and gasped with wonder at the beauty that was drawing him in. Looking into her eyes was like watching a tiny version of a spectacular firework show in the night sky.

When he tasted the food he found that it was overwhelmingly delicious and he closed his eyes to savour many of the mouthfuls more intensely, grinning from ear to ear with sheer delight. He flitted from one plate or bowl to the next, savouring each course and deciding that each spoonful was even more delicious than the one before.

The more he ate the wider the smile on the motherly face grew. She began to chuckle and the wide expanse of her crisp apron began to shake as she broke into a great belly laugh. The more pleasure she took in Flum's enjoyment the more he wanted to lick, munch, swallow and cram each superbly tasty morsel into his mouth while looking towards the cook to gauge her reaction. As her amusement grew so did his pleasure in the food.

His open mouth now stretched from ear to ear and he shovelled more and more food into it, partly to gratify his own enormous appetite and partly to provoke more pleasure in his hostess. Now he joined in the laughter and much of the food escaped from the sides of his mouth and dribbled down his chin.

He could not tell how much he ate or for how long he gorged but there came a point when he collapsed onto the floor and gave himself up to hysterical laughter.

He rolled around clutching his fat belly, dribbling, belching, farting, hiccupping and putting himself in serious danger of choking.

At last, completely exhausted, he lay still and at first his face wore a comical grin but then this goofy expression was replaced by an amiable dreamy stare. Then fatigue overcame his limbs, his eyes grew heavy and he knew that he was falling into a deep and blissful sleep. He was vaguely aware of being picked up by soft podgy arms and clasped firmly to an expansive comforting bosom.

He felt himself being rocked gently in the chubby arms of his motherly benefactress and she was crooning a lullaby. As she sang she carried him across the room and lowered him gently into a large and extremely comfortable bed. The snowy white sheets were silky smooth and they smelt of the fresh wild flowers that grow on the moor. The coverlet that she drew over him was as soft as thistle down and, as he snuggled into it, he felt that he was sinking slowly and gently down, down, down and there was no end to his falling.

Before long he was fast asleep and dreaming of the delights of spring in Dingle Dell. He smelt the scent of apple and cherry blossom and heard the throbbing sound of millions of industrious bees buzzing from bloom to bloom. He heard the birds trilling their ancient songs as if to stir the trees out of winter slumber and into a full canopy of glorious green.

He saw the leaves unfurling and lifting themselves up to be kissed by the sun once again; rustling and bustling for space and air; fluttering like green flags; resuming the magic of photosynthesis in the spring sunshine and like little factories opening up after the winter break, with no disputes or strikes to stop them, they began to wind up life's miracle to full throttle again. The dormant life that had survived the winter chill began to throb anew and pulse with fresh new vigour.

Flum dreamt that he was back at home surrounded by friends and family and all of them were just as safe and happy as before.

Chapter 17

"So, you think Pim is only pretending to become an imp," Sylfia said, looking at Cudlip with hope in her eyes. "It really is comforting to believe that. I only wish Flum had stopped long enough to hear you say it."

"We'll find him and put him straight, don't you worry," Cudlip reassured her. "Now, what else have we got to do?"

He rose from the table to rummage in a drawer and from it he pulled out a pad of paper and a pencil. Sitting down again, he licked the end of the pencil, shrugged out his elbows and prepared to scribble. He looked from one anxious face to the other and said cheerily, "I always think it's good to have a list."

Hornbeam marvelled at his coolness. Sylfia bit her lip and then burst out crossly.

"You make us sound like humans just popping down the shops on a Saturday morning. How can you be so insensitive? These are our friends in peril, not a pound of apples and a packet of cornflakes!" An angry flush suffused her cheeks.

"That's much better!" Cudlip beamed at her across the table. "Fire and spirit! That's what we need, not sobs and tears!"

Sylfia glared at him for a few seconds and then relaxed back into her chair.

"You're right, of course. It's time to be brave. Carry on, please, I'm listening."

She looked over at Hornbeam. He nodded in agreement and smiled his encouragement.

"I understand you both," the old elf told them. "I don't blame you for your tears Sylfia. You wouldn't be the fairy you are without them but Cudlip is right. We have to show even more courage now. Our friends are in great trouble and they need our help, not our pity."

"Right then," said the ever practical Cudlip. "What'll we have for number one?"

"Rescue Tansy, of course," Sylfia said. "And at the same time release Pim from his whatever it is – enforced apprenticeship?"

"Got that," Cudlip said as he scribbled a couple of lines. "Obviously those items of the plan will need a bit of fleshing out later. What do you say, Hornbeam?"

Hornbeam was hesitant. He looked from one to the other unsure of how his point would be received.

"Don't get me wrong ……" he started and then stopped to clear his throat. "I agree, in principle, that freeing Tansy and Pim should have top priority but I think there is something else that we should do first. We *must* set the bees free."

"Good, good," Cudlip said, scribbling away.

"Why is that so important now, rather than later when we have everyone together again," Sylfia asked him.

"Because the bees are being farmed for their products and without them the enterprise will be worthless. When the bees have gone the imps will have no business here."

"They might just start again," Cudlip remarked.

"Which brings me to number three," Hornbeam continued.

"Oh yes, and that is?" Cudlip's pencil was poised over the paper.

"Scare the imps away in such a way that they'll never return. At the same time destroy that wizard – he is the overlord who controls everything, I'm sure of that. We have to eliminate him so that his power over the imps is annihilated!"

"Phew!" was the only sound that whistled from Cudlip's lips. His pencil remained motionless as he took in the enormity of their task.

"Yes, I see," Sylfia murmured. "Otherwise he will just persuade more gnomes to collect more bees and force the imps to start up again and –" she hesitated this time, "– and he will take his revenge on us. I mean *all* of us ......" Her voice trailed away and she shivered.

"Don't dwell on that, Sylfia. I've got enough ancient elf magic to deal with a wizard like him. The only trouble is,

before I can use it, I must make sure that both he
and I are outside the mountain. I must fight him in the
open air, not underground. The magical fallout from his
venomous spells combined with the ancient incantations
of generations of elves cannot be confined underground.
It would blow the mountain apart and all of us with it.
Anyway, Cudlip needs to have his mountain home
cleared of uninvited guests, not demolished."

"That's for sure," the boggle agreed. "But how do we
go about freeing the bees?"

"I know how to do it," Hornbeam said.

"You do?" Cudlip looked up from his list in surprise.

"Tell us!" Sylfia cried.

"We'll build a rocket," Hornbeam told them, as calmly
as the coolest cucumber.

"It'll have a long fuse and a charge of black powder.
We'll take it into the hive, stand it on a platform near the
top and we'll send the bees down to the bottom where
they'll be safe. The fuse will be so long that it'll stretch
outside the hive and allow us to get far enough away
from the blast. A ventilation duct, like the one Cudlip
and I hid in earlier today, will make excellent cover.
You'll have to give me time to leave the mountain and
take up a position near the summit, hidden behind some
boulders or somethinng. When I'm in position one of you
will light the fuse to set off the rocket and it will blast
a hole through the floor of the throne room which, as
Cudlip showed me, is made of glass. Then the rocket
will continue on its flight upwards until it crashes out

through the glass roof at the top of the mountain. Where it will land no one can say but we won't need it anymore so it doesn't matter. The bees will follow the rocket as soon as the smoke clears. They will soar upwards in a magnificent swirling swarm." Hornbeam paused to savour the triumphant image.

"The imps will be thrown into chaos," he continued. "They'll flee the mountain in panic. I'll be waiting for the wizard to emerge and I'll challenge him. We'll do battle for many hours, perhaps days, but I'll win of course."

There was silence when he had finished speaking.

When an amazingly dangerous and death-defying plan is revealed for the first time it must often be met by complete and utter silence.

This may well have been the case when Hannibal revealed his plan to cross the Alps in the middle of winter. That first bit might have won him a round of lukewarm applause but, when he added something that sounded like, "Oh, and did I mention the elephants?" we can imagine a chilling interval of quietude. This must surely have been one of the biggest 'Did I just hear a pin drop?' moments of all time.

So it was that, when Hornbeam had finished the description of this plan and was sitting before them with shining eyes and a complacent smile on his old nut-brown face, the other two had nothing to say for a significant period of time.

Sylfia's mouth had dropped open and, although she tried several times to frame her tongue and teeth into the correct positions to produce coherent sounds, absolutely nothing came out.

Cudlip rolled his eyes to the ceiling and covered his face with his hands. Following that, he fell forwards so that his forehead rested on the table in front of him and his hands covered his ears. He looked as though he might be waiting for the explosion.

At last, the silence was broken by the old elf himself.

"Are there any questions?" he said.

"Plenty!" Cudlip wailed, raising his head from the table and gazing at Hornbeam with a mixture of pity and disbelief. "Just give me enough time to think of them all!"

"Well, while you're thinking I might as well put the kettle on again. Who else wants another cup of tea?" Hornbeam stood up and walked towards the hob.

"Question one," Cudlip said, turning to a new page to begin another list. "What about the other three fairies? Even if we manage to pull this off how can we be sure that they're going to be safe?"

"We'll make sure that they are nowhere near," Hornbeam replied. "Sugar anyone?"

The other two shook their heads.

"Question two," Cudlip went on "Have you ever made a rocket?"

"Well no, but I know how it's done," Hornbeam said, as he returned to the table and resumed his seat.

"That's not the same as actually making one."

"No, but it can't be that difficult. All you need is a tube with a cone on the top, some fins to give it stability and a generous helping of black powder."

"Black powder? What's that?"

"Er – I believe that humans call it gunpowder."

"Oh, that. But if it's so easy why do humans say, 'It's not rocket science,' when they want others to believe that something is not difficult? That would suggest that rocket science *is* difficult."

"Is that question three?"

"Er – yes – I suppose it is." Cudlip wrote it down hurriedly and then looked up to hear the answer.

"Or it could be four and 'What is black powder?' could be three," Hornbeam observed.

"Three? Four? Who cares?" Cudlip exclaimed, throwing down his pencil. "And don't say that's five, six and seven. Just explain the rocket thing, if you can."

"Human's are confusing," Hornbeam reminded him. "They see simple rockets flying about when they have firework displays so they should know it's not complicated. It's not the same as flying to the moon. Now that *is* complicated. You need more than a tube with a cone and a charge of black powder for that. You need other special materials and mathematics and rocket fuel and teamwork and courage and self belief and ……" his voice faded away.

"It could easily go wrong." Sylfia had found enough of her voice to make this statement in a croaky sort of way.

"Not if we're careful," Hornbeam assured her. "I hereby swear to observe all health and safety regulations, wear my goggles and not play with matches!"

Hornbeam smiled a little smile, hoping that they would smile too. They did not.

"Moving on to my next query," Cudlip continued, swallowing hard. He had abandoned his list but his head was still full of questions. "Where will you get black powder from? I haven't seen any under the mountain and I've visited all of their stores."

"Ah, yes. Well now," Hornbeam went on. "I did anticipate the possibility of having to take forceful measures to liberate the captured insects and so I packed some of the ingredients for making the explosive mixture. In the wagon we have two bags of charcoal and one bag of brimstone. All I need now is one bag of guano."

"And what is guano when it's packed in a box and tied with a ribbon?" Cudlip sighed.

Hornbeam answered, "Bat droppings."

Sylfia shuddered at the mention of bats.

"What a delightful ingredient! Unfortunately, when I last checked my pantry I found that I was all out of bat pooh!" Cudlip roared.

He was beginning to get a little bit excited. Hornbeam's knowledge of explosives was a revelation. The first glimmer of hope that this daring plan might work was sparking up in his brain.

"But, you're in luck, Hornbeam, there are plenty of bat caves in this mountain." He spoke seriously now.

"I expected that," Hornbeam nodded. "I'll collect it because Sylfia's nervous around flittermice. She had a nasty experience. I'd like you two to check on Tansy and, at the same time, find Flum. They should both know what we're doing and what we think about Pim. It would be better if Pim doesn't know anything, though. The less he has to hide from the wizard the better. It must be very difficult to keep up the pretence."

"I don't mind collecting bat droppings, Hornbeam," Sylfia interjected. "The bat that I collided with didn't mean any harm. I wasn't used to the terrain and we just bumped into each other. Anyway, if each of us three is given a separate job the plan might come together sooner."

"That's true, Sylfia. In that case I could start on the rocket straight away. Have you got a room that I can turn into a laboratory, Cudlip? I don't want to make a mess of your beautiful kitchen."

"I have the very place, Hornbeam. When my people left I had plenty of space and time on my hands. There were also a load of useful bits and pieces lying about and since they weren't needed anymore I decided to take up some hobbies. Help yourself to whatever tools and materials that you need. It's all through here."

Cudlip took his guests out of the kitchen and down a short corridor. At the end of this there was an up-and-over garage door. This door was made of aluminium and painted with bright canary-yellow paint. The boggle yanked the door open to reveal a very untidy workshop. The contrast between this and the clinically clean and well ordered kitchen was astounding. There was every type of tool scattered about. Some of them were rather rusty and none of them was in the right place. There were shelves along the walls and rows of hooks had been screwed into the edges of the shelves. Labels had been stuck beside all of the hooks and also along the walls above the shelves. Anyone who cared to read the labels would see that they told you where every item should have been stored but the labels had been quite obviously ignored.

On a large workbench running the length of the room there were pots of paint, cans of oil, tubs of grease and filthy rags. There were glass jars in which screws, nails, bolts, keys and many other small metallic objects were all jumbled up together. On the floor underneath the workbench were boxes in which spanners were mixed up with screwdrivers, G-clamps were tangled up with wrenches and, sticking out at rakish angles like flowers in a pot, were rulers, hammers, spirit levels and other lengthy items. Large wooden boards, sheets of corrugated metal, panes of glass and planks of wood leant against the walls in a higgledy-piggledy jumble. Jagged off-cuts of every possible material known to boggle, elf, fairy or human littered the floor and mixed with oil spills to create a hazardous mess.

It was every handyperson's nightmare but Hornbeam beamed with pleasure and, when he caught site of a blowtorch and a cylinder of gas, he rubbed his hands together with sheer delight.

"This will do very nicely," he chuckled.

Chapter 18

Doris and Burt were bored. It was ages since they had had any decent entertainment.

Burt had tried visiting the outside of the hive to bully the overworked imps as they scurried up and down the stairs. He had held out a great big stopwatch and fooled them into thinking that they were not collecting the goods fast enough.

Then he'd been to the dining room and spent an idle thirty minutes flicking ink balls at the clean white aprons of the waiters as they were setting the table for Their Majesties' dinner.

Now he mooched into the throne room and demanded to know where his wife had gone. An Imperial Guard told him that The Impress had dressed up as Calamity Jane and was out on the mountain side singing "The Deadwood Stage" whilst firing bullets at the crows.

"Her Excellent Regalness has been out there for some time," he was told. "She has managed to put a hole through an old boot and shoot the helmet off one of the guards who was coming back from border patrol."

"But no crows?" Burt asked.

"No crows, your Imperial Supremacy."

"She'll be in a bit of a mood, then," Burt muttered gloomily and proceeded to throw himself onto his throne. He slouched over to the side supported his elbow on the upholstered arm and rested his head in his hand.

"What we need is some *real* fun!" he groaned.

There was a clatter of metal as the guards stood to attention and Macciovolio swept into the room.

"Fun, your Imperial Supremacy, is what I bring!" Macciovolio declared. "You, guard! Go and fetch the Impress. She's going to love this."

"What ya got this time, Mac?" Burt asked, without much enthusiasm. He did not sit up to address his Lord Chamberlain, nor did he sound very excited for experience told him that he should not hold out much hope of being entertained by 'Macciovolio the Merry' as he and his wife sarcastically called him.

Macciovolio clicked his fingers and two more guards entered. Between them they carried a cylindrical cage and inside the cage was Tansy.

"Oh no! Not another fairy, Mac. What happened to the other one, by the way? I thought you were doing something with him."

"I certainly am, sire," Macciovolio replied, some-what peeved. "Here he comes now."

The Chamberlain beckoned in the direction of the

open door and Pim strode into the room. He was very pale now, like an imp, and his dark eyes had lost their lustre but some subtle make-up had been applied to his face making him look extremely handsome, for an imp. As the new prince walked slowly and gracefully towards the throne, Burt saw that his tall figure was clad from head to foot in magnificent clothes and his bearing was just as aristocratic as it had been on their first meeting.

"Blimey, what a toff!" The Imperor gave a whistle of appreciation and sat up. "Wait 'til Doris sees this!"

Pim stopped a few feet from Burt and, removing his fine hat which was adorned with a snow-white and very tremulous plume, he performed a deep and gracious bow.

The wizard looked almost gleeful.

"Your majesty, I give you His Highness Prince Pompous Pernickety. He who was a posh and snobby fairy is now a top class imp!"

Just then a gun went off in the corridor making everyone jump and the voice of the Impress was heard cajoling the officer who had gone to fetch her.

"Oops, there goes another helmet. What's that ya say? An ear as well? Oh well, never mind, you've got another one."

Doris bustled into the room sporting some cowgirl gear and holding two revolvers, one in each hand. She blew on the smoking end of one of her guns.

"Sometimes these things go off without consulting me. Worra cheek!" she complained, looking at the firearms as if they were children who had got up to some harmless piece of mischief.

"You there! You with the drip on the end of your nose take your friend to Slimy the Shoemaker and get his ear stitched back on."

The footman with the runny nose scuttled out of the room to attend to the guard who was squirming in the corridor.

"So, what's going on, Mac?"

She advanced across the room, swaggering as cowboys are supposed to do in Wild West films, but when she caught sight of Pim she gave a little squeal of delight and scampered like a young girl for the rest of the way.

"Oh, isn't he lovely. You've done a good job, Mac. I could kiss and cuddle and eat him all up!"

"Steady on, Dor!" Her husband sprang off his throne and jumped down to stand between his wife and Pim. "I might get jealous. I might have to chop his posh little head off."

"Course you won't. You can have such good fun with him, too. We can make such fun of him! That'll teach his family to be so high and mighty!"

"That's true, I suppose," her husband concurred. "Hey! We could send some pictures back to the fairy palace and demand a ransom. They won't pay it, of course, but they'll be mighty cross. They'll be fuming and snorting for days. I like it. It's my best plan so far."

Burt rubbed his grubby palms together and sneered into Pim's expressionless face. He became impatient when Prince Pernickety did not react.

"What d'ya think of that, ya pompous popinjay."

Pim stared back at him and swallowed hard.

"You are very inventive, Your Supreme Imperialness. One cannot help but be impressed by your unusual ideas," he managed to hiss through clenched teeth.

Burt was completely taken in and took this as a form of extreme flattery.

"Mac! Ya've done a good job so far. He's coming on nicely." Turning to his wife he said, "Now what d'ya make of Mac's other little gift?"

Without removing her eyes from Pim, Doris allowed her husband to take her by the elbow and steer her towards the cage. It was only when they had got very close to it that she was forced to stop looking at the new prince in all his glory. Her husband turned her to look at Macciovolio's prisoner. Tansy was sitting on the bottom of the cage, her legs straight out in front of her, her arms crossed and a deep frown on her face.

"Not another bloomin' fairy! Mac, I think ya must have got some sort of obsession like that Professor Higgins in 'My Fair Lady'! What'll ya turn this one into? She doesn't look very promising. A bit sulky, if ya ask me."

"There is no need to turn her into anything, Impress, because she is already very entertaining and, by her own admission, she is an enchantress."

"Enchantress? In a cage? I don't believe it. You can't keep one of those in a cage. You're mad. Isn't he, Burt? No one keeps an enchantress in a cage. It's no wonder she looks cross, Mac."

Doris was rather alarmed. There was room for only one enchantress around here, she thought. They already had The Sorceress and that was quite enough.

"You'd better take her outside and let her go before our own Mistress gets to hear of it," she told the magician, "or, before she starts some magic of her own. There could be all kinds of trouble, mate."

"She's not a *great* sorceress like our own Mistress," Macciovolio snapped impatiently. He wanted to add "you fool" but held his tongue.

"She's only got one type of special magic and, anyway, she's in an iron cage and that renders her powerless."

"What if you let her out?" Burt asked.

"Well, you see, she and I have come to a very special agreement," the wizard told him, looking smug.

"What sort of agreement?" Burt asked, suspiciously.

"This beauty, my lord, is a Dancing Fairy. She's one of the very best. She has agreed to amuse you by displaying her skills and, if you wish, she will teach you to dance."

"Oo! Lovely," Doris exclaimed. "I've always wanted to dance, just like Ginger Rogers!"

"How d'you know that we're going to be safe when she's let out of the cage?" Burt asked suspiciously, still pursuing his line if inquiry.

He needed to be convinced that he was not going to be carried off to fairyland where some seriously magical punishment would be exacted on his person as revenge for his miserable treachery.

"Worry not, Your Imperialness. I have told her that,

with her great talent, and my power she will become the most famous dancer in the universe. She will be adored by all. She will be loaded with riches and I will introduce her to The Sorceress herself. Under the patronage of our glorious Mistress, this talented fairy will gain limitless power and influence. No creature will be able to resist her charms and her performances will become the stuff of legends."

Macciovolio looked from one royal imp to the other and saw that they were caught in his web of words.

"Just think. You two will be able to say that you were the ones to discover her. You'll become famous, too, and The Sorceress is bound to reward you. We will all become more powerful, just you wait and see. I'm sure of it."

He could see that Doris was already dreaming her own day dream and was revelling in the possibilities of life as a celebrity. Burt, however, was a little more cautious.

"She doesn't look very happy at the prospect," he observed.

"Oh, that's because she hates the cage and is stiff from lack of exercise," Macciovolio assured them. "You can't keep such a great artist locked up for long before they become tetchy. When she is unable to practise her art she becomes depressed. Don't expect her to look happy until she is dancing."

He kicked the cage. "Tell them how excited you feel, Miss Dancing Butterfly Fairy. Your future is golden is it not?"

"If you say so," Tansy mumbled. "Just let me get this

hideous audition over with," she added, more to herself than to those who were peering at her through the bars of the cage.

The truth of the matter was that, if she did not perform for the Imperial Imps, Macciovolio was going to slice off Pim's head. That was the real deal that had been struck and much as she raged against it, Tansy was not in a position to refuse.

Macciovolio's real plan was to see just how good a dancer this fairy enchantress could be and she would not dare to try anything if her "beloved" was under sentence of death. Macciovolio had realised that, even if she had lied about loving the pompous prince, she was not the type to stand by and let anyone to be killed if she had the power to prevent it. Even an evil magician can recognise a noble soul when he bumps into one.

There was one thing that he had not told Tansy and it was that if she really was an exceptional performer and could cast spells by dancing her audience into a stupor, he was going to turn her over to the Sorceress alive, to be her slave.

"O.K." Burt said. "Let's see what she can do, but stand by, Doris, in case she tries any funny business."

The Imperor retreated to the other side of the room and placed himself between two of the Imperial Guards who were standing to attention on either side of the double doors.

Tansy was released from the cage and shook herself. She did some bending and stretching exercises to relieve the stiffness and then she began to dance, slowly at first, circling the glass floor. She looked downwards and was shocked to see the enormous hive beneath her feet and the shapes of innumerable bees within the dimly lit interior. She thought that she could also see other strange creatures moving about and they appeared to be robbing the bees of their honey and wax.

Macciovolio snapped his fingers and she looked up to see his hypnotic eyes glaring at her. He pointed at her and banged his staff down on the floor.

Tansy brought her mind back to the task and began to engage in some intricate steps, performing them with great delicacy. The music was inside her head and she gave herself up to its rhythms and melody. She began to weave through the air, whirling and twirling, faster and faster, rising up to the glass ceiling and swooping down to skim over the glass floor. All the time her delicate body made subtle shapes in the air and a glittering trail of twinkling lights followed her.

Macciovolio was extremely pleased with her performance. He was not entranced, of course, because he was too strong a wizard for that but he was certainly enraptured.

Tansy gave herself up to her art, her troubles fell away and nothing else mattered for the duration of the dance. Macciovolio saw that she was no longer sulky and defiant but very beautiful and utterly charming and he was surprised to find himself strangely affected by her. He had to admit to being almost spellbound and he glowed with pride to think that the Sorceress would be impressed too.

The Imperial Duo were spellbound also and gasped with delight at Tansy's beautiful performance they began to dance together, hesitantly at first, but with growing confidence until they covered the floor with great thumping strides.

"Wantwits! Nincompoops!" thought Macciovolio. "How dare they interrupt my exquisitely talented creature's performance!" He scowled at them and tapped his staff on the floor to signal his impatience.

To his even greater annoyance, Tansy grabbed Pim and began to dance him around the floor but before the wizard could break them apart Doris did it for him.

"Teach us, teach us!" she cried. "Teach us some proper steps!"

So Tansy had to take hold of Burt and show him very slowly and deliberately how to do a fairy waltz.

Doris watched very carefully and then, squealing with delight, she enveloped Pim in a smothering embrace and stomped about the room in a poor imitation of Tansy.

"Music! We must have music!" she declared and raced out of the door, along the corridor and into her boudoir. Within seconds she was back with an LP record of the soundtrack to 'The King and I'. A domestic worker imp staggered behind her under the weight of an old wind-up gramophone.

"Wind it up!" she ordered. "Be quick about it, numbskull! Hurry"

The poor domestic was all fingers and thumbs but

somehow he managed to get the old machine working and the sound of 'Will You Dance?' blared out.

Taking giant strides, just like the King of Siam had done in the film, she set off at a gallop around the room.

Pim found it very difficult to partner her because she became more and more enthusiastic and her changes of direction became even more erratic. He was greatly relieved when Burt lifted the needle from the record and the music came to an end.

"Put him down, Doris," he said, peevishly. "Ya're not dancing. Ya're making a fool of yerself!"

"You're the fool!" she retorted. "You're a silly old jealous fool and you can't stand to see me enjoying myself!"

So the royal pair fell to bickering more and more ferociously and they became so engrossed in their arguing that they did not notice how Macciovolio grabbed Tansy and threw her back into the cage. The wizard then signalled to two of his Imperial Guards to take her away. Nor did the royal couple notice that the wizard took Pim firmly by the arm and marched him out of the room in the opposite direction.

Not even the wizard noticed the shadowy figure that lurked in a dark corner behind one of the thrones.

Cudlip had seen everything. He had been thrilled by Tansy's dancing, impressed by her beauty and star-struck by her awesome talent. He had also chuckled at the pantomime performance of Burt and Doris as they blundered about in their inept version of a dance. In spite of all that, he could not fail to be chilled by the wild-eyed wizard and his shabby treatment of both Tansy and Pim. He found that most upsetting.

At least he had found two of the fairies that he was looking for and he could tell Hornbeam that they were still alive. Unfortunately he would have to report that they were both, and Tansy especially, being treated very badly.

Pim looked more like an imp with each passing hour and that was a worry because at some point pretence could turn into reality.

As for Flum, he could not find him anywhere. He would have to organise a much wider search because, if he could not be found in this part of the mountain, it probably meant that he had gone off in the wrong direction and was well and truly lost.

Chapter 19

Sylfia picked her way through the bat cave. It was wide and high and very, very dark. There were hundreds of bats roosting above her head. They covered the ceiling and lined the walls, hanging side by side like furry brown sardines. They chattered in their ultrasonic language and Sylfia knew that they must be talking about her. She thought they must be wondering what she was doing there and every now and again one would break away from its huddle and flutter across the cave, swooping close to her head, but never colliding with her. The first time this had happened Sylfia nearly jumped out of her skin but she knew that these creatures meant her no harm and their radar guidance system would not allow a collision, even in the deepest, darkest cave.

All the same, she was glad that, outside on the mountain, dusk would not come for many hours. She would not like to be here when the whole colony, moving as one huge clattering mass, would fly out for the hunt.

Cudlip had brought her here after breakfast, along a narrow tunnel which had opened out into this very deep cave containing one of the largest bat roosts on this side of the mountain. Far away in the distance Sylfia could see the opening that gave onto the mountainside and a shaft of sunlight was there, slicing in through the darkness. Before starting work she had flown down to the cave entrance and peered out, standing as if in a trance, breathing fresh air and feeling the spring sunshine warm on her face.

Before breakfast she and Hornbeam had rummaged in Cudlip's workshop until they found a sack without holes, a ball of string and a small shovel shaped like a trowel. Hornbeam had estimated that the sack would hold enough guano to mix with the other ingredients of black powder that he had brought with them in the wagon.

Her job was to shovel bat droppings into the sack until it was full. Then she had to carry the bag back into the tunnel and wait there for Cudlip to return and guide her home again.

He had left her here so that he could go looking for the other three fairies. She tried not to think what the news might be when he returned.

"At least he might bring Flum back with him," was one of her more comforting thoughts. "That would be something to cheer us up and we could persuade him to look more kindly on Pim."

To keep up her spirits she hummed a little tune as she worked. Her fairy glow showed her where to find the best heaps of dung and the sack filled up quite quickly.

Sylfia estimated that it was nearly lunchtime when her bag was full. Taking the string from her pocket, she tied the top securely and dragged her precious cargo back to the tunnel entrance. She carried it some way along the passage but when there was no sign of Cudlip she sat down to wait.

It was not long before she heard a noise coming from further along the tunnel.

"That's good timing, Cudlip. I just finished a few minutes ago," she called into the darkness. "I've got a nice big bag of top quality bat droppings. Just what Hornbeam ordered."

There was silence.

"Cudlip? Here I am just where you left me," she called again.

Still there was no answer.

"I must have imagined that noise," she said to herself, without conviction. The truth was that she no longer felt completely alone.

She stood up, shivering, and peered into the darkness. An icy cold wind blew into her face and it became difficult for her to breathe. She heard the rustle of a satin cloak and the smell of the sea filled her nostrils, reminding her of home. A spinning disc of blinding white light whirled before her eyes and, just when she thought that her eyes were going to burn away, the light fragmented into a phantasmagoria of brilliantly coloured fragments. Every colour that you can imagine, and many more besides, popped and darted, exploded and spluttered in a twinkling display. Then, instead of fading away as a firework display will do, the colours began to swirl around like a giant Catherine Wheel and when this whirling slowed down they began to fuse together and turn into a translucent golden ball. The ball stopped spinning but kept on shimmering as it bobbed up and down in the air just an arm's length above Sylfia's head.

She reached up to touch the gorgeous sphere but it bobbed out of her reach. As she gazed deep into its interior, she saw an image that made her simultaneously gasp with delight and sob with relief. She saw that the ball was really a floating bubble, and inside, bathed in the shimmering golden light, was the beautiful face of her mother.

As she gazed in speechless wonder at this unexpected vision it spoke to her in a tinkling, far away fairy voice.

"Dearest daughter, there you are. I've been looking for you everywhere. What a terrible time you're having. I've come to take you home, my darling, back to the high cliffs where the gulls hang in the salty air and dive like arrows down into the glittering ocean. Come sit with me among the purple thrift and breathe the healing ozone. Throw your cares into the salty breeze. Watch all your troubles blow away over the vast and restless ocean. My poor girl, come back to the place where you belong and your fairy people will sing you to sleep in a warm and loving embrace."

"Oh, yes please, mother, I've missed you so much. Take me home." Sylfia lifted her face to be kissed and her eyelids closed as she drifted into a world of dreams.

She became enveloped by the bubble and felt her mother's gentle arms folding softly around her.
The bubble seemed to float through the bat cave, out of the opening and into the sunshine of a brilliant spring day. The whole world seemed to have been made anew and it was blazing with glorious sunshine.

The bubble soared higher and higher into the clear air so that it could cross the mountain peaks. After that it dropped down to float on over the Moaning Moor. When it reached the Windy Heath Sylfia found that she was flying low enough to smell the carpet of purple heather as it tossed about in a gale.

The bubble, however, was not influenced by the wind. Instead of heading south, it took a left turn and followed the Rumbling River all the way down to the coast. It was here that it landed softly among the marram grass on top of a sand dune. It bounced up and down a few times and then slowly rolled down the dune on the seaward side until it came to rest in a shallow depression in the soft white sand of the beach. It was then that the bubble burst with a gentle sploshing sound.

Sylfia had seen the whole journey in her dream and now she relaxed in the belief that she was back home. As she lay on the sand she could hear the familiar sounds of the waves lapping on the shore, the rustling of the dry grasses as they bent to the caress of the off shore breeze and the calling of the gulls high up in the air above her head.

It came as a great shock to her when, without warning, the sand gave way and she felt herself falling. She did not fall very far but it hurt a great deal when she landed with a sharp smack on hard cold rock. She groaned and painfully rolled over. She tried to move her arms in order to rub the places that hurt but they seemed to be stuck to the sides of her body. What's more, her legs seemed to be stuck together as well so that she could neither sit up nor stand. As for flying, it was out of the question. Any attempt to spread her wings caused her deep distress because they were held in a vice like grip down the length of her back.

The bright spring day had gone and she was back in the darkness of the tunnel that led to the bat cave. It was far blacker now than it had been before because, to her horror, she found that she had lost her fairy glow.

Was she dead? For a moment it seemed to be a possibility but then she thought she must be alive after all because she had too much feeling in her body. She hurt all over, her head throbbed and her mouth was dry.

The realisation came to her that she was wrapped from neck to toe in some sort of sticky, but extremely strong, material and it was bound around her very tightly so that she resembled a cocoon. That was why she could not move properly and, no matter how hard she squirmed and wriggled, she could not get free.

The noises of waves and grass and gulls had been snuffed out and she became conscious instead of the sounds of two creatures scuffling and arguing very close to her in the tunnel.

One of the voices belonged to Cudlip but the other one she did not recognise.

It was a harsh female voice and it was swearing at Cudlip using a great deal of bad language which will not be repeated here. Suffice it to say that her haranguing of Sylfia's boggle friend included phrases such as "Leave me alone you heap of old donkey guano!" Other insulting phrases included "Give me back my property you frigging sneak thief or I'll break your ugly flea-ridden head!" and "Gerrof me and mind your own blasted boggling business!"

"Now then, stop it," Cudlip urged but his opponent kept on struggling. Unexpectedly she elbowed him in the stomach and with difficulty he only just managed to hang on to her.

"Oof! Keep still you discombobulating old witch," he gasped.

The witch, for so she was, made a final desperate effort to escape and just managed to squirm out of Cudlip's grasp. She ran towards Sylfia and bent down to pick up the bundle of fairy but Sylfia bit her hand. The witch shrieked and was about to lash out at her captive, using her fist, when Cudlip, catching up with her, grabbed her round the neck with one of his arms and round her middle with his other. In this way he managed to restrain her.

He pulled the witch away and they tumbled together out of the tunnel and into the bat cave. They rolled over and over before crashing into the wall on the opposite side of the cavern.

A flurry of bats flew off the ceiling and walls and whirled around the heads of the combatants. The witch sprang to her feet first and snarled at them while Cudlip was slower to rise and appeared to be rather dazed. The witch struck him with her clenched fist and, when he dropped to the floor again, she stood over him triumphantly. She raised her arms above her head, her eyes glowing red and her shimmering satin cloak swirling around them both. She and Cudlip were enveloped in the glowing fabric which rippled like water and displayed a kaleidoscopic pattern of iridescent colours. In a loud crackling voice she began to intone a hideous spell. It was a spell designed to send her boggle foe into oblivion.

All seemed lost when, out of nowhere, a huge muscular figure materialised and launched itself into the fray by means of an impressive flying rugby tackle. The witch had her feet whipped out from under her and she was thrown to the ground. She landed with a sickening thud and the spell died in her throat. Her head met the rocky floor with a resounding crack, she gave one long groan and, as the black blood began to flow from a gash across her forehead, she lay still.

The newcomer towered over the unconscious body, breathing hard. His fists were clenched in case the witch should spring up again and resume the fight but time passed and it became clear that she was either dead or unconscious. She remained in a heap at his feet.

Cudlip got up, shaking all over. He looked down at the witch and then up at his rescuer.

"Thanks neighbour," he said. "I don't know what brings you inside the mountain but I'm very glad to see you."

His rescuer grinned and touched his forefinger to his temple indicating that he was pleased to be of help.

Cudlip bent down and very warily checked the witch's pulse. He felt a faint irregular throb at the side of her throat.

"Still alive," he said. He reached into his pocket and pulled out some of his own magic. Actually, it was some of Hornbeam's magic. It was a reel of invisible elfish thread. Sylfia had unloaded it from the wagon and left it in his kitchen. He had been intrigued by the pretty stuff because on the reel it looked like glittering tinsel and yet, as it was unwound, it became lost to sight. First he had played with it and then he had "borrowed" it, "just in case", because "you never know".

Now he quickly got to work, winding it round and round the unconscious witch to wrap her up tightly in a cocoon, just like Sylfia.

When he had made sure that the prisoner was bound fast he asked his companion to keep an eye on her while he went back into the tunnel to check on Sylfia.

He was used to seeing in the dark and he had his own dull red glow but it was very difficult to find Sylfia in the darkness. Her fairy light was very low and what remained had been obscured by the mysterious sticky threads that encased most of her body. He searched about for her on his hands and knees.

"Is that you, Cudlip?" she whimpered. "I'm over here. I can't move. I can't see. My light has gone."

Guided by her voice, he soon bumped into her helpless form and set to work to release her. He clawed at the gooey threads and unloosened them enough for her fairy glow to start penetrating the gloom around her. He took a clasp knife from his pocket and used it to cut away more of the witch's string. Eventually enough of it had been peeled away for Sylfia to start moving about again. As soon as her arms were completely free she started to pull the bonds away for herself. Cudlip could sit back on his heels and rest, as the fairy unwrapped herself completely.

"How do you feel, my dear," he asked.

"Very strange," she replied. "Woozy and sick. My head hurts as though I've been hit with a hammer."

"You have, in a way. You were hit by a whopping great hammer of a spell, like a magical anaesthetic. I'm glad I came back when I did. You weren't under her charm for very long so you'll still have your brain in tact."

"What happened, Cudlip? Who is she?" Sylfia asked, as she worked to free herself.

"She's a witch, that much is clear," Cudlip answered. "I think it must be Sycodelia. I've heard the imps talking about her. She's very powerful and scares them all stiff. They try not to get lost in the mountain in case she stalks them."

"Stalks? You mean she hunts them?"

"Yes, that's another way of putting it and when she finds one, alone and lost, she fills their minds with images of whatever they long for most or whatever their weaknesses may be. She makes them believe that they are living their most precious fantasies."

"I know!" Sylfia exclaimed. "I dreamt that my mother came to rescue me and she took me home!"

"Quite so," Cudlip said, looking at her sympathetically. "I'm sorry for you, that it's not true I mean."

Sylfia looked back at him, with sorrowful eyes.

"One day," she sighed, looking away into the darkness. "One day."

By this time the last of the rubbery strands had been peeled away and Sylfia was sitting with her back against the wall of the tunnel, very limp and completely exhausted. There was silence while they both contemplated their narrow escape.

Soon Cudlip got up, went to the end of the tunnel and looked into the cave.

"She wraps up her prey like a spider," he murmured. "I wouldn't mind betting that somewhere in this mountain she has a pantry full of cocoons, all hanging up together, dreaming away to themselves. Then one day when she feels hungry its time for her to crunch and munch some of them! She goes and sinks her fangs into a selection of the living meals that are hanging there, still nice and fresh you see, not dead, just dreaming! She'll suck the goodness out of 'em, just like a spider sucks the goodness out of its prey and all that's left is a desiccated, crinkly husk."

"Must you go into details?" Sylfia asked, shuddering.

"Sorry!" he said and returned to where she was resting, her back still supported by the wall of the tunnel.

"Don't worry," Syfia told him. "I need to toughen up and I think I am. I was in enormous danger wasn't I? Thank you for rescuing me. You were wonderful."

"I suppose I was," he joked and Sylfia smiled back, rather wanly.

"I can't take all of the credit, though," he went on. "Someone had to save *me* in the end! Show yourself, you old troglodyte!"

The newcomer was too big to get into the tunnel and when he showed himself at the entrance only half of his face was visible but Sylfia recognised him immediately.

"Lummock! You're back! I'm so glad to see you!" she cried.

"Lummock is glad too!" he grinned. "So is Mr Boggle!"

"Do you two know each other?" Sylfia asked Cudlip.

"I was just wondering the same thing about you!" Cudlip answered. "I only knew him slightly but now I hope I can count him among my growing number of new friends!"

"Yes! Lummock has lots of friends now!" the troll said proudly, beaming at them. His face, which, was framed in the entrance to the tunnel, was a picture of contentment.

"Yes you have, Lummock. Lots of new friends," Sylfia agreed with him. "I don't know what we'd do without you."

Lummock almost burst with pride. He sat on the floor of the bat cave beside the unconscious witch and chuckled to himself.

He told her, in his own simple way, how he had returned to his home on the mountainside because he had missed it and because he thought that he might be able to help his friends some more. He had been wandering on the mountainside all morning looking for signs of them and when he rested for a while near the mouth of the bat cave he had heard a commotion inside. A cloud of excited bats had flown out of the cave right past his head and he knew that was a very strange thing to happen in the middle of the day so he had come into the cave to find out what was going on. He had seen Mr Boggle being threatened by a terrible big bat and so he had thrown himself into the rescue.

"What wonderfully good luck that you were looking around on this side of the mountain, Lummock. We can't thank you enough," Sylfia told him.

"D'you know what I've been thinking?" she went on, turning back to Cudlip. "If that prisoner of yours likes to devour imps so much then she must have been delighted to come across a fairy. There's far more 'goodness' in a fairy!"

Cudlip laughed at her joke and was glad to see some colour coming back into her cheeks. Lummock was delighted to see the beautiful fairy again, especially since she had thanked him so prettily and called him a friend.

Cudlip stopped laughing and remained silent for a

long time, deep in thought. Something about Sylfia's words had struck a chord and deep in his subconscious, a niggling concern started to grow. It grew into a worry and the worry started to gnaw at him, even though he could not quite put it into words.

It was when she spoke again that Cudlip sat up with a start.

Sylfia simply asked him how he had got on in his search for the other three fairies.

"Oh my," he said. "Oh yes, of course! What a slow and stupid boggle I am! Don't you see? If she likes to hunt imps then she'll love to hunt fairies!"

He leapt up, banged the sides of his head with his fists and started to hop up and down in the manner of Rumplestiltskin doing a jig. He hopped from one foot to the other, kicking the air with each of his lower legs when it was not in contact with the floor.

"That must be it. She must have got him. He got lost and she got him," he said to himself over and over again.

"Cudlip, what are you talking about?" Sylfia asked anxiously. "Tell me who did she get?"

Cudlip stopped leaping about and stood right in front of her so that she could see him properly in her own light.

"I saw Pim and I saw another fairy, a female, a wonderful dancer. That must have been your friend Tansy," he told her.

His face was pale and his expression was very mournful.

"Yes, I'm so pleased but go on," she nodded at him.

"They were in the throne room with the wizard. He was showing them off to the Imperor and Impress. I looked for Flum as well but I couldn't find him anywhere. I looked all around that part of the mountain. I decided that he must have misread the map and got lost but now I'm thinking that, if he was lost, there's a good chance that he ran into Sycodelia and she's got him wrapped up somewhere."

Sylfia's face lost its colour again and she turned whiter than when she had been in the cocoon. She stared back at Cudlip, aghast.

"What if it's true?" she whispered. "Can we rescue him? It's not too late is it? He'll still be alive won't he?"

"I don't know but we'll have to find him as soon as possible."

Cudlip bounded along to the end of the tunnel and back into the cave. Lummock had been told to keep an eye on the witch and that was exactly what he was doing. Sycodelia had come round to see his face very close to hers and his large watery eyes staring at her without blinking. She lay very still, not daring to move a muscle. As she gazed back at him, apprehensively, she tried to wriggle further away.

Cudlip came and stood over her as well, nudging Lummock slightly to one side.

"Is your name Sycodelia?" he asked.

She transferred her gaze from the troll to the boggle but did not answer.

"I'll take that as a "yes". How many fairies have you

caught today and yesterday?"

"What's that to you?" she snarled.

"Your life may depend on it, that's what," Cudlip snarled back.

"Undo this elfish string and we'll talk," she wheedled in a slightly friendlier voice.

"No way. I'm not an idiot," was Cudlip's response. "You'll stay like that, with this good troll as your guard, until we decide that you have been rendered harmless. By the way, Lummock, you can stop staring if you like."

"Thanks boss," Lummock saluted and moved back a little.

The witch winced and wriggled but the more she jiggled around the tighter the elvish thread nipped and squeezed her.

"Tell us where to find your stash of food and, if our fairy friend is in a fit state to be rescued, then Lummock will take you to Mulberry Wood. He'll keep you on a lead until you learn to be a good witch. You'll have to cook ordinary food in a cauldron and make spells and potions that help and heal."

"Ugh! You must be joking," she replied. "I'd rather die!"

"Well, that can easily be arranged. Those elfish threads can be made to squeeze the life out of you, slowly, painfully and without mercy." Cudlip looked his sternest, as though he really meant it.

The witch bit her lip and thought deeply for a minute or two.

"O.K." she resumed. She sounded more resigned now.

"Just suppose I tell you what you want to know, no promises mind. I haven't decided for sure."

Cudlip raised his eyebrows and put his head on one side in an inquiring manner, willing her to go on.

"Just suppose I tell you where my lovely, juicy pets are, then I will need this great lumbering troll to take me to the Wizard of the West. He'll set me free and give me work to do. I don't want a namby-pamby life in some fairy wood. It would drive me insane. You must see that."

"Is that alright with you Lummock?" Cudlip asked.

The troll nodded amicably, happy to do anything for his new-found friends.

"Good. That's agreed. Now tell us, before it's too late, and if it is too late that's the end of you!"

Chapter 20

Macciovolio had marched Pim out of the throne room and, straight back to Grim and Glum.

"Show him everything," he ordered. "I want him to learn the business but I don't want him near the other fairy. Do you understand? I don't want them to meet unless I am there to hear everything they say. Is that clear?"

"Yes sir!"

The two Imperial Guards saluted and marched off down the corridor with the unresisting prince between them.

The wizard turned on his heel and swept back to his office.

He supervised the transfer of Tansy from her cage to the prison cell and locked her in himself.

"Where is Pim?" she asked, scowling at her captor through the bars of the cage. "How do I know that you haven't harmed him? I won't dance again unless I see him safe and well!"

"Of course you won't, my pretty little prize. You'll see him, in this magic mirror, busy at his work. Here you are," he purred, passing her a looking glass through the bars of her cell. "I just don't want *him* to see too much of *you*. It might distract him from my purpose."

"Your purpose?"

"Yes. It's nothing much. I'm turning him into a royal imp, you see. He's going to take my place when we're away."

"We? Am I included in that 'we'?"

"Indeed you are my precious little magic ballerina! I have such ambitions for your extraordinary gifts."

"You're going to turn me into a slave of the Sorceress and my friend Pim into a puppet ruler?"

"That just about sums it up. So clever, as well as gifted, what a find you're turning out to be!"

"And what if I refuse?"

"Oh, the same arrangement as before, your lover boy loses his head. Quite simple isn't it? But so effective!"

The wizard rubbed his hands.

"I can't wait to show you off to my glorious Mistress!"

Macciovolio smiled a spine chilling smile and settled himself at his desk.

"Now shush, while I make my plans! There's a lot to think about before we can leave."

The wizard busied himself not only with pen, paper and ink but also with a wand, a crystal ball and a creaky old abacus. His plans, apparently, involved looking into the future, doing calculations and casting small spells.

Tansy supposed that the spells were needed to check his arithmetic as a little desk wand would hardly be sufficient for making world shattering changes to the future.

Tansy looked into the mirror and saw Pim, accompanied by Grim and Glum, being guided around Imps and Insects Inc.

She gasped and squirmed at the horrifying treatment endured by the poor innocent insects and she wondered how Pim managed to keep his composure. Either he was a terrifically good actor or he really was turning into a cold, unfeeling imp.

She studied his eyes, looking deep down into their shining ebony depths and looked for signs of compassion, a hint of warm fairy feeling, a flicker of the old Pim who was always imperious but always fiercely loyal. Was that a glimmer of his old self or did she just imagine it?

She spoke to him silently, moving her lips but making no sound that Macciovolio could hear.

"Stay with us Pim," she mouthed. "The others will get us out of this. Don't let the imps have you. You belong to us. You're a fairy, don't ever forget that!"

She sent out her thoughts with every wave particle that her imagination could summon and with all the strength that her will power had to spare. She was rewarded by a slight turn of his head and the flicker of a smile as he glanced back at her for an instant from the other side of the glass. She knew that he could not see her but his expression seemed to change slightly and, just for a microsecond, she thought that she caught the ghost of a wink on his otherwise expressionless face.

He looked very much like a royal imp now. His skin was chalky white but there was colour in his cheeks provided by theatrical powder and paint. His expression was sullen, disdainful and cold but he also looked vulnerable and surprisingly handsome. He said little to Grim and Glum as he walked, ceaselessly maintaining his haughty demeanour with his head in the air and a sneer on his lips. His height and bearing made him an ideal candidate for the Imperial Guard but Macciovolio preferred him to dress like royalty and act out another part.

She sighed, put the mirror down, turned her back on the wizard and lay down on the bench to sleep.

Hornbeam had been working all morning sawing, hammering, moulding, welding and riveting.

He had sawn off part of an old metal drainpipe which became the cylindrical body of the rocket and then he had fashioned a nose cone. First, he had cut a circular piece of sheet metal then sliced it from the edge to the centre so that he could bend it round to make the shape of a cone. This shape was held in place by a line of rivets.

He had found another sheet of metal hidden behind some wooden panels that were leaning against the wall and he was busy cutting this into a set of triangular tail fins to give the missile some stability when Cudlip staggered into the workshop carrying the unconscious body of Flum.

Sylfia, still a bit light headed and unsteady on her feet, followed behind with the sack of guano in her arms.

"He was caught by a witch, Hornbeam. I think she's called Sycodelia. He's still alive but deeply unconscious," Cudlip panted.

Hornbeam used his arm to sweep clutter from the table onto the floor.

"Lay him down here. Where did you find him?"

"He was hanging in a cave on the west side of the mountain. He must have got lost and walked straight into her parlour."

"What can you do for him, Hornbeam?" Sylfia asked tearfullly. "Can you bring him back?"

Hornbeam bent over Flum's inert body and lifted his eyelids to stare into his pupils.

"He's deeply enchanted. I'll have to try a spell of my own with a healing potion on top. While I prepare things, you finish removing those sticky threads and rub his arms and legs to get his blood circulating then you can turn him on his side and gently unfold his wings. Wipe them well and flex them. He'll be glad of that when he wakes."

Hornbeam bustled off to the kitchen to sort through his herbs and potions and prepare some medicine while the other two did as he had instructed.

Sylfia sang very softly as she gently caressed her friend's poor crumpled wings. The plangent song that she sang was a nostalgic lament for times gone by but each verse ended with a lyrical chorus that expressed hope for the future.

Cudlip massaged Flum's limbs energetically, muttering encouragement in a trembling voice and all the time sounding a bit cross.

"Come on, lad. You can do it. Come back to us. We need you. I'm sorry I let you get into this mess. I should have told you about all the exits from my house, but still, you shouldn't have gone off on your own, you know. You need me to take care of you under the mountain."

Hornbeam returned with a bowl full of effervescent magic potion. There was a clear emerald green liquid at the bottom and a pale green foamy layer floating on top. Bubbles rose through the liquid and burst at the surface giving little puffs of purple smoke which drifted up into the air to form billowing clouds just below the ceiling.

The old elf raised Flum's head and administered the potion while intoning a spell in the ancient elfish tongue. The other two looked on anxiously.

Flum's glow began to return as he swallowed small sips of the potion.

"Look he's smiling," Sylfia cried. "That medicine must be very good, Hornbeam."

It was true that a beatific smile had spread over Flum's face but Hornbeam did not seem to share her excitement.

"He's still dreaming, Sylfia. That probably means that he's still in the witch's thrall. It looks as though it's going to take him a long time to shake off her magic."

"Should we still be worried?" Cudlip asked. "I mean he's not going to die is he?"

"I don't think so," Hornbeam replied. "But it was a good thing that you got to him when you did. He could have sunk so deeply into the realm of sycomagic that it wouldn't have been possible to bring him back."

When Flum had swallowed most of the potion Hornbeam picked him up very gently and carried him with the utmost care to the nearest bedroom. He laid him down on the bed and covered him with the counterpane.

"All will be well and all will be well," he whispered to his patient. "Now all *we* can do is wait for as long as it takes," he told Sylfia who was standing by, still looking anxious.

"He'll probably drift in and out of a state of sycobliss but, as long as he keeps his glow, he should come back to us eventually."

"I'll keep an eye on him," Sylfia said, settling down in an old chair by the bed and taking Flum's hand in hers. "You two have a lot of work to do."

"Where's the witch now?" Hornbeam asked Cudlip as they left the room.

"With Lummock," Cudlip told him.

"He's back is he? What a good-hearted fellow he is."

"We left him standing guard over her in the bat cave. He appeared out of nowhere and floored the witch as though he was swatting a fly! I couldn't have captured her without him. It was a miracle. Then I tied her up with your magic thread which I'd 'borrowed' from the kitchen, just in case."

"Of course," smiled Hornbeam. "You never know when it might come in handy."

Cudlip had to tell Hornbeam about the bargain he had struck with the witch.

He was relieved when Hornbeam nodded his head and agreed that it had been the best course of action, especially since Flum needed to be rescued as quickly as possible.

"I'll go and see Lummock now and thank him," Hornbeam said. "I don't know about letting him take the witch to The Wizard of the West, though. He can be a very unpleasant magician with a terrifying temper and anyone who approaches him has to know the best way to do it. What's more I need to have a word with this witch of yours as soon as possible. It sounds probable that she was bitten by an enchanted spider, one that was infected with a virulent strain of sycomagic. It would solve the problem of what to do with her if I could concoct an antidote to turn her into a vegetarian but, whatever happens, we can't let her go until we know that Flum is fully recovered. We may need her help to bring him back to normal."

While Hornbeam was away Sylfia sat beside Flum's bed, humming softly and watching him anxiously.

After a while Cudlip came in with refreshments and told her that Hornbeam had made great progress with the rocket.

"How we'll get it into the beehive is quite another

thing," he said. "The imps are working there day and night and Imperial Guards stomp around watching them all the time."

"Hornbeam told me that the hive is on many floors," Sylfia murmured, keeping her eyes on Flum, for she did not want to miss any signs of change. He said that he wants to position the rocket on the top floor of the hive and send the bees down to the lower levels out of the way. The imps will have to go down to lower levels as well, if that is where the bees are to be found."

"True, but someone has to go in there first, with all those imps and guards still swarming around in order to speak to the bees," Cudlip said. "If Hornbeam did it he would be spotted and arrested, maybe even killed."

"He won't even get in there before they notice him," Sylfia said. "Someone smaller in size, more like an imp, will have to dress up in a protective suit to sneak into the hive without being suspected."

She turned her beautiful eyes on the boggle's anxious face and he saw that a realisation had dawned in them.

"It'll have to me, won't it? Imps and fairies are all about the same size. Hornbeam is an elf and therefore far too big. You are thin enough for an imp but too tall. I'm certain that Flum would have volunteered but now he's far too ill. Don't worry," she went on, as Cudlip opened his mouth to protest. "We fairies are trained to talk to insects and bees have always been a favourite of mine. They seem to respond to my voice in a very good way and, anyway, I'm glad to do my bit to help. This will be a proper job at last, my best contribution to the plan so far, but until then I'll stay with Flum, if you don't mind. We fairies don't know much about hammers and chisels!"

Cudlip gazed at her in admiration and for many minutes he was lost for words.

"You fairies are amazing," he said, at last. "You all look so dainty and ephemeral but every one of you is made of very stern stuff. You're all so brave and determined."

"We use good magic, that's all." Sylfia told him. "We put our trust in doing what's right. If one of us comes to an end the rest of the fairy world goes on without us but firmer and stronger than ever. All we have to do is keep faith with the good magic."

Cudlip nodded but finding no more words to convey his immense regard for fairy wisdom, he merely patted her hand and turned, like her, to gaze at the blissfully sleeping Flum.

Chapter 21

Lummock was very pleased to see Hornbeam.

And so was the witch. She had had a very uncomfortable time lying on the cold hard floor of the bat cave even though she had soon realised that Lummock was a simple troll, basically affectionate, keen to be of some use in the world and, as long as his friends were not being threatened in any way, ready to get along with anyone.

She had tried a few escape spells but the invisible thread was too strong for her. It was deeply infused with the ancient magic of elves and would not allow the interference of any flummery from an ill-mannered witch. She had screeched her magic in vain and each time a spell failed she had cursed mightily inducing the threads to tighten their grip just a little bit more.

Then she had tried to coax Lummock into loosening her bonds but he had steadfastly refused to budge on that one for he had been given no instruction about letting her go. He had been told to guard the witch while the boggle and the beautiful fairy went to find one of their other friends and that was exactly what he was going to do, come hell or high water, come rain or shine, come anything else that springs to mind as a way of indicating loyalty and admirable faithfulness. He merely smiled a foolish smile and shook his big shaggy head.

In the end she gave up both screeching at the bonds and nagging at the troll and took to lying perfectly still. Blood still trickled from her forehead and, truth to tell, she was feeling both dizzy and sick, although a cornered witch would never admit to any sign of weakness.

Lummock, who had been towering over her, bent down to see why she had fallen silent. She looked up and saw concern on his big flubbery face so she decided to try moaning slightly, in order to evoke even more sympathy. It worked because Lummock lifted her up into a sitting position and propped her against the wall of the cave. He left her there while he went outside and down a slope to where a spring gushed out from the mountainside. He returned with a handful of wet moss, applied it as a dressing to the cut on her forehead and in this way he managed to staunch the flow of blood.

"That's better," he told her. "Nice'n quiet. That's the way."

"Hello, Lummock," Hornbeam called to him, as he stepped into the cave from the tunnel. "I'm glad you came back. You were just in the nick of time, I hear."

Lummock grinned down at him as they shook hands, Hornbeam's gnarled old one completely enveloped by

Lummock's great big knobbly fist. Hornbeam had to leap up onto a boulder to do this and the troll had to bend double, so great was the difference in their heights.

"How is Mulberry Wood?" Hornbeam asked.

"Very nice Mr Hornbeam. Mr Hootsmon, too. Very kind he is, but ……" and his voice trailed away as he ran out of ways to express his feelings.

"I know, old fellow. You're a mountain chap, aren't you," Hornbeam finished for him. "Woods and forests are all very well but you need the heights, don't you? A bracing wind in your face, rocky paths under your feet, the call of the eagle overhead, all that sort of thing, that's what you call home."

Lummock nodded vigorously and looked as though he would clap Hornbeam on the back but, when he realised it would knock the elf off the boulder and send him flying, he scratched his ear instead.

Hornbeam turned his attention to the witch. He went over to and examined her closely.

"Who're you?" she snapped. "You're an elf aren't you? Are these your pesky threads around me, you old man of the woods? Get them off me before I curse you into the back of beyond."

Hornbeam stiffened when he heard her insults.

"Then you'll be in a pickle yourself, wrapped up in those threads forever. They won't come off without me, you know. The threads won't hear me from the back of beyond, will they?"

He did not often adopt a sarcastic mode of speech but

the witch was so rude, she made him feel very indignant.

"What a charming lady you are, to be sure," he went on. "I hear that you have a detestable taste in food and a very unusual larder."

"Mind your own frigging business!" she retorted. "What I eat is my own business and where I get it from is none of yours!"

"Oh yes it is!"

Hornbeam was almost shouting now.

"When you choose to enchant my friends and turn them into half dead carcasses in your dreary, smelly pantry then that most certainly is very much my business!"

The witch snarled at him and looked away.

Hornbeam composed himself and went on in a calmer, quieter tone.

"How long have you been like this? Did it start when you came to the mountain or have you always had murderous arachnid tendencies?"

She whipped her head round again to stare at him full in the face.

"What do you mean by that?"

"I mean what sort of witch did you used to be? Where did you come from? Did you suddenly turn into this sorry creature or was it a slow process that turned you into a monster?"

Hornbeam was dominating the conversation now.

"What's your game?" she asked, looking at him suspiciously from under a furrowed brow.

"I won't beat about the bush," Hornbeam sighed,

rubbing his chin thoughtfully.

"Can we change you back into a decent sort of witch who gets on with life without interfering with others? Or have things gone too far? Should we just carry you back to the Wizard of the West, all wrapped up in those threads like a birthday present. He'll look on you as such a failure won't he? He'll probably turn you into a battered old crone, with a pointy black hat, who mixes his potions in a cauldron all day and sings croaky songs about 'eye of toad' and 'tongue of newt'?"

Hornbeam had hit the spot now, for he had worked out that this was one of the Wizard's seven daughters, one of the Seven Searchers. He had spotted the family resemblance as soon as he saw her.

Her father had sent all of his seven daughters out into the world to become great witches and achieve magnificent feats of magic wherever they went. Only then, when they had become famous for their magic, would he count them worthy to be called Witches of the West and invite them to share in his power and glory.

"He'll be as cross as that?" she asked, so quietly that her words were barely audible.

"I expect so, perhaps even more furious than that!" Hornbeam was laying it on thickly now.

"What can I do?" asked Sycodelia, for that was her name.

"Come with me and undergo some sycotherapy," Hornbeam suggested. "I may find a use for you in the days that lie ahead but in the meantime, you need some counselling in anger management, some proper food and a more comfortable place to sleep. You'll be under lock and key for now, of course, but who knows how you'll turn out? You may be able to render us a great service when my plan takes off and we might find a glorious part for you to play. Maybe it'll be something that even your father can be proud of!"

The witch continued to stare at him but she said nothing for some time. What could she say? This old elf seemed to know all about her and it was useless to deny anything. Everything he had been saying had struck a chord. It was not a case of finding out what he was going to do *to* her but what he was going to do *for* her.

"Lummock, old friend," Hornbeam said. "Thank you once again. You've been invaluable so far. Can I count on your help again, before this adventure is over?"

The willing troll nodded his head vigorously and bent down again to shake Mr Hornbeam by the hand.

"I'll come to find you when the time is right is that OK?"

Lummock beamed and nodded again.

"Yes, Mr Elf. That will be wunnerful."

"Well done. You're a true friend, Lummock. Goodbye for now!"

So saying, Hornbeam picked up the bundle of witch, threw her over his shoulder and disappeared into the dark tunnel.

"Oh no! That's the bloodsucking spider witch!
Why have you brought *her* here?"

A dismayed Cudlip was staring at Hornbeam's burden
as if she were a giant cow pat about to be dropped on his
spotlessly clean kitchen floor. "Don't let Sylfia see her for
heaven's sake. It'll make her ill and what about Flum?
That thing might eat him up when we're not looking!"

"Not if I lock her up somewhere. Have you got a
secure chamber in this rabbit warren, Cudlip?"

The boggle sighed and saw that it was useless to stand
in the way of Hornbeam's juggernaut determination.
He took a bunch of keys down from a hook on the wall.

"Follow me, then, but not too close! She's looking at
me as though she'd like to bite my head off."

"You're so right!" growled Sycodelia, gnashing her teeth
at him over Hornbeam's shoulder.

Cudlip took them down a corridor and showed them
into a chamber that had been a storeroom but was now
bare except for some straw and a few packing cases.

"Will this do?"

"It looks fine," Hornbeam said, putting his burden
down in the middle of the floor and walking over to
examine the lock. "Where's the key?"

Cudlip flipped through the bunch and held up one
of the larger, more rusty-looking keys. He passed it to

Hornbeam who tried it in the lock. It hadn't been used for a long time.

"It works but it could do with a spot of oil," he said.

"Yes sir!" Cudlip stood to attention and gave a mock salute before tripping off to the workshop to find a small can of machine oil.

"What are you going to do with her?" he asked on his return.

Hornbeam took the key from his friend and, after oiling the lock with a couple of drops, turned the key back and forth several times until it moved quite smoothly.

"I think she could be useful to us if I can turn her back into a normal witch."

Cudlip adopted his most quizzical look.

"A *normal* witch? I didn't think there was such a thing."

"I mean one that hasn't been infected by sycomagic, one that lives above ground and is capable of weaving spells that are just as powerful as sycomagic but more useful. Did you realise that this is one of the Seven Searchers, wandering witches who are all daughters of the Wizard of the West?"

"No! Really?" Cudlip's eyes widened in surprise and then he gave a wry smile. He could not resist the opportunity of mocking his recent foe.

"What would your daddy say about you living underground and creeping about like a spider?"

She hissed and spat venom at him. Fortunately he had been sensible enough to keep his distance.

"She's all yours, old friend. I'll be keeping well away

and, if it doesn't work out, don't say that I was the one who encouraged you in your madness. Best of luck!"

In the days that followed both Cudlip and Hornbeam worked hard to finish the rocket but Hornbeam also spent a great deal of time with the witch.

He had reduced her bonds so that she was free to move around the cell but not before he had twisted a bundle of elf threads into a rope. He fastened this rope around her waist and tied the other end to a metal hoop that he had driven into the floor.

Naturally, she attempted to undo this rope from time to time but the old elf magic proved too strong. Whenever she tried to untie the knots, they simply wound together even more tightly than before.

He had persuaded Cudlip to help him carry a bed into the chamber. The boggle performed this task with extreme caution and left immediately afterwards, without even looking at the prisoner for fear of being cursed by her.

Hornbeam turned the packing cases into a table and a couple of chairs. He supplied his prisoner with a chamber pot, a basin to wash in, hot water every morning, soap, towels, blankets, knives, forks, spoons, good wholesome food, fresh water to drink, books to read and, most important of all, his conversation.

After lunching alone one day, Cudlip was returning to the workshop when he bumped into Hornbeam in the passageway. He was surprised to see that the old elf was carrying what looked like a bundle of brushwood under his arm. On closer inspection he noticed that the bundle was made up of several individual brooms.

"We don't really have a lot of time for cleaning," Cudlip said sarcastically. "Why do you need all those besoms?"

"I'm making progress with Sycodelia," Hornbeam replied. "She told me where she had stashed her collection of broomsticks and so I went to fetch them for us."

"For *us?*" the boggle frowned with astonishment. "You'll never get me onto one of her old flying twigs!"

"Oh, you never know ......" Hornbeam began.

"...... when they'll come in useful," Cudlip finished, with a laugh and a shake of his head. "Quite so, old friend. Now let's go and finish that rocket and then you can show me how to mix black powder."

Chapter 22

Ever since Cudlip had carried him home from the witch's pantry, Sylfia had devoted herself to the care of Flum.

He was still in his own dream-world but as the days passed he opened his eyes more and more often. Each time this happened he looked straight at her and after a time she knew that he had begun to recognise her. When she spoke to him he answered by mouthing some words of incomprehensible speech before drifting back to sleep. She had not been able to understand any of his babbling monologues but it was enough that he was trying to communicate again.

She told herself that he was on the mend and talked to him constantly, even when he was fast asleep. She told him all the news about the rocket and how Cudlip was sneaking about at night to keep an eye on Tansy and Pim.

She also told him repeatedly how they all expected him to make a full recovery very shortly.

Hornbeam had told her about how he had brought

the witch back and had locked her up somewhere in the house. She had been dismayed by this and, attempting to allay her fears, he had taken her to the storeroom and showed her the lock. He explained about the rope that he had woven from elfish threads and tried to convince her that the old magic was too strong for Sycodelia to break them. He had then invited her to look inside, not only to see how Sycodelia was secured, but also to hear how subdued the witch was now but Sylfia had refused to go inside and had raced back to Flum's bedside, trembling and fearful. She had spent the rest of the day singing quietly not only in the hope of entertaining Flum but also to keep her mind occupied and off the subject of witches.

In the evening Cudlip came in to sit with the two fairies. He told Sylfia that Hornbeam had a lot of weird ideas but there was nobody else who was wise enough to take the lead and they had to trust to the old elf's knowledge and experience to get them through.

"It's obvious that he knows something about this witch and where she comes from. He may be going to use her for something."

"You're right," she answered, smiling wanly. "I haven't known Hornbeam for very long but I know that he is an exceptional creature and deeply magical. We have to trust him and hope that everything will work out. What news of Tansy and Pim?"

As she spoke these names Flum stirred in his sleep and muttered a faint, unintelligible sentence or two.

They both bent towards him but neither could catch

any coherent or sensible meaning. Sylfia sighed and answered him in tones that were gentle and encouraging.

"Keep trying Flum. We're here for you. You're coming back to us, I know you are."

Cudlip told her how Macciovolio had become obsessed by Tansy. Every day he took her to the ballroom to dance. He had dressed her in fine clothes and was giving her exotic royal food to eat.

"He's like a circus trainer exercising a rare and expensive animal. He's expecting his Mistress to be mightily impressed with Tansy, so much so that she will keep her as a pet, I mean slave, and that will bring him reflected glory. It's horrible," Cudlip complained.

"At least she's being looked after physically and isn't in any immediate danger," Sylfia reminded him. "That's a great relief to all of us but especially to Hornbeam. I know that he feels dreadfully responsible for all the things that have gone wrong. What about Pim?"

Flum stirred in his sleep again.

"He's still strutting around as if he owned the place. Last time I saw him he was without his escort of grim-faced guards. Macciovolio must really trust him now. He's leaving more and more of the running of the business to Pim because he can't think of anything else but Tansy. He can't wait to present her to The Sorceress."

At this Flum sat up in bed. His eyes were wide open, his fists were clenched and he threw punches in the air. He was shouting something over and over again.
It sounded as though it might be "Treachery! Kill him!"

It took both Sylfia's soothing words and Cudlip's strong grip on his shoulders to calm the young fairy. He was staring past them as though he saw an ugly ghoul or hobgoblin on the other side of the room and, for once, Sylfia was glad when he closed his eyes and lay still again.

"It seems as though he's following our conversation and remembering how Tansy has been captured. If he can recall what happened before he met the witch that's a good sign isn't it?" Sylfia said.

"It certainly is," the boggle replied. "It's very promising."

Nevertheless, Sylfia thought that they should change the subject to avoid distressing the invalid any further.

"What about the rocket?" she asked.

"Finished" said a voice from the doorway.

Hornbeam stood there, his hands filthy, his face streaked with grime and grease and his clothes looking as though they were only fit for the rag bag. Even though he was exhausted and ready to drop, his bright eyes twinkled and gleamed triumphantly.

"Come and see."

They followed him to the workroom and at the door he stood to one side to let them pass.

As Sylfia and Cudlip walked into the room they immediately stood stock still, gazing up at the construction.

Cudlip, of course, had been involved in all stages of its development and knew what to expect but now the expression on his face showed that he shared Hornbeam's pride and exultation.

Sylfia gazed in wonder. "I didn't realise that it would be so- so- beautiful," she said at last.

"Thank you, my dear," Hornbeam whispered. "I'm so glad you like it."

He had painted it in horizontal yellow and black stripes to represent a bee and, around the lower part of the rocket's cylindrical body, he had used up a whole pot of silver enamel paint to write some elfish runes in large and beautiful symbols.

Cudlip saw that Sylfia was trying to read the magic letters.

"I think I know what Hornbeam's written there," he said proudly. "I think it says 'LIBERATOR'. Am I right?"

The old elf nodded.

"Of course," Sylfia said, smiling at them both. "That's exactly what it should say."

The very next day Cudlip and Sylfia crept along a tunnel towards one of the rooms in which the imps stored their protective clothing.

The boggle had chosen a time of the day when he knew there would be no changeover of work force but they still had to move cautiously and be on the look out for Imperial Guards.

The clothing was hanging up on rows of pegs just as it does in a school changing room. Sylfia went to a peg that was very close to the door and quickly pulled on a pair of overalls, as well as special boots and gloves. Cudlip helped her with the head gear and together they worked out how to fasten it down. Now she looked like any imp dressed ready for the hive. They had agreed on a sign that would allow Cudlip to distinguish her from the rest of the workers and she made that sign now. She curled the first finger and the thumb of her right hand to make the shape of an O and touched it to her eye. Then she hid herself among the folds of hanging clothes and settled down to wait.

There was a changeover of workers every hour and on every level. Cudlip said that only those who had gathered enough honey or wax would be allowed to leave but he was sure that he could smuggle her out through a ventilation shaft when she had finished communicating with the bees.

Cudlip made sure that Sylfia was out of sight among the clothing before he left the room. He did not go far into the tunnel but hid himself in a fissure in the rock wall quite near to the door.

The minutes ticked away. Sylfia rehearsed the words that Hornbeam had told her to whisper to the bees. They were magic words designed to persuade the bees to grant her an audience with their Queen. She held her breath when a guard came through a door to the hive and paced across the room to the door that led into the corridor.

Outside the room, in his hiding place, Cudlip bit his nails and sharpened his wits.

At last the noise of marching feet further up the tunnel told him that a changeover party was on its way. The imperious voice of a guard shouting "Quick march" and "Eyes Front" resounded down the passageway and reached the ears of the boggle.

"This is the tricky part," he told himself.

The door to the changing room opened and the guard who had come from the hive looked out.

"Twelve!" he shouted up the tunnel. The party halted and the accompanying guard counted twelve imps to go forward and in through the doorway. The remaining imps were wheeled around and marched back to their quarters.

The guard who had called for twelve imps counted them in and shut the door.

Once the unwanted imps and their guard were out of sight Cudlip left his hiding place and pressed his ear to the door. When he was sure that there was no creature close to the other side he opened the door a fraction and peeped in. The imps were all occupied in putting on their protective suits and, fortunately for our spy, the guard who was watching them very closely had his back to the door.

Very soon the door at the far end of the changing room opened and twelve weary imps limped inside. The guard hurried over to guide them into rows where they would not be able to communicate with the fresh workers.

While the guard was busy in this way, Cudlip took

his chance. He opened the door wider, dived in, grabbed the nearest imp and dived out again. This one had not yet put on her helmet and he was able to clamp his hand over her mouth.

As the door banged shut other imps turned around to look. They saw a figure standing in front of the door and she was already clothed from head to foot in protective gear.

They assumed that it was one of the imps that had marched in with them.

"It was draughty in here," she said as she bent down to pick up the stray helmet. She replaced it on its peg and held her breath, hoping with all her might that the other imps would not notice that the peg had no other items of clothing hanging on it.

In fact, each of the other workers was too busy worrying about the dangers that lay in store inside the hive so they all shrugged and turned back to the business of protecting themselves against unpredictable bees.

Outside the door, Cudlip was struggling with his captive. This imp did not want to go into the hive but neither did she like being abducted. This unknown creature that had grabbed her was very skinny and bony and, at the same time, very strong and determined. It could be anything, from a goblin to a demon.

Cudlip was finding it very difficult to restrain her and he needed to drag her into his hiding place as quickly as possible. If he loosened his grip for an instant she could wriggle free, escape up the passageway and alert the guards.

He pulled her with all his might towards his hiding place but she dug her heels in and sank her teeth into his hand which caused him considerable pain. He managed to hang on to her, gritting his teeth and merely giving out an angry grunt.

It was then that he felt a hand on his shoulder and his blood ran cold.

"Can I help?" the newcomer asked.

Cudlip's head buzzed, his heart pounded and his mouth dried up. He turned around very slowly and apprehensively, fully expecting to find himself gazing into the cruel eyes of Macciovolio.

To his amazement, he found that he was looking into the face of one who was just as capable of inspiring awe but thankfully did not inspire knee-buckling fear.

Cudlip silently dropped the imp and when she too looked into the face of the newcomer she did not flee. She bent her body into a low bow and murmured "Your Highness".

"You're not needed here today," said the prince. "There has been a mistake. Leave the protective cloth-ing with me and return to your quarters. Tell them that Prince Pernickity has given you the day off because it's his birthday."

The imp rapidly divested herself of her outer garments and, mumbling her thanks to his Most Regal Wonderful-ness, fled up the tunnel and out of sight.

Cudlip's face settled into a lopsided grin and he raised one eyebrow quizzically.

"Pernickity?" he spluttered.

Pim shrugged and shook hands with his friend.

"All part of the Big Act, you know. I have to thank *you* for the idea that has saved my life and, what's more, I'm getting quite used to all this regal stuff. It suits me don't you think?"

Cudlip's grin disappeared and wrinkles of amusement were replaced by worry lines.

"Really?"

"Only joking," Pim assured him. "But I expect all my friends believe it of me. I've always been – well – pompous, you know."

"I'm sure they all *want* to think the best of you, but *can* they really?" Cudlip asked.

"So, you're saying that they're not sure? Even though Tansy is in the clutches of that demon and those insects are being exploited for his greed and vanity they think I'm enjoying myself? While my friend is the slave of an evil magician and hundreds of other living things are suffering just to please his Beloved Mistress, The Sorceress, they think that I would turn traitor? How can they believe that, even for a moment?"

He spoke bitterly now and looked utterly dejected.

"Cheer up, lad, I mean Your Highness. I'll tell them that it's not true. They'll believe me, I'm sure. Those others are my friends now as well as yours and we have a plan! A good plan! It's just that Hornbeam thought it was best not to tell you anything."

"Not to be trusted, eh?"

"No! No! Not at all, my lad! Hornbeam is a very wise old elf, you know that. He just thought that the less you knew the less you'd have to tell and the better it would be for you. You have to pretend so much when that fiend Macciovolio is about. It must take enormous concentration."

"I see, but I think I should know the plan now, don't you? I've already covered up for you here in this tunnel. I bet there's a lot more I could do."

There were noises further along the tunnel and Cudlip looked alarmed.

He made for his hiding place but before he disappeared from view he had time whisper. "For heaven's sake, keep yourself and Tansy out of the throne room. It's going to blow up!"

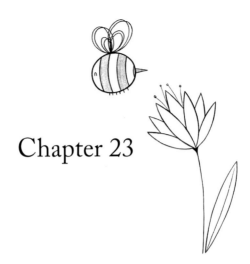

Chapter 23

Sylfia followed the other imps out of the changing room and onto the circular platform that surrounded the hive at that particular level.

She was handed a bucket by one of the guards and told to collect honey. Inside the bucket there was a small knife and a ladle for that purpose. She guessed that the knife was to slice into the comb.

Without further ado the party of workers filed through the revolving glass door and into the hive.

The noise was tremendous. The combined buzzing of hundreds of thousands of bees produced a number of decibels worthy of a jet engine.

It was also very hot in there and the sweet smell of oozing honey and sticky nectar was overwhelming.

Sylfia was glad that most of her face was hidden inside the protective helmet, not only because her fairy features were hidden from view in this way, but also because the other imps could not see how she was moved by the sight of industrious bees being robbed by so many plundering hands.

She grasped the bucket firmly in her left hand and, using her right hand and arm to help maintain her balance, she edged her way forward. She stepped slowly at first along one of the wooden platforms that ran through the honeycombs and as she brushed past the working bees she spoke the soothing sounds that helped her fairy race to communicate with the insect world.

It was not long before she could make her way more quickly through the combs. It was as though the bees were creating space for her and she could sense that they were speaking to each other about her. They did not pause in their activities, however, so the imps did not notice any difference in their behaviour. However, the pitch and tenor of their buzzing changed in a subtle way that only Sylfia could detect and it meant that her presence was being discussed. Then Sylfia noticed that one elderly bee had left her work on a honeycomb and had started to follow her.

As she rounded a corner between two combs she found that another bee was standing in her way and two others approached, one from the left and one from the right. Then all four bees stood still using their wings to waft air over her from all directions. None of them had drawn a sting and Sylfia knew that she was safe and could breathe more easily using the movement of air that the bees created over her. All four bees stayed in position, lowered their heads and hummed soothingly.

Sylfia looked around for imps and saw none. The bees had guided her to this place and were now recognising her as a friend so, using the air that the bees wafted over her, Sylfia took a deep breath and uttered the magic words that Hornbeam had taught her.

The bees hummed appreciatively and when she had finished they ushered her down, through a maze of combs and platforms, deep into the hive and into the presence of the Queen Bee.

Sylfia removed her gloves so that she could stroke the Queen's fur as a sign of friendship and respect and she whispered more of the magic words that Hornbeam had given her. In return the Queen touched the fairy gently with her front legs and used her giant tongue to lick off the honey that was adhering to her protective clothing. As they tenderly groomed each other Sylfia told the Queen Bee of Hornbeam's plan to liberate the hive explaining that he was going to blow the top off so all the bees must get as far away as possible down into the depth of the hive.

The Queen listened intently, nodding slowly. Then she turned away and danced her instructions to her attendants who all this time had waited patiently around her. When she had finished her dance the courtier bees crawled away in all directions to pass on her instructions to the whole hive.

She had told them that the whole community was to move lower into the hive, as far down the mountain as they could, so that the upper levels would be abandoned.

Sylfia knew that the number of bees in any hive thinned out towards the top because the upper storeys were mainly honey stores. The nurseries were always nearer the bottom of the hive where the ventilation was good and where more bees congregated to feed and clean the developing young.

The bees would have to resist the urge to work and would have to crush together into a very tight pack. This meant that they would have to rest more, eat sparingly and spend the time grooming each other for flight. They would also have to tend the combs that contained the pupae of new queens because when it was time for The Great Release the new queens would have to fly off in all directions followed by their own swarms. Each swarm could then establish a new colony in a new place.

Sylfia knew that many bees would die in The Great Crush. Some adults might run out of air and many grubs and larvae would be abandoned when the bees escaped.

In addition, there was no way of knowing how the imps would be commanded to react. Sylfia feared that if the Imperial Guard tried to break the bees' strike many more of the Queen Bee's subjects would perish.

Sylfia managed to find the words to promise that The Great Release would happen as soon as possible, to avoid too much suffering, and the Queen Bee hummed her thanks with honeyed breath. Her fur was dreamily soft and her delicate droning sent Sylfia's imagination racing back to her home on the downs by the sea.

Full of pity for the captives, and stabbed by nostalgia for her family, she was longing to free these insects from slavery and send them back to their proper lives in the outside world.

Before the bees led their visitor back to her level of exit they filled her bucket with honey so that it overflowed.

Sylfia murmured her thanks and left the hive. She looked around for signs of Cudlip and spotted the tip of his green hat hanging from the end of a ventilation duct. She made the sign that they had agreed, first checking to make sure that no guard was watching. Then she mounted the stairs to the big honey vat and added her cargo. Up here there were two stern-looking guards watching every movement that she made.

She kept her head down and descended the stairs as quickly as possible, clutching the empty bucket.

At the bottom she stopped and, glancing back up, she was alarmed to see that the vat guards were looking straight at her. She wondered if she had done something out of the ordinary that had raised their suspicions.

Two more guards left their positions near the hive door and advanced purposely towards her.

"What did I do wrong?" she thought. "Can I speak like an imp and bluff my way out? Should I turn and run?"

These thoughts were still running through her mind when, with giant strides the two guards reached her and roughly moved her out of the way.

"Can't you see? His Highness wants to descend. Get out of the way!" one of them hissed in her ear.

She was pushed roughly to one side and the guards stood to attention as Pim came down the stairs and strode away over the platform. Sylfia saw that they hurried after the prince and when they reached his side they danced attendance on him and hung on his every word.

Pim waved a regal hand to acknowledge their presence and immediately engaged them in conversation about the work rate of the imps and the yields of honey and wax for that day.

Sylfia took the opportunity to slip out of sight under the stairs. Here she removed her protective clothing and stowed it away in a dark corner, along with her bucket.

She was ready, when the coast was clear, to fly at the speed of light up to the ventilation shaft and in through the opening where she had seen Cudlip's hat hanging as a sign. Slowly Pim and the two guards moved away, deep in conversation while following the path around the circular wall of the hive, until at last they were out of sight.

She crawled out from under the stairs and looked up. Two imps had just taken up their buckets of honey and the guards were watching as they carefully poured the contents into the vat. At this moment there were no other workers on the platform or the stairs so she took her chance.

The guards in the vat room above and two of their comrades who were just marching into view from behind the hive were temporarily blinded by a flash. They blinked and rubbed their eyes. When they asked each other, "What was that?" no one could supply a sensible answer.

"There's something wrong in the hive!"

Macciovolio was watching Tansy in the throne room when Grim rushed in to report this fact. After her exercises to limber up, his precious hostage was just beginning to give a dazzling display.

Without turning his head the wizard asked in a rather bored voice what could possibly be so urgent that it would warrant this irritating intrusion.

"The bees have left the top of the hive, sir," Grim panted, trying to catch his breath. "They've all gone down to the lower levels, sir, and they seem to be – erm," Grim cleared his throat. "They seem to be – well – on strike, sir."

Macciovolio turned slowly to study the face of the soldier, one of his most loyal and sycophantic servants.

"Is this some sort of joke, Grim? If it is, it's in very poor taste and you run the risk of incurring my most spiteful wrath."

"No, indeed, sir, it's the honest truth, sir, on my word of honour."

Macciovolio sighed deeply.

"I'm surrounded by fools, dolts and idiots! If I turn my attention away for a moment the organisation falls to pieces!"

"It occurs to me that nothing like this ever happened

until that prince came on the scene, sir," Grim said slyly, giving the word "prince" a sarcastic emphasis. "Maybe he wasn't ready for such a lot of responsibility, sir. Shall I fetch him, sir?"

The wizard glared at Grim with a look of deepest contempt on his face.

"You're enjoying this!" he snarled. "You'd like nothing better than to see him fail. You think he's usurped your position, I suppose? Jealous fool! Let me remind you that he was my idea and if *my* ideas fail it makes *me* look very silly. Do you think I would enjoy looking silly? Do you? Answer me!"

"No, sir, not at all! You would not like to look silly, sir! I would not like you to look silly, sir!"

"Well then, I suggest that you go and find Prince Pernickety and the two of you can discuss together what might be going on to make the bees behave in such a way. When you've decided on the cause then you can set about putting it right! Together! Understood?"

The wizard's voice had increased in volume while he was making this speech. The final few words were screeched into the face of the unfortunate Grim who, looking even more saturnine than ever, saluted and marched very briskly away.

Tansy had stopped performing when the shouting had begun and now she was staring down into the hive through the glass floor beneath her feet.

"What are you waiting for? Carry on!" Macciovolio shouted impatiently.

"Bees are mysterious creatures," she said, turning towards the wizard and ignoring his bullying manner. "Hundreds, even thousands, work together as one co-operative unit, serving their community together, like well-oiled cogs in a living machine. Individuals stop when they die, of course, and the whole hive will hibernate when the weather it is very cold but to have them stop all together and so abruptly for no apparent reason is very intriguing. There must be some great magic at work here."

"Nonsense!" the wizard exclaimed angrily but Tansy gazed at him steadily and he began to feel very perplexed and greatly troubled.

"That'll do for today," he snapped. "Get back in your cage. I suddenly find that I have a number of things to do today."

He turned on his heel and briskly marched out of the room. The folds of his cloak rustled stiffly as he went and his staff rang like a bell when, with each stride, he banged it down hard on the stone floor.

Two guards took Tansy by the arms, threw her back into her cage and locked her in. As she was carried out she looked down through the bars to see a swarm of imps, all wrapped up in their protective clothing, clearing away the last of the honey and wax from the top levels of the hive. There was not a bee to be seen anywhere and she realised why her visit to the throne room today had seemed so strange. She had missed the distant and, until now, endless drone of the bees.

Chapter 24

Cudlip was overjoyed by Sylfia's success with the bees.
Before they started back for home they looked out from
their hiding place high up in the rock wall and saw that
there was already a change within the hive. They observed
that large numbers of bees had already deserted the upper
levels and were moving down, out of sight, into the lower
regions of their glass prison.

"Well done, Sylfia. You were terrific," he told her.
"Are you O.K?"

"Yes, fine. The bees were the terrific ones. They and
their Queen were so very gentle and understanding."

"Excellent! Let's go and tell Hornbeam. He'll be
delighted. Maybe we can move the rocket tonight,
under cover of darkness!"

With that they backed out of the ventilation shaft
and the boggle led the way back home.

When they reached his house he burst in through one
of the many front doors, shouting at the top of his voice.

"It's done! The bees are on the move! Sylfia was great!"

There was no answer.

"Hornbeam, where are you?"

There was still no answer.

"Did he say that he was going out?" Sylfia asked.

"No, he didn't. He was going to fix up some trolley wheels to transport the rocket" Cudlip moved quickly down the hallway that led towards the workshop.

"I expect he's so engrossed in his work he can't hear us."

Cudlip strode into the workshop, flushed with excitement, and found that a trolley had been fixed up and it was parked beside the rocket, waiting to be loaded. He could not, however, see Hornbeam anywhere.

Next, Cudlip ran down a long corridor to the room where Sycodelia had been kept under lock and key and finding that the door was standing open he looked in with great fear and trepidation. There was no sign of either the witch or of Hornbeam.

When Sylfia heard that Hornbeam was not in the workshop she ran down another corridor in the opposite direction and knocked on the door of Flum's room. There was no answer. She opened the door quietly and peeped in, expecting to see her friend still fast asleep in his bed, but to her consternation, she saw that the bed was empty. She went in and searched around but there was no sign of any living creature, not among the rumpled bed clothes, not under the bed, not in the wardrobe nor anywhere else in the room.

They met in the kitchen and, when Sylfia heard that

Sycodelia had gone and Cudlip heard that Flum was missing, their joint concern turned to massive dread.

They slumped down into chairs and stared straight ahead. Their imaginations worked overtime as they invented their own theories to explain the disappearances.

Neither dared to tell the other what they pictured in their heads as the possible fate of their friends.

Both jumped when they heard a front door slam. They stared at each other, rigid with fear, unable to move except to grab the edges of the table in front of them.

Footsteps approached. Cudlip grabbed a large copper pan from its hook on the wall and leapt into position behind the half open door. Sylfia looked around desperately and then caught sight of a large bread knife in a wooden block on the side bench. She grabbed the knife and moved at the speed of light to join Cudlip behind the door.

The footsteps advanced at a leisurely pace down the corridor and stopped outside the kitchen. The door was pushed open a little wider.

Cudlip raised the pan above his head. Sylfia gripped the knife in both hands and held it straight out in front of her. They both stood perfectly still, holding their breath.

A figure moved into the room and Cudlip brought the heavy pan down onto its head while Sylfia screamed.

The body of Hornbeam lay stretched out on the floor at their feet.

Pim was standing on a platform near the top of the hive. He was staring in through the glass wall, wondering how much of the bees' behaviour was due to his friends' activities and when he looked up through the glass ceiling that was also the floor of the throne room he wondered how on earth it could be blown up. He needed to keep Tansy out of the throne room and he had no idea how he could do that.

Imps were coming out onto the platform at this highest level carrying empty bags and baskets because there was no longer any honey or wax left to collect. The bees had gone down into the mountain and the harvest had dried up.

Grim, reluctantly obeying Macciovolio, came looking for Prince Pernickety and together they went down to the next level. It was the same story there. There were no bees, no wax left and no honey to collect. Some imps stood around waiting for further orders while others had been marched back to their living quarters.

They descended further. At lower levels imps were still collecting some wax and small amounts of honey but their buckets were not even half full. Many of the imps staggered out of the hive in a state of exhaustion after long spells of digging and scraping for every morsel that was left.

As they neared the bottom of the hive the Prince and the Guard could see the bees crowded together in vast numbers moving only their wings to help with ventilation but otherwise keeping very quiet to conserve energy.

"They're waiting for something," thought Pim. "They must have been told that something is going to happen."

At the very bottom of the hive those imps whose job it was to go in and sweep out dead bees found that they could no longer gain access because the bees were pressed so close together that any intruder would be crushed. Indeed, a few of their unfortunate colleagues had not made it out in time and their faces could be seen squashed up against the glass, mouths and eyes wide-open with horror.

"What're we going to do?" Grim asked abruptly.

"I hadn't realised that it was up to us." Pim replied complacently.

"Oh, yes. Macciovolio has given this task to the two of us. It's our reward for being his special favourites."

Grim sounded bitter but at the same time he took pleasure in causing what he thought would be his rival's extreme discomfort.

"I see."

This was a disappointing reaction for Grim. He wanted some ranting and railing and stamping of feet so that he could tell the pompous prince that it served him right for muscling in on his patch.

"Have you not got any ideas? You must have worked

with insects in the old days," Grim said gruffly, hiding his disappointment.

"Bees weren't my concern. I was more of a butterfly watcher. One thing I do know is that this is only the start."

"What d'ya mean?"

"Those bees are waiting for something."

"Don't be daft. What can they be waiting for? A day at the sea side? A trip to the circus? We can't hang around while they decide. What they need is a kick up the backside to get them going again. I vote that we light a bonfire down here and drive them back up again."

"You'll kill them with the heat and the smoke will rob them of oxygen," Pim told him. "Bees can't be forced like that. We need to tap into the communal instinct."

"Oh yeah? What's communal instinct when it's wrapped in tinsel and tied up with a bow?"

"They all behave as a team. They take instructions from the Queen but she must have given them new instructions, different to normal."

Grim grimaced and sucked air through his teeth.

"If she's anything like our Queen Impress she'll be the silliest fool in creation," he moaned.

Pim thought hard for a moment

"We should send out gnomes to collect a new Queen. That should revitalise the bees and get them going again. There's nothing like a bit of rivalry is there?"

Pim was stalling for time and that was the best he could think of, but it worked.

"O.K." Grim agreed. "You organise that and I'll tell Macciovolio what you're doing. If he likes it then it's *our* plan. If he doesn't like it then it's *yours*."

Pim smiled as though that was a good joke and Grim was annoyed yet again that he had not been able to goad the Prince into anger.

Pim watched the Guard march off in search of the wizard. Grim started to climb on the west side of the hive taking one set of stairs after another, moving from one platform onto the next, until he had climbed out of sight. Pim waited for only a few moments before starting up the stairs on the *east* side if the hive. He was determined to find Cudlip and get to know exactly what was going on.

Hornbeam was stretched out on the kitchen floor staring at the ceiling.

He could see the faces of Sylfia and Cudlip gazing down at him anxiously.

Their voices sounded as if they were coming from the far end of a long tunnel, hollow, echoing and distant.

Sylfia was patting his hands and face and seemed to be saying "Hornbeam? Can you hear me?"

Cudlip was kneeling on the floor, wringing his *own* hands and wailing. His words sounded like "I'm *so* sorry!

Please forgive me. Don't die old friend! Have I killed him Sylfia? Tell me I haven't! I'll never be able to live with myself! *Never!*"

Hornbeam groaned and tried to sit up. He groaned again, even louder, as gongs and kettle drums began to sound between his ears. He lay down again.

"Take it easy, old fellow. Stay still," Cudlip told him. "Take your time. Thank goodness he's alive, Sylfia! What can we do for him? How can we help him?"

"Here, put this on your head," said Sylfia. "No, not you Cudlip, it's for Hornbeam's head. Don't try to get up, Hornbeam. Wait until you feel better."

Somehow Sylfia managed to remain calm in the face of the boggle's panic. Her voice was soothing as she gently placed a cold wet towel around the old elf's head.

A number of minutes passed and, during this time, Sylfia turned her attention to Cudlip, consoling him and telling him that everything would be alright.

Eventually, Hornbeam was able, with the help of his two companions, to sit up.

They propped him against the kitchen wall and watched his face intently. He looked back at them with a dazed expression which was to be expected under the circumstances.

"What happened?" he asked.

"I hit you with a pan because we thought you were the witch coming back to get us," Cudlip blurted out.

"I see. I should have left a note."

"To tell us not to hit you?"

"No! To say that I had let her go."

"Why in fairydom did you do that?" Sylfia asked, wonderingly.

"She was ready. She had to go home. It was time. Any way, she's taken important information from me to her father, The Wizard of the West. He'll be very pleased to get it. We're going to release the rocket soon so there was no point in detaining her."

"What about Flum?" Sylfia asked.

Hornbeam looked puzzled.

"Isn't he in his room?"

"No! We thought that the witch must have got him again. That's why we were so scared!"

Hornbeam was in pain. His head throbbed, his face was pale and he looked even older than usual. Now to add to that his face furrowed even more deeply as it took on a worried frown.

"I left him sleeping, or at least I thought he was sleeping. He must have got up and wandered off! This is not good. He must be found. We need to account for all four fairies when the rocket goes off."

"I'll go," Sylfia volunteered. "He listens to me. I think I know where he'll be. He'll be looking for Tansy, I'm sure. Let's just hope that no one else finds him first. Will you be alright with Cudlip, Hornbeam?"

"Yes, yes, my dear. A couple of cups of nettle tea and I'll be as right as rain."

Both Sylfia and Cudlip looked doubtful.

"Don't do anything silly, either of you," Sylfia urged.

"You're both in shock and Hornbeam, especially, needs to take it very easy."

She wagged her finger in a matronly fashion.

"Don't do anything strenuous until I get back!" she ordered.

"No ma'am!" they chorused like schoolboys. "We'll only be drinking tea and eating toast for the rest of the day."

Sylfia prepared to leave and then looked down at the bedraggled pair sitting on the kitchen floor.

"Promise you won't do anything silly?" she said, one last time.

"Never!" they chanted.

"I wish I didn't have to leave you two alone," she hesitated.

"Go!" Cudlip urged. "You need to find Flum before he gets into even bigger trouble than we can by just sitting here!"

"Right, I'll be back as soon as I can. Take care!"

She left at the speed of light and they heard one of the front doors close with a bang behind her.

Cudlip turned to Hornbeam.

"I really can't tell you how sorry I am."

"I know you are, old friend, but what's done is done. Now, where's that tea?"

"Peppermint is it?"

"No nettle would be best, I think. Then I'll have a little lie-down."

Cudlip helped Hornbeam to bed. By the time he returned with the tea the old elf was fast asleep.

"Best thing for him," the boggle murmured and sat down on a chair to watch over his friend. He sipped the restorative drink himself and, exhausted by emotional tension, nodded off in the chair.

Chapter 25

Some hours passed and then there was a slight rap on Hornbeam's bedroom door. When there was no answer from inside the room, a visitor stepped tentatively inside. "Mmm! No fairies, just these two sleeping beauties."

When the newcomer touched Cudlip on the shoulder the boggle woke with a start, spilling the tea down his front.

"Pim!" he gasped. "How did you get in here?"

"I was wondering where to find you when Sylfia came across me and told me how to get here. I offered to help her find Flum but she said she should go alone. I'm not his favourite flavour at the moment. If he saw me out there and started a scrap it would be difficult for all of us."

"Won't you be missed?" Cudlip wondered as he dried himself on a cushion.

"Maybe. In fact it's very likely, but I'm on a pointless mission to find a new Queen Bee. It'll be easy to make up a flea and wasp story. I had to know what's happening, you see. Maybe I can help. Why did you say that the throne room would blow up?"

Cudlip jumped up, his eyes shining with pride.

"Come with me," he whispered, taking Pim's arm and glancing at the old elf to make sure that he had not been disturbed.

He led Pim down the corridor until they stood outside the door to the workshop.

"Look in here," he said, opening the door.

Pim stepped through the doorway and gasped with surprise. He stood very still and stared with round eyes and a wide open mouth.

"Amazing!" he breathed, genuinely impressed by the beauty of the machine. "Absolutely amazing! What does it do?"

"What does it DO, my boy? What does it DO? Can't you see what it does? It's a rocket! A one-hundred-percent-elf-and-boggle-hand-crafted-rune-painted-high-class-whizz-bang-exploding rocket!"

Pim's mouth opened and shut several times as the cogs of his brain ratcheted around.

"Don't you see?" Cudlip cried gleefully. "Yes, of course, you do! It's simple isn't it?"

"Simple? What is?" Pim asked in wonderment.

"It will blast through the top of the hive and the bees will be able to escape!"

"Ingenious! That's why the bees have moved! They know!" Pim exclaimed.

Cudlip explained how he had just been introducing

Sylfia into the hive when Pim came across him in the corridor and how he had been struggling with the 'left over' imp.

"You four have been very busy. I'm very impressed!" Pim told him.

"Well, actually just three of us," Cudlip told him. "I'm afraid Flum had an unfortunate encounter with a witch who was masquerading as a spider. He nearly got desiccated and his brain is still a bit addled. Now he's gone walkabout and I wouldn't say that he's one hundred per cent 'with it' yet."

"That must be why Sylfia was so keen to find him without delay?"

"Yes and she was right not to involve you. Flum needs to be told that you're still one of us. He hadn't been told that before his run in with the witch. He's after your blood"

"I see. Quite so, if he doesn't know that it's all a ruse. What's wrong with Hornbeam? Is he sick?"

"Yes. No. I mean not really," Cudlip demurred. "I hit him on the head, accidentally, of course. I thought he was the witch coming back. It's a long story and I'd rather not tell it just now, if you don't mind. I'm too ashamed."

The boggle shook his head and sighed deeply.

"What can I do?" Pim asked eagerly, fervently hoping for a part in this stage of the adventure.

Cudlip looked up quickly as an idea came to him. He smiled and rubbed his hands together.

"It's a great stroke of luck – you finding us here.

Hornbeam's going to be weak and wobbly for some time but *you* could help me move the rocket. We need to put it in place on the top platform of the hive. If you help me to do that we can leave Hornbeam to rest. He needs to be ready for his next ordeal."

"Next ordeal?" Pim asked in alarm.

"Dealing with Macciovolio, Pim. There's no point in freeing the bees if the wizard is still here to start the whole sorry business up again."

Pim whistled and spoke his thoughts aloud.

"Can an old elf deal with that much evil magic?" he wondered.

Cudlip looked startled. He had never thought about the elf like that before. When Hornbeam spoke of his powers he always sounded so confident. Cudlip had never seriously doubted him, at least not for any length of time. He had marvelled at his new friend's big ideas and, although he would readily admit to a certain degree of scepticism at first, it had been short lived. Hornbeam had managed to inspire him with hope and enthusiasm.

Now Pim had sown some seeds of doubt.

"I believe he can," he told Pim airily. "We have to believe it. We have no other plan."

"You're right," Pim exclaimed, rubbing his hands together. "Let's get started then. Is that the trolley?"

The boggle and the fairy loaded up the rocket. They found Hornbeam's stash of bubble gum very useful. They chewed pieces to wedge underneath the rocket so that it would not roll about. They covered it with a patchwork quilt and, with Pim pulling and Cudlip pushing, they manoeuvred it out of the house and into the system of tunnels that led to the top of the hive.

They moved slowly because the trolley was heavy and cumbersome. From time to time they were passed by groups of imps and pairs of Imperial Guards. Cudlip melted away into the rock face at the sound of foot steps and Pim stood still, staring imperiously at all who passed by.

Worker imps were obviously curious and would like to have asked questions but Pim was too important so they simply shuffled past, looking at the ground.

Guards were another matter. They stopped to stare and would have asked a lot of awkward questions but Pim used his most ringing voice to bark out commands and orders to march on.

"This is secret business known only to the Lord Chamberlain and myself. Any interference with this consignment will result in severe punishment."

When one particularly nosy guard stretched out his hand to lift the quilt Pim moved at the speed of light. The guard was unconscious on the rocky floor before he or his companions had a chance to blink.

"Next time you ignore my instructions your head will part company with your body. Understood?"

"Yes sir …… of course, your highness …… please forgive …… stupid fool …… let us drag him out of the way, sir …… sorry sir ……"

Pim and Cudlip progressed down the winding tunnels

until they emerged onto the top platform of the hive. They came to a stop in front of the revolving glass doors and, on Pim's advice, Cudlip went to hide in a ventilation duct.

"How are we going to get it in through those doors?" Cudlip asked from his hiding place.

"No bother," his accomplice whispered.

Pim called loudly and imps appeared from all directions, from wherever they had been working on that circular level, inside and outside the hive. There was no reason for them to wear protective clothing now because the bees had gone from up here but they still carried buckets and they wielded brooms as well. These workers were still busy gathering every morsel of honey and wax that might be left in the hive and that included sweeping it off the floors.

"This is a new cleaning machine," Pim told them. "Take off those doors so that I can wheel it inside."

The imps jumped to this task with alacrity. A machine to do the job for them! This new Prince was turning out to be a good fellow after all!

They even took over the job of pulling and pushing the trolley into the middle of the hive.

"Leave it there!" Pim ordered. "Report for duty on the lower levels but say nothing about this because I don't want silly rumours spreading. The machine might not work and if it doesn't The Lord Chamberlain will be very cross. Do you want to take the blame?"

The heads of the imps shook vigorously, along with

their shoulders and knees. Pim had learnt that the merest mention of Macciovolio could engender fear and panic.

When they had gone Cudlip came out of from his hiding place and together he and Pim lifted the rocket from the trolley and stood it upright in the middle of the hive. Bubblegum was indispensable here too.

It was very quiet inside the hive and, to add to the light provided by the flaming torches, electric lights had been switched on. They looked up and noticed that it was night and through the glass roof they could see a canopy of stars sparkling in the night sky. There was no one in the throne room.

"It must be supper time, or even later," Pim said. "It might even be bed time. This would be a good time to set it off."

"Steady on, young fella. We need to lay the fuse first," Cudlip told him. "I'll have to go back to tell Hornbeam that it's ready because he wants to be outside on the mountainside when it goes off. He's probably not fit enough yet and, anyway, he needs to know that the rest of us are safe."

"Wilko," Pim chirped. "Let's lay that fuse and then you can go and consult the boss. I'll just stay here and guard the rocket from prying eyes."

Cudlip beamed at him.

"You're enjoying this aren't you?"

"Sure thing," Pim grinned back. "This whole sorry adventure has just taken a turn for the better. It's been pretty grim so far but now I can't wait to burst that wizard's balloon or should I say blow his glass roof off!"

They fitted a box of black powder into a special fuel compartment that Hornbeam had made in the base of the rocket.

Cudlip produced the reel of invisible elfish thread that he had been keeping in his pocket all this time. He lovingly fingered the gorgeous stuff and then carefully dipped the end into the charge box. There was a clip on the inside that gripped the fuse and made sure that it stayed in contact with the explosive mixture. Holding the reel loosely between his hands he backed out of the hive, across the wooden platform and up to the wall of the cavern. In this way the fuse was laid and only an occasional scintillation showed where the magic thread was lying across the floor. He stored the reel with its unused thread inside the nearest ventilation duct.

Cudlip helped Pim to put the door back on the hive so that it was more difficult for someone outside on the platform to see the rocket inside. The magic fuse was thin enough to pass underneath the door.

When all was ready Cudlip turned to leave.

He jumped with fright when he found that his way was barred by a crazy-looking Flum.

"Hello young fella. You look cross. Now just let me explain what's going on," he said cheerfully.

Flum took no notice. He looked straight past Cudlip as if the boggle was not there. He only had eyes for Pim and his face was like thunder.

"There you are you blastardly daggard! You treacherous

turncoat. I've been looking for you everywhere."

As he growled the last few words he flew at high speed across the platform and launched himself at Pim. He began throwing punches in wild, abandoned fury. The speed and ferocity of Flum's attack was such that it caught Pim off guard and made him stagger backwards, crashing into the glass wall of the hive.

Cudlip tried to separate them but when he grabbed one of Flum's arms his only reward was a sharp crack on the cheek bone from the furious fairy's elbow.

Cudlip's interference did give Pim enough time and space to leap away from his opponent and prepare to defend himself. He regained his balance just in time for, as soon as Flum had freed his arm from Cudlip's grip, he pounced again. Pim was ready for him this time and side-stepped with great nimbleness.

Flum was carried by his own momentum towards the rock wall of the cavern. To avoid a collision with the wall he swooped upwards and crashed instead into one of the brackets that carried a flaming torch. A slim fairy would have merely rattled the thing in its holder but the impact from a portly fairy like Flum was enough to tip the torch out of its socket and send it crashing to the floor.

In his fury Flum hardly noticed what he had done and he turned in an instant to fly into Pim again at the speed of light. The pair rolled over and over on the floor.

Only Cudlip saw the disaster as it started to unfold.

The flaming torch fell onto the magic fuse. The thread glittered joyfully and flared up with chuckling glee.

It sparkled and crackled and a coloured flame began to zip along its length. Cudlip shrieked and leapt on top of it. He danced up and down on the flame, in an attempt to smother it, but he only succeeded in scorching his feet.

"Stop it, you fools," he yelled. "Help me put this out!"

Pim would have helped without hesitation but he could not disentangle himself from the furious Flum and Flum only had one thing on his mind and that was to kill the treacherous Pim.

Sylfia, who had been tracking Flum in an adjoining tunnel, caught up with him at last. As she flew into the cavern she saw immediately that Cudlip needed help and joined him in stamping on the fuse. The harder they stamped, however, the brighter and hotter burnt the flame. After all, this was a magic fuse and, once alight, it would take a very strong spell to dampen its ardour.

"Can we cut it?" she asked. "Could we do it with scissors? Or an axe?"

"I'd have to go to the workshop," Cudlip replied.

"We haven't got time! It's nearly up to the hive!"

It was true. The progress of the flame was inexorable. It reached the door of the hive and disappeared underneath.

"That's it!" Cudlip groaned. "Take cover! You two! Stop brawling and follow me!"

He grabbed Sylfia's hand and pulled her over to the cavern wall. He found the opening to a ventilation shaft and pushed her in. He followed her inside and together they crouched down with their hands over their ears but the other two still wrestled on the wooden floor.

Pim had seen Cudlip and Sylfia disappear into the air duct and he tried to follow but Flum's chubby arms were firmly locked around his neck and the heavy fairy's weight dragged him back.

"Stop it you fool," Pim shouted. "We have to take cover. There's going to be an explosion!"

No sooner had he got these words out when there was a roar from the gun powder in the charge box as it caught alight. Red and orange flames licked out from under the door of the hive. Pim managed to drag himself and his assailant away from the spreading flames, towards the wall of the cavern, but not before their clothes, wings and hair were singed.

The wooden platform started to shake and, with sickening creaks and groans, it began to collapse.

At last Flum saw the danger, through the red mist of his fury, and felt the flames as they began to scorch his extremities. He looked around and, observing his impending doom, he allowed himself to be dragged by Pim. With every ounce of his remaining strength Pim managed to pull them both across to a place in the rock wall where they could hang on. They could see that the entrance to one of the tunnels was gaping not far above them in the rock wall but the wooden steps up to it had fallen away. They fluttered their poor singed wings but could not make much progress towards the comparative safety of the tunnel and what's more currents of hot air were swirling around the cavern blowing them against the wall. Their damaged wings were not strong enough to beat against the blast and carry them to safety so all they could do was hang on tightly to the bolts and brackets that had fixed the wooden platform to the wall.

The noise inside the hive rose to a deafening pitch and the intense heat began to crack the glass walls. That part of the sagging wooden platform nearest to the hive was burning fiercely now.

The rocket shuddered and rocked, rattled and creaked. The noise changed from a roar to a piercing shriek and Liberator began to lift off. The noise intensified and the craft seemed to hover for a few moments in the empty space at the top of the hive until suddenly, with a whoosh, it was gone.

The glass floor of the throne room shattered, as did the roof above, and the walls of the hive started to disintegrate with a fearful splintering sound. The evening sky became clearly visible and cold night air flooded into the mountain. Shards of glass showered down into the throne room from the shattered roof. Some of it piled up on the shelf of rock that ran around the chamber and had supported the dance floor but most of it joined the broken glass floor that fell down into the depths of the cavern.

Broken glass cascaded down like a waterfall, down, down into the depths of the hive until it came to some wooden platforms that were far enough below the blast to have stayed in place. There the glass landed like sharp hard snow and built up into tinkling, glittering drifts on top of those imps and Imperial Guards that had not had time to run away into the tunnels.

Pieces of broken and charred wood fell on top of the drifts of shattered glass and sooty smoke rose from the smouldering heaps.

As soon as the last shard of glass and the final splinter of wood had landed an eerie silence fell but not for long. The groaning and coughing of survivors soon broke out and then an unearthly rumbling noise began to rise from the deepest depths of the mountain.

The noise grew and grew and the debris began to shiver and shake as vibrations began to ripple through the whole mountain. The imps and guards who were still alive were already scared out of their wits but when the mounds of debris began to ripple, roll and undulate under their feet their panic knew no bounds. They fled in every direction open to them, pushing their way through the ruins of the hive, crawling, limping and yelling until every imp that was fit enough had disappeared down the tunnels into the mountain. Some had guessed what was coming next and believing that enough was enough for one day they fled as fast as their injuries would allow, leaving the dead and dying behind.

The heaps of tinkling, smouldering rubble began to quiver more urgently and bees emerged in their hundreds and then in their thousands. As they emerged into the empty spaces above the debris they immediately took flight and headed on upwards towards freedom. A buzz-ing column of furry bodies rose up at top speed to fill the upper reaches of the cavern.

The column of bees became denser, faster and louder and soon spread out to fill the whole cavern from side to side. They soared upwards with unstoppable purpose and determination and the volume of the noise they made rivalled the blast of a jet engine. It made hearts pound and ears ring. In their hiding place Cudlip and Sylfia heard the steady drone of the flight to freedom and wept with joy.

Pim and Flum clung to the rock wall with all their might and were overcome with gratitude when they realised that the bees were taking a curving flight around them so as not to knock them off their perches.

The unstoppable surge for freedom went on for many minutes until at last the numbers thinned out and the column became a wisp of very young or very old bees struggling to keep up but showing just as much determination to escape.

When the last bee had buzzed crazily out of sight the air gradually stopped its vibration and became still again. Pim was able to use the strength that remained in his large but tattered wings to fly both himself and an exhausted Flum up to the mouth of the tunnel.

He looked back to see Cudlip's long thin arm waving from the ventilation shaft and he waved too.

Flum looked at his companion in wonder. Pim had so recently been his deadliest foe and could easily have left him to die in the blast but instead his acknowledged enemy had saved him. He did not think he would have survived without Pim's help. For once in his life Flum was lost for words, plain or jumbled. Pim, however, had just one word to say.

"Tansy!"

Flum nodded and they set off together down the maze of tunnels that would lead them to Macciovolio's headquarters.

Chapter 26

Hornbeam woke in an instant and sat bolt upright, clutching his bruised and thumping head.

Now something else was wrong. What was that terrific noise?

The bed underneath him was trembling. He swung his legs over the side and stood up but this felt no better because the rock walls of Cudlip's house were shaking too and the floor was undulating beneath his feet.

He could hear the distant crashing sound of the glass floor and roof of the throne room as they fell down into the depths of the cavern. A light went on in his brain and a sudden dawning filled him with cold fear.

All went quiet for a short time and he waited, with wide eyes and bated breath for another deafening noise. It was like the sound of an aircraft taking off. It was a tremendous humming, buzzing, throbbing wail as thousands of bees took flight, making a gushing torrent upwards through a confined space.

Hornbeam, still clutching his poor sore head, staggered down the corridors to the workshop.

"I don't believe it," he gasped when he saw the empty space where the rocket used to be. "Why did they do that? Why did they not wait for me?"

He spent some time searching the house.

"Cudlip? Sylfia? Flum? I don't believe it! Why did they do that? Am I still asleep? This is a nightmare? I want to wake up now!"

Sylfia found him sitting on the kitchen floor, slumped against the wall, in much the same place and position as she had left him.

He seemed dazed and confused.

"Hornbeam! What happened to you? Did you get knocked out again? Speak to me! How can I help you?"

"What happened yourself," he said. "*You* tell me what's going on! They set it off didn't they? Why did they do that without me?"

"They didn't mean to, Hornbeam," Sylfia told him, sorrowfully. "It was Flum's fault. He attacked Pim while he was helping Cudlip to set it up, that's all. They were going to come back and tell you and wait for you to choose the time but Flum rushed into the cavern from the tunnel and flew at Pim in a rage. I'd been following him but I had to hide from guards for a while. By the time I arrived Pim was fighting back and he side stepped so that Flum hurtled past him, knocked a flaming torch out of its bracket and it fell down onto the fuse."

Hornbeam stared at the floor, shaking his head.

"Cudlip laid the fuse without me," he muttered sadly. "Why couldn't he wait? That was wrong of him."

"Oh, Hornbeam, I know, but you should have seen them. The bees I mean. They were awesome. I'm so sorry you missed it," she added sympathetically. "When I saw them racing for freedom, like a throbbing tornado, it was ...... it was ...... spectacular! It was mind-blowing!"

"Yes. It must have been wonderful" Hornbeam murmured and got to his feet wearily.

"Only thing is, I still have to stop that wizard!"

He sighed and abruptly left the room.

Sylfia followed after him and saw him opening the door to a cupboard in the hall. As he rummaged in the dark interior of the closet she heard him muttering to himself.

"I put them in here. I know I did. Don't say they've been chucked out. Oh no, here they are. That's a relief!"

He emerged, covered with dust, sneezing and rubbing his poor tired eyes.

"Better take these. Just in case, you never know. We might need transport out of here."

He was carrying a bundle of Sycodelia's broomsticks and, without making any further comment, he headed in the direction of the nearest exit.

"Hornbeam!" Sylfia called after him. "Wait! You're not strong enough! Where are you going?"

"I'm going out on the mountainside where I should have been when the rocket went off. Someone has to deal with that wizard and persuade him that it's all over!"

He turned around and looked at her more kindly, as though he had just remembered who she was. He smiled and held out his hand looking a little more like his old self.

"Come with me, Sylfia." he said gently. "We'd better stick together and on the way you can tell me about the others. Are they all safe? Where are they all? Who has gone to get Tansy?"

Sylfia went with him down the tunnels that led to the bat cave and from there they stepped out onto the mountainside.

It was heavenly to be out, breathing the cool night air and seeing the stars glittering in the indigo sky. Cudlip's house had been a good home, a safe haven, but what a relief to leave the dank, mouldering tunnels with their ability to smother magic and drain fairy energy.

She felt like a proper fairy again and Hornbeam felt the strength of generations of elves pouring into him on the invigorating night breeze.

Cudlip, she told him, was safe. She described how he had pulled her to safety.

When all was quiet again they had agreed that she should go back to the house to find Hornbeam while he kept an eye on the rest.

Pim and Flum had had a bad time, she told him, but they had clung on to the fixtures that had held the disintegrating staircases to the wall. She was able to report that she saw them both make it back into the tunnel, scorched and dishevelled, but still alive.

"Still fighting?" Hornbeam asked.

"No, I don't think so," she replied. "They were both too shocked and hurt and Pim had helped Flum to suvive."

"Maybe the experience brought Flum to his senses," Hornbeam mused.

"A drastic remedy," Sylfia observed.

"True, but remedies can often be cruel and sometimes worse than the sickness. The important thing is that both the cause and the cure come to an end."

As they stood on the mountainside, getting their bearings and enjoying their new feelings of freedom and power, they saw scores of imps running about in panic and confusion. Unfortunately, there was no sign of a wizard.

"I hope I haven't missed him." Hornbeam said, a worried frown passing across his old face.

Neither he nor Sylfia had ever seen Macciovolio but they knew that they would recognise him from Cudlip's graphic descriptions.

They did, however, see the Imperor and the Impress emerging from the gaping hole that used to be the glass roof of their throneroom. The two homeless rulers looked extremely sorry for themselves as they limped down the mountain path, their wigs askew and their painted faces streaked with soot, sweat and tears.

Doris was grumbling as usual.

"You were a fool to buy that newfangled picture making machine," she moaned. "I knew it was dangerous as soon as I saw it. Little buttons going click and vicious flashing lights to blind you. I knew there was an evil demon in there gathering enough bad magic to blow us all to bits!"

"How do you know it was my fault? You always blame me! I never did a thing," Burt moaned defensively.

They continued on their way, arguing at full throttle, totally unaware that their voices were carrying across the whole mountainside.

Suddenly, they were stopped in their tracks as a huge bulky creature stepped out from behind an outcrop of rock and barred their way. This figure loomed over them like a monumental statue.

Doris and Burt shrieked with fear and Sylfia gave a little shriek of joy.

"It's Lummock!" she cried and she flew up the mountainside to stand on the troll's vast shoulder and hug the lobe of his ear. That was one feature of the bulky troll that was just about small enough for a fairy to encircle in her arms.

"Oooo! So happy is Lummock that you be safe," he murmured, blushing deeply.

Sylfia could see that the Imperor and Impress were staring up at them, undecided as to whether they should flee or faint.

"A blooming troll," Doris bleated at last.

"And another tricksy fairy," Burt hissed with contempt. "One too big and strong and the other too fast and frisky! What'll we do?"

'This!' Doris decided.

She threw herself to her knees and, clasping her hands together, she held them up in a theatrically pleading manner. Her husband followed suit.

"Don't hurt us, please, Mister Troll. We're poor homeless souls! We've just been blown up! We've just been made homeless!" Doris begged in a quavering, black-and-white movie voice.

"It was a most uncomfortable experience. You have such a kind face, Mistress Fairy. Don't you think that we have suffered enough for one night?" Burt joined in, using his best wheedling tone.

"OK, that's enough. Keep your performance skills under wraps for now. You don't fool us," Hornbeam told them as he walked slowly up the path to join his friends.

"Blimey, an elf as well. The whole world has come out to see us done for!" Doris wailed.

"Sssh!" Burt whispered. "It's Hornbeam from Mulberry Wood. Don't you recognise him?"

If he had hoped to silence her with this reminder it didn't work because she jumped to her feet and grabbed the elf's hand. Shaking it vigorously she exclaimed her delight that they were meeting again and asked if he remembered her from the old days.

Hornbeam looked at her coldly and released his hand from her grip.

"Only too well," he replied. "This isn't the time or the place for remembering the havoc you caused in a peaceful community. Are you in charge of these imps?"

"We are the Imperor and Impress Under the

Mountain, if that's what you mean," Doris replied sulkily.

"Not any more," Hornbeam snapped. "However, we need you to take charge of these wandering imps and lead them somewhere and let it be somewhere where they will not do so much harm. Before you do, though, I need some information."

"Why should we tell you anything?" Doris asked ignoring the restraining hand that her husband had placed on her arm.

Hornbeam looked at her inquiringly and Lummock took one step closer, his arms stretched out. Each of his gigantic hands was ready to grab one of the pathetic imps and imprison them in an iron grip.

Doris and Burt backed away.

"What do you want to know?" Burt hurriedly asked.

"Where's the wizard? Is he still inside the mountain or has he gone?"

"Macciovolio, you mean?" Burt asked. "Erm ...... dunno, to be honest. D'you know, Doris?"

"He was going to leave but he got detained," Doris explained helpfully. "There was some trouble"

"Trouble? What sort of trouble?"

"Let me see ...... oh yes ......, he was after one of those boggly troggly things. I thought we'd got rid of all those a long time ago, Burt. It just goes to show you don't know what's lurking under yer own feet."

Sylfia flew down from Lummock's shoulder to hover in front of them.

"Who else was involved? Was there a fight going on?"

she demanded clenching her little fists.

"We didn't stick around to see," Burt answered, backing away warily. "There were Imperial Guards all over the place and we wanted to get out before they blocked the exits."

"Round up your imps and take them further down the mountain," Hornbeam ordered, as though bossing royalty around was an everyday task for him. "Run away if you like but you'll be hunted down eventually. Stick around to help and there may be benefits for you and your clan when this is all over. The choice is yours. Go!"

The royal pair made off down the mountain path, skidding as they went and tripping over small rocks that were strewn in their way. As they went, imps crept out from behind boulders and crags to follow them, at a respectful distance.

As the two displaced rulers negotiated the track that led down the mountainside a considerable band of frightened and disoriented followers joined their train. By the time they turned a corner and were lost to sight about two hundred imps were tiptoeing after them.

"Let's go," Hornbeam hissed urgently and all three set off for the top of the mountain.

Chapter 27

Pim guided Flum through the tunnels that led them towards Macciovolio's headquarters. Their progress was impeded by worker imps running about in panic as they tried to locate the nearest exit onto the mountainside. From time to time they had to steer a course around falls of loose rock and the air was thick with smoke and dust. The atmosphere under the mountain had never been pleasant but now it made them cough and their eyes, which were stinging badly, watered profusely.

At last they stopped at the entrance to the courtyard and saw Macciovolio's office on the other side. The courtyard was a mess. Statues had toppled over and smashed and the rubble was covered with dust but at least the area seemed to be deserted.

Pim signalled to Flum to conceal himself behind one of the pillars that had been left standing while he himself picked his way through the rubble to get to the office door. He knocked but there was no answer. He opened the door and looked inside. There was no one there. The cell which on previous occasions had held himself or Tansy had no occupants at the moment and the door to the cell stood open.

Pim stepped inside the room and walked around. He checked behind and underneath the desk but nobody was hiding there.

"Is this what you're looking for?" a voice behind him asked.

He spun around to see Grim standing in the doorway and in his arms he carried the cylindrical cage that contained Tansy.

"Macciovolio is preparing to escape, Pim," she said. "Grim is taking me to him now."

"You weren't there when you were needed, Princey" Grim gloated. "I'm his chief assistant now and what's more *we* won't be requiring your services any longer."

There was a horrible self-satisfied leer on Grim's face and with his next remark he looked positively exultant.

"In fact," he went on. "There's really no need for you to exist at all!"

With that he placed the cage upright on the floor and drew his sword.

"It gives me great pleasure to dispatch such an irritating bighead as you!"

He advanced with the point of his weapon aimed directly at Pim's heart.

Pim stepped backwards until he was pressed against the wall and could retreat no further.

Grim was sneering triumphantly as he approached and Pim was looking around for a possible weapon with which to defend himself when there was a thud. Grim's mouth dropped open, his eyes rolled up into his head and he groaned. His legs gave way so that he dropped onto his knees and then he fell forwards, flat on his face, and deeply unconscious. As he fell he knocked over Tansy's cage so that it rolled across the floor with Tansy in it and it did not stop until it collided with Pim's feet. He took hold of the cage and turned it upright so that the two fairies stood close together, face to face, separated only by the bars of the cage. They smiled at each other.

"I knew you'd turn up," Tansy said.

"I knew you believed that I would," Pim said.

Pim tore his gaze away from her and looked over to the doorway. Flum and Cudlip were standing there looking very pleased with themselves because between them they had managed to lift a large lump of rubble and hurl it at Grim's head with enough force to knock the guard out cold.

"Well done, my boy, you're stronger than you look," Cudlip said to Flum, shaking his hand.

"You too," Flum said to Cudlip, clapping him on the back. "You've a bong arm for a stroggle!"

"Thanks, both of you!" Pim cried. "But what just happened here? Where did Grim come from?"

"Macciovolio sent him to fetch Tansy and I followed," Cudlip said. "I saw him go in to raid the pantry before going back. I was hiding over there."

He pointed across the room to a spot that was some distance from the entrance.

"I wasn't close enough to speak to you before you set off across the courtyard and I didn't want to shout, he might have heard, so I just crept round to where Flum was hiding. Then he came out of the pantry and noticed that the office door was open. You know what happened next."

"Good thinking!" Pim said. "Now all we need is the key to this cage and we can get out of this infernal place."

"Only Macciovolio has a key to this," Tansy told him, unable to hide the note of despair in her voice.

"Oh no he hasn't!"

All eyes turned to Cudlip.

"Who's that?" Tansy whispered to Pim.

"A spy, a story teller and a good friend but I don't know what he's talking about," Pim whispered back.

"I use the same words as our unconscious friend, the one who is currently impersonating a floor mop, when I say 'is this what you're looking for?'"

Cudlip held up a tiny key on a gold chain.

"That's it!" Tansy cried. "How did you get it?"

"While I was checking on our wizard, before I followed old Grim down here, I took the liberty of 'borrowing' this from the wizard's belt. After all you never know when something like that will come in useful!"

"You're a wicked thief but we love you!" Pim told

him as he accepted the key and released Tansy from her iron cage.

"Thank you! Thank you all!" she cried, hugging Pim and then Flum. At first she shook Cudlip's hand in a formal manner then she gave him a hug too.

Sadly their joy was short lived. They had only taken a few steps towards the door when the voice of the wizard rang out across the courtyard. All four companions froze in fear.

"Hurry up you laggards, before they get away!"

He was close, very, very close.

Their blood was already running cold but it almost iced over when they realised that he was picking his way across the rubble strewn courtyard, surrounded by Imperial Guards, all of whom were armed to the teeth with bristling spears and glittering swords.

"Oh no," Tansy gulped.

"What blithering idiots we've been to think he wouldn't know," Pim croaked as he looked around desperately for a means of escape. There was none.

"Humming blell!" Flum moaned. He made a move as though he was going to peep around the door and gain his first sight of the wizard but Pim grabbed his shirt and pulled him back.

"Hide," he whispered. "He doesn't know you. He doesn't even know you're here. Quick!"

Flum did as he was told.

Cudlip was the next to react. Why he chose to confront the wizard instead of melting into the background in his usual way will remain a mystery forever. He could never explain it, not even to himself.

He stepped out of the office and stood face to face with the wizard. He was only half the height and an eighth of the width of Macciovolio, so skinny and bony was he, but when he drew himself up to his fully extended height he could just about peer up into the wizard's face.

"It's just me here. Can I help you?" Cudlip asked.

He saw the icy stare, recognised the wizard's desire for revenge and steeled himself for the onslaught.

"So here you are, boggle thing. I always knew there was at least one of you hanging around being nosey, poking that particular appendage in where it doesn't belong. I was prepared to overlook you and conserve my energies for more important matters but now you have gone too far! You're not just a sneak you're a sneak thief. No one steals from Macciovolio!"

The wizard stretched out an arm and pointed one fore-finger at Cudlip's head. There was a flash and a crackle as a streak of brilliant white light zipped from the end of his finger nail.

Cudlip gave a loud cry and disappeared in a puff of smoke. Within a fraction of a second he was no more. All that was left was a small pile of ash on the floor and a few flakes of fabric debris floating in the air. The boggle had been exterminated.

Pim gulped and choked back his tears. Tansy looked at him with deepest sympathy, recognising that this boggle had been a good friend to him.

Flum peeped out from his hiding place behind the big desk and, seeing their distress, guessed that a great disaster must have overcome Cudlip.

He crouched down with his head in his hands and his shoulders shook silently.

"Come out at once you two!" Macciovolio ordered

Tansy and Pim had no choice but to step out of the office and confront their fate.

"What happened to Grim?" their tormenter snapped.

"The boggle hit him on the head with part of a statue," Tansy replied, truthfully.

Macciovolio looked sceptical.

"All on his own?"

There was silence.

"O.K." Pim said. "I admit it. I helped to knock him out. He taunted me, told me I was no longer needed. I saw red."

After this piece of deceit the rest of the conversation flowed quite easily for Pim. He warmed to his subject, a worthy pupil of his recently exterminated boggle mentor and proud to have been his friend.

Tansy stood silently beside him, her hand squeezing his very tightly. She looked nervous and tearful and inside she felt that she would like to collapse on the floor and weep herself to sleep.

"Why did the boggle steal the key?"

"I asked him to. I wanted to take Tansy away to freedom. It tore me up to see her in a cage, a slave to your whim and pleasure!"

"I should kill you," Macciovolio snarled. "You've dece-ived me. You're a liar and a traitor."

Pim swallowed hard. He could see some justice in the wizard's accusation. Turning to look at Tansy, for what he thought would be the last time, he smiled tearfully. He studied her sad face and waited for the wizard to strike.

The blow did not come. The wizard was thinking hard and his face bore its cold, malicious smile.

"However," he said slowly. "You make an entertaining pair so I'll take you both. The Sorceress may be amused by a fairy prince and I will have extra pleasure seeing you squirm as your precious darling becomes her slave as well as mine!"

Swirling around, his cloak swishing like the wind through dry grass, he ordered his guards to escort the prisoners to the throne room.

They marched the two fairies out of the courtyard, with Macciovolio leading the way Many of the guards secretly rejoiced in the fall of the pompous prince but no one gave the inert body of Grim so much as a backward glance.

Flum followed at a distance, shaking with grief and, at the same time, marvelling at Pim's courage. He was no longer an enemy, an adversary or a pompous fool. He was a hero and Flum was deeply ashamed of the way he had behaved.

Not only had he, Flum, brought about the release of the bees too early which had spoilt the plan but now Cudlip had been wiped out. As well as that, two fairies, one his best friend and the other a brave comrade, were in the greatest danger. He would have to follow them and do whatever it would take to make amends for his great foolishness.

Chapter 28

When Tansy and Pim were marched into the throne
room they saw for the first time Macciovolio's magical
means of travel.

He had conjured up a spinning disc of white vapour
and it looked as though he had captured a cloud and
formed it into a circular magic carpet. It was powered by
a mysterious energy source and it hovered over the gaping
hole where the glass dance floor had once been. It hung
in mid air as though suspended by invisible threads and
it was positioned so that it was level with the rocky floor
that still ran around the walls of the chamber.

The marble thrones were still in place, blackened and
covered with soot now and without their velvet cushions
which had been burnt to a crisp. As we have seen,
Burt and Doris had managed to clamber out onto the
mountainside. They had been sleeping in their royal
apartments along the corridor when the rocket had broken through, wreaking havoc and destruction as it went.

Macciovolio jumped on board the cloud craft, dragging his two fairy prisoners with him. Their wings had been bound so that they could not fly away and each had a strong rope tied tightly around the waist. Macciovolio held the loose ends of these ropes in his iron grip as he shouted the spell of command for the flying cloud to take off.

It began to rise up through what remained of the throne room making for the hole where the glass roof used to be.

The wizard, still grasping the ropes in his steely grip, looked down imperiously on the massed guards who had arranged themselves all around the remaining circle of rocky floor and were gazing up in amazement as the vehicle ascended. He shouted his commands down to them. They were to clean up the mess and make sure everything was shipshape and Bristol fashion for his return. They answered by saluting in a half hearted fashion.

Once the cloud craft had cleared the hole in the roof it continued to rise up above the mountain and once he was out in the cold night air the wizard breathed deeply and whooped with glee.

Hornbeam and Sylfia saw the wizard rise out of the mountain standing as they were near the hole in the top and they first gasped in amazement at the sight of the magic craft but then they groaned with despair at the sight of their two friends on board, bound as prisoners. Their dismay was compounded when they saw Flum shoot out of the mountain in pursuit of the magic craft and its evil inventor. He was travelling at the speed of a hunting falcon, like an unusually chunky aerial predator whose sight is fixed unerringly on its airborne prey. Their terror was complete when they saw Flum the hunter catch up with Macciovolio, his prey, and attempt to prize the fairy captives away from him.

The wizard was taken by surprise at first and could be seen to step back. There was a sharp intake of breath from Hornbeam and a shriek of fright from Sylfia when it looked as though all four figures would fall over the side of the craft but Macciovolio would not have let this happen. He recovered his balance very quickly, soon regained a firm footing even though he was now right on the edge of the disc and roared with anger. There was more gasping and shrieking from the watchers when they saw him dangle both Pim and Tansy over the side hanging from the ropes that he held tightly in his fists. If he let go they would fall down into the centre of the mountain and, with their wings tied up so that they could not fly, they would have had very little chance of survival. Flum had no other choice than to hold up his hands in surrender and Macciovolio lifted his cargo back on board. He dropped both Pim and Tansy into a mist that bubbled up from a depression in the centre of the craft and once they were completely enveloped by the vapour they fell into a hypnotic trance. Their knees buckled and, sighing deeply, they both collapsed into the bowl-like depression and lay completely motionless in a deep sleep.

Macciovolio then advanced on Flum. The fairy was given no time to take to the air and fly to safety, so fast and sudden was the attack.

There was another blinding flash from the wizard's deadly finger and Flum just managed to dodge a direct hit but he was caught by the edge of the powerful ray. He felt the destructive force spreading through his body and it was enough to render him helpless. He was blown, reeling and tumbling, over the edge of the cloud craft and down into the darkness. He fell so quickly that he would have disappeared into the gaping hole in the top of the mountain had not a bulky figure raced to the edge and, just in time, stretched out his muscular arms to catch him.

Hornbeam and Sylfia rushed up to find that Lummock was still precariously balanced on the edge of the hole, gently cradling the inert body of Flum in his huge hands.

The Flying Cloud Carpet continued to rise higher and higher until it was just a fuzzy white speck in the night sky and then it stopped ascending and started to travel in an easterly direction. During his ascent the magician had time to take his parting shot, sending a bolt of his magic lightning straight down to the spot where the friends were gathered on the edge of the hole. It struck the ground next to Lummock's feet and the fragile new debris that had been created by the flight of Hornbeam's rocket sizzled, glowed and slowly began to slide downwards into the chasm.

Lummock rocked backwards and forwards for a few moments then finally lost his precarious balance.

He managed to throw Flum's inert body to Hornbeam before sliding away from them to be lost from sight in the cavernous black hole.

There were clattering sounds followed by shouts, groans and screeches and then the commotion was followed by silence.

Hornbeam shouted down into the darkness.

"Lummock! Can you hear me?"

There was silence.

He tried again.

"Lummock! Are you alright?"

A faint reply floated up.

"Yes, Mr Hornbeam. Lummock thinks maybe he is."

"Where are you?"

"Hanging on, sir. Urrgghh! Lummock is climbing up now," he groaned.

"Urrgghh! On a ledge now," he panted with relief.

After another pause Lummock resumed the conversation.

"Lummock has company, sir. Little imps in shiny suits. Lummock landed on some. Very sorry. Knocked some off the ledge. Very sorry, he is. Others running away now. Bye, bye!"

There was more silence.

"Impies gone now, sir. Lummock all alone. Very sorry!"

"Don't worry, they're Imperial Guards, Lummock and it's a good thing that they ran away," Hornbeam shouted. "Watch out, in case they come back. You might have to stay on the ledge until morning."

"Yes, Mr Hornbeam. Lummock will climb out when he sees the way."

Meanwhile, Sylfia knelt on the ground and cradled Flum's head in her lap.

"Oh, Flum. You poor, brave fairy! What did you do that for? You didn't have a chance!"

Her tears dropped down onto his lifeless face.

"Look at you! Nearly dead for the second time! Dear, funny Flum. What will I do without you?"

She kissed his brow and stroked his hair. She rocked him tenderly in her arms, sobbing all the while.

Flum opened his eyes and smiled at her.

"Dear, brave, funny? Wow! I'll have to skive out of the die more often!"

"You're alright!" she shrieked, her grief turning to joy in an instant. She held his face between her hands and looked stern.

"Don't you *dare* dive out of the sky *ever* again because dear old Lummock can't always be there to catch a *great idiot* like you!"

"Great idiot? That's more like it!" Flum said as he sat up. "It's great to have my magic back, out here in the open air again."

"Sometimes, I think that you're determined not to survive, lad," Hornbeam said, interrupting their fond reunion. "That was probably the silliest of all your little escapades!"

This brought Flum back to reality and, as he remembered his resolution to make amends, a fresh wave of shame washed over him.

"I wanted to make up for my stupidity, that's why I went after them, that's all."

Quickly and meekly he related what had happened under the mountain and how Macciovolio had taken Pim and Tansy as prisoners once more.

They all wept together over Cudlip's fate until Hornbeam brought their crying to an end. He squeezed his eyes with the thumb and forefinger of one gnarled old hand and, lifting his head, he took a deep breath through his nose.

"We'll have to mourn properly for Cudlip later. We're losing time. I have to catch up with that wizard and deal with him once and for all."

"I'm coming too," Flum told him, firmly.

They looked at each other. Hornbeam hesitated for a moment and then he nodded.

"Yes, lad, of course you must, but only if you do as you're told from now on!"

Turning to Sylfia he tried to smile reassuringly.

"Don't worry, my dear, I'll bring him back. I'll bring all of them back. Look after faithful old Lummock, won't you? He'll help you. There's such a lot to do here and he'll keep those guards at bay. There may be many of the other insects still alive. See if you can set them free."

While he was giving her more instructions, some of them rather muddled in his haste to get on his way, he was choosing the two best broomsticks from the bundle that he had brought out of the mountain. He selected what looked like the strongest and tried it out, flying low over the rocks at first, but gradually wheeling higher and higher above Sylfia's head. Flum joined him in this practice and after a great number of wobbles and a few unexpected dives they began to feel competent enough to set off after the Flying Cloud Carpet.

They hovered over the gaping hole so that they could shout their thanks and goodbyes down to Lummock.

"Take care, Mr. Hornbeam," he answered, his deep voice echoing around the cavern. "Good luck, Mr. Flum. Lummock will look after his beautiful fairy friend."

The beautiful fairy friend had to be brave now even though her heart was full of anguish and felt as heavy as lead. She grieved deeply for Cudlip and trembled with fear for all her other friends; Pim and Tansy in the evil wizard's clutches; the ancient elf looking so very frail as he hovered there in the silvery moonlight; her dear, funny, tubby fairy looking very clumsy and ill at ease riding on a broomstick for the first time in his life instead of flying with his own spectacular wings. In spite of her grave fears, however, she would say nothing to detain them.

She knew the magnitude of what they had to accomplish and, even though the task seemed impossibly difficult, there was nothing she would do to hinder their departure.

She hovered close to them so that she could hug each of them tightly and whisper her own keeping-safe spells in their ears. Then she let them go.

They took off and rose rapidly into the night sky.

Sylfia flew with them at first as they soared higher and higher but all too soon they were high enough to catch sight of the reflected moonlight on the restless surface of the distant ocean. The pair on broomsticks knew that it was time to turn towards the east and with much waving of hands and blowing of kisses they pointed their flying brooms towards the coast and flew off eastward, after the wizard.

Sylfia descended slowly, turning from time to time to watch the retreating figures.

She did not alight on the mountain top but flew straight into the blackness of that newest of mountain features which would from now on become known as The Gaping Hole. She searched in the darkness until she found the warmth and comfort of Lummock's shoulder and there she stayed, worried and forlorn. She snuggled into the troll's shaggy mane of hair and hid there, shaking, shivering, occasionally sobbing and waiting for daybreak.

 # Chapter 29

As Macciovolio drifted along on his magic Flying Cloud Carpet he was preparing a speech. In this speech he was explaining to his Mistress that there had been a bit of trouble at Imps and Insects Inc. The project had been sabotaged but, although this was a bit of a nuisance, it was not too serious. His guards had been organised to clean things up.

"The organisation will be up and running in no time," he would assure her.

"In the meantime," he said to himself, practising his most soothing sycophantic voice, "I have brought you a couple of amusing gifts. One is a unique Enchanted Dancing Fairy and the other is the Chief Suspect in the Act of Sabotage.

"This despicable saboteur, My Supremely Beautiful Mistress, can be made to suffer by watching the total enslavement of the aforementioned Dancing Fairy. Why will he suffer? Well, My Beloved Mistress, it is very simple she is, you see, *his* one and only beloved and he will squirm deliciously at every stage of her humiliation.

"When we – sorry, I mean when – *you*, My Dearest Most Sublime Mistress finally tire of this amusement *you* will be able to choose how to exterminate both of the worn out playthings."

The wizard was pleased with his composition and looked down malevolently on the two unconscious prisoners who were still curled up in the central bowl of the cloud craft, each in a deeply enchanted sleep. His admiration for Tansy was nothing compared to his devotion to The Sorceress.

Not for a moment did he imagine that he was being followed. As far as he was concerned there was no effective opposition that could track him through the skies and no power strong enough to put an end to his ambitions (or to his love of self).

He was flying into a splendid dawn. Over the course of an hour the sky in the east had turned from dark indigo to a bright rosy pink and now it was streaked with ribbons of shining silvery mackerel clouds. Each layer of cloud was reflecting the rays of the rising sun to produce a cascade of bright gemstone colours. There was the shining blue of aquamarine, the yellowy pink of topaz, the red of carnelian, the purple of amethyst and the surface of the sea turned a sparkling pink. This was better than that dark smelly mountain, he told himself.

He passed over the port of Mistanmurk which was

shrouded, as usual, in early morning mist and fog.
He flew over the estuary and out to sea where an off-shore breeze buffeted his cloud craft and caused it to pick up speed.

This was better than that dank foisty heap of rubble known as Bulzaban Mountain which was full of idiotic fawning creatures, each with the capacity to irritate him beyond measure. He rejoiced in his own power and cleverness, as the cloud craft sped along.

He was free! He was on his way to Isolagloria to see his beloved Mistress and once there he would shower her with gifts, well a couple of unusual items of interest anyway. It was better than going on an exotic summer holiday. It was even better than the end of the last day at school. He gave a spontaneous, exultant cry that was taken up by a number of herring gulls that had risen early in order to scan the sea for shoals of fish.

He knew that a ship setting out from Mistanmurk would take about three days and three nights to reach the island of Isolagloria. He calculated that by flying at this altitude and speed he would be there in six or seven hours. He would land in time for a late lunch, how delightful!

He smirked with self-importance and decided to wake up his prisoners so that he would have a captive audience to listen to him crowing with self-satisfaction.

Tansy and Pim sat down near the leading edge of the travelling cloud and rubbed their weary eyes with cold damp hands. Beads of moisture clung to their hair and clothes and they shivered in the chilly morning light. To them the wind was too cold, they had missed the glory of the dawn and the uncertainty of their future weighed heavily on their minds. They gazed ahead solemnly, occasionally glancing down at the ocean to notice jolly little fishing vessels chopping through the waves, or schools of playful dolphins leaping and diving in formation as the whole convoy made progress towards an unknown destination, a destination to which only generations of wisdom could lead them. The fairies could not help but envy the animals their liberty and joy in life. They could find no comforting words for each other and so simply wrapped an arm around the other's shoulders and pressed close together for warmth.

The cloud was bobbing along in a free and easy holiday fashion and not one of the three cloud travellers thought of looking behind them. The wizard had no reason to believe that a rescue party might be pursuing him and the two fairies had no reason to hope for one. If they had looked back they would have noticed that they were being pursued by two broomstick shaped flying machines which were advancing at top speed out of the west. The pursuers were travelling at a superior rate of knots and so were steadily gaining on Macciovolio's cloud.

The time passed and then quite suddenly the wizard stopped his whickering self-congratulations and drew himself up to gaze ahead intently.

"Yes!" he was heard to cheer with excitement. "There she is!"

He punched the air and pulled sharply on the ropes that were still tied around the fairies' waists.

"Look ahead you two. Isn't she glorious?"

The two fairies peered ahead. The sun was high now and all around them fluffy white clouds scudded across an azure blue sky. It was a fine spring day and the sea water gleamed with silvery reflections while the little white foam tops to the waves rose and fell as they were blown along on a stiff breeze.

Looking towards the horizon the fairies saw the island of Isolagloria rising out of the glistening water. The towers and pinnacles of a palace, which had been fashioned from the purest, whitest marble, shimmered in the sunshine.

Tansy and Pim gasped to see that the buildings were encrusted with precious stones – diamonds, rubies, emeralds and sapphires – and the glittering prismatic jewels threw out brightly coloured rays to create hundreds of little artificial rainbows in the sky.

If the Flying Cloud Carpet had flown over the island they would have been able to look down on the palace gardens and then they would have seen how the sparkling buildings were surrounded by immaculate lawns of velvety green grass across which peacocks and golden pheasants strutted. They would have seen borders full of gorgeous flowers, glasshouses full of luscious fruits, spectacular fountains gushing water spouts high into the air and a swan lake that twinkled in the sunlight. Beyond the pleasure gardens they would have gazed down on luxurious woodland where unicorns, deer and wild boar roamed free. The island was an enchanted paradise, a treasure store of riches both natural and cultivated.

The fairies did not see any of this in detail, however, because their time on the cloud was drawing to a close and they were destined to arrive on the island in a very different fashion to the one that the wizard had imagined.

There was the swish of a broom and the sound of a familiar fairy voice hailing them as Flum drew up alongside.

"Hello there!" he cried out cheerily. "What a chase we've had! How are you two? You've woken up I see. You shouldn't have brushed me off you know," he said, glaring at Macciovolio. "I'm very cross now." Tansy could hear that he was because he was not getting his words mixed up.

"You!" the wizard bellowed. "I thought I'd got rid of you!"

"Sorry to disappoint you," Flum shouted back. Macciovolio raised his hand to shoot him out of the sky but this time Flum was too quick. With an expert touch on the broom and a sideways movement of his head he disappeared from sight underneath the cloud.

Macciovolio strode to the edge to take another shot but as he did so he was struck on the backside by the twiggy end of another broom. He whirled around and found himself face to face with a wizened old elf.

"What the ......?" he bellowed in disbelief.

"Time to take on someone your own size," Hornbeam

told him calmly and, with those words, he deftly wielded his broomstick like a Samurai sword and slammed it into the wizard's midriff, winding him badly and making his victim double up with pain. The blow made Macciovolio drop the ropes that were tied around his captives' waists so that he could clutch at his wounded abdomen with both hands. Flum reappeared close to the edge of the cloud where the other two fairies were sitting.

"Quick! Jump on!" he shouted.

Tansy seized her opportunity without hesitation and leaped daintily onto the broomstick. She settled herself behind Flum and called to Pim.

"You can do it, Pim. Jump!"

Pim was much less agile than Tansy. He was taller, heavier, and his feet were not trained to make precise dancing steps. He jumped with great panache but without accuracy. Although one foot made contact with the broomstick the other did not. To maintain contact with the broom handle he grabbed the end as he fell and this tipped the whole thing straight up in the air. He was now hanging from the end of the broom with both legs dangling towards earth.

"Hang on tight," Flum cried out. "Thank goodness he didn't high up your tands!"

Tansy could hang on for she was sitting, like Flum, with her legs wrapped around the wooden handle but Pim only had a tenuous hand hold on the end of the broom and here the wood was very smooth. There were not even any twigs attached to act as a brake and provide grip. He could feel his hands steadily slipping downwards and he had no way of stopping them.

"I can't!" he groaned. "I'm too heavy. I'm going!"

With that he lost his hold on the very end of the broom handle. It parted company with his clenched fists and he began his fall downwards towards the ocean far below.

Flum did not hesitate. With a final and quite unnecessary exhortation to Tansy to "Hold on" he left the broomstick and dived after Pim. He unfurled what was left of his fabulous rainbow wings and flapped them with maximum force so that they drove his body downwards at great speed. He stretched out his arms, like a diver, to reduce air resistance and in this way caught up with Pim who had automatically formed his arms and legs into an X-shape in order to increase his surface area and slow him down.

Flum first grabbed the rope that was still dangling from Pim's waist and then he spread his wings like a parachute. Although singed and rather tatty round the edges his remarkable wings were still a wonderful sight with the rainbow colours shining in the sunlight. Even though they were gossamer thin and light as a feather they were as strong as silk and wide enough to create an effective canopy.

Flum tied the free end of the rope around his own waist and with both hands he worked hard to unpick the tangled threads that Macciovolio had used to bind up Pim's own spectacular wings into a tight bundle.

Flum could sense the sorcery that had been employed to secure the inelastic bonds. He ran through all the untangling spells that he had ever learnt but not one of them worked.

Time was running out. Both fairies saw that they were just moments away from plunging into the ocean. They could feel the spray on their faces and taste the salt in the moist air. They were eternally grateful for a westerly breeze that picked them up for a while and carried them along, parallel to the surface of the water.

Tansy had quickly learned how to control the broomstick with her knees while gripping tight to the broom handle with her hands and now she flew alongside, desperate to help in any way possible. She knew that woodland fairies never learnt how to swim because they had no need to, not until now that is.

She joined in the intoning of spells to unwrap Pim's wings but experienced the same difficulty as Flum. It was not easy to counter Macciovolio's magic.

Flum thought that the bonds were weakening and that he was going to be able to unfurl one of Pim's wings, but no sooner had the thought taken hold than the breeze dropped and they fell straight down towards the water.

Flum fluttered his wings frantically but it was no good. He and Pim tied together were too heavy and when the next wave broke over them both fairies dropped out of sight beneath the foam. They felt themselves being dragged down into the cold, fast moving sea where their clothing, and the rope that tied them, became waterlogged very rapidly so that it was increasingly difficult to fight their way up to the surface. They both struggled desperately, waving their arms and legs rapidly, in order to break the surface and gulp air before the next wave engulfed them.

Tansy watched helplessly and cried out in her despair. She decided that she would have to land the broomstick on the sea in the hope that the other two would be able to grab hold of it and keep their heads above water.

The drowning pair kept struggling to break the surface and breathe air but it was becoming more and more of a struggle and they were tiring fast.

Tansy prepared to land the broomstick in an attempt to save them even though it was a very risky manoeuvre. She could have been pulled under the water herself and then she would drown with them.

She was skimming very close to the surface of the water, preparing to land on it, when she caught sight of a beautiful streamlined shape keeping up with her just underneath the surface. She realised that a dolphin had heard her cries and was tracking the broomstick so she whistled softly to the animal and pointed to her poor drowning friends. Without hesitation, the graceful animal dived down underneath the struggling fairies and, when it rose to the surface again, it had the waterlogged pair clinging to its back, coughing and gasping.

So it was that the three fairies made landfall on the glorious island of Isogloria, not using their own wing power, but with two of them soaking wet, semi-conscious and collapsed on the back of a sleek dolphin and with the other one riding on a tatty old broomstick.

Tansy hauled her friends, one at a time, up onto the beach as the dolphin waited patiently in the shallows. After that she patted the dolphin and kissed its nose by way of thanks. It uttered a series of whistles and clicks before pushing away to make its way back to deep water.

Dazed and shocked, Pim and Flum lay face down on the pure white crystalline sand, while Tansy slapped their backs to make them cough up the briny water. Then they stretched out on the sand, completely exhausted, to dry in the sun.

Tansy resumed the chanting of untangling spells and very slowly the bonds loosened. After awhile she was able to free Pim's wings and spread them out in the sun to dry. Then, over a considerably longer period of time because she was working with both hands behind her back, she eventually succeeded in freeing her own wings.

After that she sat on the beach close to her friends looking up at the sky and waiting for them to recover. She was not drenched to the bone like Pim and Flum but she was wet from the spray and wading into the sea to haul the half drowned pair ashore. As the seawater dried it left a coating of salt on her skin and she had a very unpleasant taste in her mouth.

The other two were drying nicely but they were so encrusted with salt and sand that they looked like a strange new species of beach crab.

The salt made all of the survivors very thirsty and they

would all have loved to swallow deep draughts of cool fresh water. In the event, however, Tansy was far too engrossed in the drama unfolding overhead to go and look for a stream.

Chapter 30

Macciovolio had recovered quickly from Hornbeam's second blow and before long he straightened himself up to stare, open mouthed, at his opponent. At first he scowled and hissed with undisguised fury but then curiosity and even amusement crept into his expression. It seemed that he was being attacked by a frail old elf and, what's more, the decrepit old creature looked as though a strong puff of wind would blow him clean away. The wizard smirked scornfully and turned to say something sarcastic to the fairies.

It was then that Macciovolio realised that Pim and Tansy were not there. He bellowed with rage.

"You'll pay for this, you old thief!" he yelled and pointed a deadly finger at Hornbeam's head. Sparks flew but, to the wizard's amazement, they simply bounced off the elf. He seemed to be protected by a magical shield through which the wizard's deadly evil could not penetrate.

"What the ……" Macciovolio began but never finished.

The venerable old Hornbeam had suddenly changed before the wizard's eyes. Now he looked like a shining young elf, taller, straighter and stronger, with smooth skin and a very handsome face. His eyes, which had always twinkled, now shone more intensely with a piercingly bright light and his face was framed by thick, glossy hair which tumbled down onto his shoulders as it had done in his youth. From deep in his throat an ancient incantation rang forth and the words burst into the air like machine gun fire. They rattled the wizard's thoughts and blew them away in the same way as a rushing wind in autumn scatters the rustling dry leaves.

The wizard reached for his ebony staff which, as well as being his symbol of authority, was also another source of his magical power. Hornbeam saw what he was doing and barked out an order that woke the slumbering spirit inside the wood. It was an order that could not be ignored by the spirit and the staff slipped from Macciovolio's grasp. It launched itself over to Hornbeam and settled with a sigh into his waiting hand.

It was not long before the wizard discovered that his power was ebbing away, his knees buckled and his magic aura faded. Although it was cool on the cloud, Macciovolio became feverish and his clothes were so damp with sweat that they stuck to his body. He found his voice at last but it was weak, hoarse and crackly.

"Who are you?" he whispered.

"Names are not important," Hornbeam told him.
"I have had many over the ages; The Watcher;
The Guardian; The Wise One of the Wood, The Spirit of the Forest; it doesn't matter. In more recent centuries I've adopted the soubriquet of Hornbeam. It suits my current manifestation and makes me sound like an old hedge. No matter. Now, Macciovolio, The Earth Mother has given me permission to take your power. You haven't used it wisely, you know, and so it has become forfeit."

Macciovolio's cruel eyes glittered for an instant before he shrank from the elf and hid beneath his cloak Hornbeam commenced the incantation that would finally drain Macciovolio of his mystical power.

He had almost finished when a strong wind blew up and the elf, young and strong as he now was, struggled to keep his balance on the undulating cloud.

Cold gusts of air whistled out of the east and tossed the cloud about like a small boat in a storm at sea. Down on the beach the fairies shivered and moved together for warmth and protection.

In the next instant lightning flashed, thunder rolled, the sky became dark and the sun turned black.

From the east there came the sound of trumpets and a huge pillar of fire rose up perpendicular to the horizon. It grew in height and breadth until the column of flame filled the upper atmosphere and streaked the heavens with red and gold.

Then there came the noise of a great chariot rumbling into battle with its heavy iron wheels clattering and its mighty war horses snorting and straining their muscular chests against the creaking leather and jangling metal of their harnesses.

The war chariot that emerged from the fire was huge and it was drawn by two magnificent black horses. Their fierce eyes rolled in their tossing heads, their glossy coats gleamed with reflected firelight and the muscles of their gigantic legs worked with the power and efficiency of a well oiled steam locomotive. Their thick manes fluttered in the rushing wind and their galloping hooves made the reverberating sound of distant thunder.

The chariot was driven by The Sorceress. She was clad in armour of burnished metal and its sheen glimmered with ornamentation of the purest gold. Her hair streamed out from under a dragon shaped helmet which glistened so brightly in the light of the flames that it looked as though it too was on fire. She clutched the reins in one hand and in the other she wielded a magnificent double edged sword.

She had received news of the rocket. She had interrogated stray imps. She had made up her mind who to blame.

Macciovolio peeped out from under his cloak and squeaked with joy.

"Over here My Glorious Mistress!" he croaked. "I knew you would come to save me," he lied. "Noble conquering all powerful goddess," he fawned.

His mistress charged nearer and the wizard rose in anticipation of being swept off his feet and carried to safety.

It was not to be. The Sorceress could see that, not only had he failed her, he was now drained of his power and no longer of any use, a creature of no value, an inconvenience, an insignificant worm, worthless and despicable.

The chariot streamed through the air and headed straight for The Flying Carpet Cloud. Hornbeam backed away, ready to hop on his broomstick and fly out of the way to avoid the thundering wheels and the glittering sword.

Macciovolio, however, stood still, waiting, with his feet planted deep in cloud vapour. His arms were outstretched and he wore an innocent beatific smile on his face. His beloved mistress was coming to save him. What joy!

The din of galloping hooves and the rattling of the chariot grew until it became a tremendous clamour. Now he could look straight into the eyes of his wonderful mistress. He could feel the hot breath of the horses on his face and he could smell their sweat.

It was at this point that his joy of anticipation turned to horror for now he could see the cold, scornful stare of his beloved Sorceress and there was a deadly intent in her glittering eyes. She drew level with his cloud and raised her sword arm. Macciovolio only had time to whimper, "No-o-o-o-o!" as the sword descended with tremendous force and the blade cleaved through his shoulder and chest. He was sent flying off his cloud to plummet down, down, down to the watery deeps below. There was a heart rending shriek that echoed through the dark stormy atmosphere then Macciovolio plunged into the dark ocean and sank without trace.

"Fool!" was all his mistress had to say and this was hissed through clenched teeth.

She had brought the chariot to a halt and, turning the horses, she trotted back to the cloud at a leisurely pace. Then she caught sight of Hornbeam.

"The Guardian!" she breathed, "or whatever you call yourself now. I should have known that you'd be in this somewhere. You should be called The Meddler. That's the name that suits you best. You've meddled in my business before but this is one time too many. It is time for me to put a stop to your interfering ways."

So saying, she transformed herself into Grimlick, the huge fire breathing dragon with impenetrable scales, cruel claws and scorching breath. The lightning flashed and the thunder rolled around her as if the storm approved of the dragon.

The elf lost no time and turned himself into St. George in shining armour, the deadly sharp tip of his platinum lance pointed directly at the throat of the scaly red serpent.

The Sorceress pulled up just in time, her soft under belly just short of the weapon's tip.

She shifted her shape again. This time she turned into a beautiful damsel with soft pale skin, angelic eyes and a pleading expression on her face.

St. George checked his advance and instead of driving in the fatal blow he took on the shape of a little scurrying mouse which caused the damsel to draw in her flowing skirts so that they tightly encased her legs. She jumped high up in the air, screeching with fear, and looked around in desperation for a chair to climb upon.

Then there was a flash and The Sorceress transformed herself into a cat. Her razor sharp claws were out, her gleaming white fangs were bared and her yellow eyes glowed with predatory expectation.

The mouse rapidly shifted his shape and became a hare. With a great leap he jumped over the astonished cat and bounded away across the sky. He ran free for a great distance until the wily sorceress changed into a falcon, the fastest moving creature in the air above the earth and, with one great beat of her wings, she was on his tail.

As the hare ran back in the direction of Macciovolio's cloud, the streamlined bird of prey, fashioned as she was like a feathery javelin of death, caught up with the hare and gripped him in her talons of steel.

The hare became limp and lifeless, one last trick employed by captured prey, in the hope that the predator will relax for a moment and allow them the chance to wriggle free.

This falcon took no notice of the old trick and lowered her beak. She gleefully prepared to rip open the hare's throat and gouge out his innards, but before she could commence her meal the bird was blinded by a brilliant flash of white light. She turned her head to one side to blink away the little coloured stars that were interfering with her vision but within seconds she had refocused.

The flash of light turned out to be a dainty, dancing fairy and the falcon was enchanted by the agility and grace of this magical apparition. She relaxed her grip on the hare. He tried to wriggle free but was not quick enough. Automatically her grip tightened like a vice and her talons punctured the hare's flanks but she did not damage him with her beak. Her attention was on the fairy and she moved her head to and fro so as not to lose sight of the entrancing image.

Tansy danced as she had never danced before. As long as she could hypnotise The Sorceress with her bewitching grace, Hornbeam would be spared that piercing, ripping beak.

Unfortunately the old elf had not been safe from the raptor's talons. He now gave up his magic and resumed his normal appearance once more looking like Hornbeam, the ancient elf of the woods. Tansy could see the wounds in his sides where the falcon's talons had pierced him. He looked deathly pale and seemed to be fainting from loss of blood.

The Sorceress saw that he had conceded defeat and dropped him onto Macciovolio's cloud. She would deal with him later but for the moment she wanted more of the delicious entertainment. She resumed the shape of a warrior queen and, with her sword in her hand, climbed back into the chariot. She laid the sword across her lap and settled down to watch the show. Her eyes glittered and a rapturous expression spread over her beautiful, wicked face.

All Tansy could do was dance, dance and dance some more. As long as she danced The Sorceress was distracted from her prey but Hornbeam was becoming paler and weaker with each passing minute. Tansy knew that she could not go on dancing forever and, anyway, she could see that Hornbeam needed help now.

Then, out of the corner of her eye, she noticed that two fairy shapes were moving about on the cloud. Pim and Flum were there and they were trying to lift the now unconscious elf onto his broomstick. She danced around to the other side of the chariot so that The Sorceress had to turn her head and eyes away from the cloud to keep watching the entertainment.

Tansy looked past her audience and could see the broomstick trying to take off in a wobbly, uncertain way. Flum was sitting at the front, so that he could steer and Hornbeam was slumped behind. The elf's eyes were closed and his head was resting on Flum's broad back. Pim sat behind Hornbeam and kept him in place by wrapping his long arms tightly around the elf's waist. This also helped to staunch the flow of blood from Hornbeam's wounds.

To Tansy's relief the broomstick managed to become airborne and Flum steered it down below the cloud and out of sight. She went on dancing to make sure that her friends could get as far away as possible and she resolved to go on until she dropped out of the sky with exhaustion.

That would give her friends the best possible chance of escape but Tansy never carried out her plan.

What followed was the most unexpected, terrifying and magnificent turn of events that she could ever have imagined.

Ever since The Sorceress appeared the sky had remained dark and threatening. Thunder had grumbled and lightning had flashed all around them. When the horses stopped their charge the cold wind that accompanied the chariot had died down and the air had become hot and humid, as it usually does in the vicinity of a thunderstorm. The column of fire had continued to flame up from the horizon, turning the sea golden but, strangely enough, the sun had stayed black.

Now an equally sudden but even more fearsome change took place. A mighty wind blew out of the east and with it came hail, snow, sleet and sharp, piercing splinters of ice. The island of Isalogloria was shaken by a terrific earthquake and the ocean around it began to boil and smoke.

The noise this time was of thousands of horses and hundreds of chariots running into battle. There was the roar of many waterfalls thundering down unseen mountains, spurting through gullies, gushing through chasms, crashing over boulders, uprooting trees and removing all obstacles with ferocious force.

Now it was that the sun changed colour again. It turned silver like the moon, then red like fire, then blue like the Morning Star.

What looked like seven silver stars appeared in the west but how could they be stars in the middle of the day and how could heavenly bodies materialise in the atmosphere and move so rapidly with direction and purpose?

Suddenly they ceased to look like stars and took on the appearance of huge birds with long necks and brightly shining, multi-coloured plumage. Whatever they were they drove on through the wintry storm maintaining great speed in spite of the howling wind and driving hail. They were impervious to the freezing sleet and unhurt by the icy splinters. The gale was not able to move these unknown creatures off course and they came on with unerring accuracy, vengeful, determined, unstoppable and fearsome.

Tansy, blown about in the wind and rain, sought shelter underneath the chariot.

The Sorceress stood up to watch the approach of the seven shapes. Her sword arm held the gleaming weapon aloft and she gripped the horses' reins tightly with her other hand. The muscles of her face became set in a look of grim determination.

"The Seven Searchers!" she snarled. "Who do they think they are? How dare they invade my air space?" She breathed hard, her nostrils dilated and her eyes narrowed in contempt.

Tansy peeped out from beneath the wheels of the chariot and whistled softly as she caught a glimpse of seven beautiful witches approaching at high speed on their broomsticks. They streamed towards The Sorceress, shimmering in gorgeous silk and satin dresses which were spangled with glistening jewels. They sparkled and twinkled as if a myriad of stars had fallen on them from the sky.

The eldest sister was in the lead and she was dressed in sumptuous cherry red silk, as fine as gossamer and trimmed with feathers from a proud peacock's tail. Her glossy black hair was entwined with clusters of rubies and sapphires and each cluster had the form of an exotic flower. The hair that was not caught up in decorations was so very, very long that it streamed out behind her like a sparkling mediaeval banner.

Behind her came two more sisters flying side by side. One was in a gown of shimmering silver trimmed with the softest white feathery swansdown and the other wore a mantle of pale aquamarine satin shot through with lustrous threads of gold and trimmed with a kingfisher's lustrous feathers.

Three more sister witches followed these. One glimmered in a gown of emerald damask studded with lustrous pearls. Another shone in a topaz coloured robe which was luminous with hundreds of translucent diamond studs. The third witch in this group was dressed in violet tulle trimmed with beads of amethysts and spangles of star-shaped silver.

Sycodelia, the youngest witch, brought up the rear wearing her finest gossamer dress in which the colours of the spectrum glowed as brightly as the dawn and, as the delicate material rippled in the wind, the rainbow hues scintillated like the suns' rays in the crystal clear atmosphere after a storm.

All seven sisters had crowns of silver filigree worn low across their foreheads. These coronets were not fashioned from ordinary silver but from magician's silver. This metal is so pure that it produces its own light, the gleam of which is forever bright and, like some distant stars, it is ever so slightly blue. This silver shines brightly, even in the darkest night, and it never tarnishes.

The witches slowed down as they drew near to the chariot and silently they gathered around The Sorceress. Their broomsticks bobbed up and down in the fierce wind as The Seven Searchers studied The Sorceress with interest. She glared back at them defiantly.

"Get out of my sight, witches. You have no business here!" she snarled.

"On the contrary," the leading witch and eldest sister replied in a voice as calm and cold as a frozen lake. It rang like a bell and cut into the Sorceress's consciousness like splintered glass.

"We are here on our father's business. The Wizard of the West is no longer your ally. We are here to conduct you back to your own country because you are no longer welcome in his."

"What nonsense is this?" The Sorceress shouted. "This is my island, my sea, my air. You're the ones who should be going back to where you come from!"

"No!" called the eldest witch and now her voice beat like a hammer on an anvil. "You have abused nature for too long! It is time to relinquish your power. You have doomed yourself!"

"And you have hurt Hornbeam," Sycodelia said quietly, more to herself.

Her oldest sister glanced across, frowning a little at the interruption.

"As from this day you are exiled from the West!"

The Sorceress gave a wild hysterical laugh which turned into a deep throated groan of fury. She could be heard plainly through the wind and hail, even on the beach far below.

She brought her sword down to slice through the head of the leading witch but it never made contact. All seven witches pointed at the blade and, in unison, intoned a spell the words of which will remain a mystery forever. The incantation was uttered very rapidly and softly in a long forgotten tongue of necromancy. The blade stopped in mid air and, try as she might, The Sorceress could not bring it down onto her intended victim. She screamed in anger as the blade trembled, gleamed with a strange violet light and then shattered into a thousand tiny twinkling pieces.

The Sorceress roared and shifted her shape. The chariot and horses were gone in an instant and Grimlick hovered among the witches breathing fire that might have singed their fine dresses had the two witches who were dressed in aquamarine and topaz not conjured up a fountain. Between them they held up a golden bowl that spurted clear, cold water. They aimed the full force of the water spout straight into the dragon's open mouth.

Grimlick's breath turned to smoke and steam.

She coughed and spluttered and her eyes sparked with anger.

She immediately turned into a swallow and began to fly away at high speed but the witches were ready for her. They caught her in a net made from steel thread that the Wizard of the West had spun himself and his daughters had woven into a trap for even the strongest magic.

Whichever shape the Sorceress became the magic net changed shape and held her fast.

The net had seven dangling ropes, three along each side and a leading rope at the front. Each witch tied one of the ropes around her waist and by this means they were able to drag the captive sorceress far away, back to her homeland in the frozen North.

The next day they chained her up in an ice cave which is deep inside a snow-clad mountain, cut off from the rest of the world by impenetrable forests and frozen rivers. She fell into an enchanted sleep and, as far as we know, she remains there still.

Chapter 31

Flum steered the broomstick, through the gloom, back down onto the beach where he and Pim unloaded the unconscious Hornbeam and settled him on some soft sand at the base of a sand dune. Pim flew a little way inland to find a stream. He brought back fresh water in a leaf.

Hornbeam revived a little when the fresh water touched his lips but then, groaning and wincing with pain, he lay back again and closed his eyes once more.

"That's right, lie still old friend," Flum whispered. "Help will come soon, don't you worry."

Where it would come from he did not know but he knew that it was important to offer reassurance to someone who is sick. He took off his shirt and, tearing it into strips, made bandages to tie tightly around Hornbeam's middle. He muttered some healing spells that his mother had taught him when he was a wee fairy and the bleeding stopped.

Pim flew back and forth fetching more and more fresh

water from the stream. He and Flum needed to drink as well. Their mouths were still salty from their time under the waves and sandy from their time lying out on the beach to dry.

Looking back, neither Flum nor Pim could remember how long they had lain on the beach recovering from their fall into the sea but when they did at last sit up and look around they found that Tansy had left them without a word.

Looking up they had seen the Sorceress drop Hornbeam onto The Magic Cloud Carpet before settling herself in the chariot to watch Tansy's dancing.

Flum and Pim had simply exchanged glances. Words were no longer necessary for communication between these two unlikely comrades. Adversity had settled their differences and brought them together in a manner that conversation would never have done.

A quick nod of agreement was all it took for Flum to pick up the broomstick that Tansy had left lying on the beach beside them. They both jumped aboard without hesitation and soared silently up beneath the cloud. It had only been the work of a moment to lift poor Hornbeam aboard. He was so light and frail, like a puppet made out of cardboard.

Now, as they tended the old elf on the beach, they were wondering how to distract The Sorceress and so allow Tansy to escape.

Even if they had thought of a plan they would not have had time to carry it out because a fierce storm blew up and the sea began to lash the beach with gigantic waves. They tried to protect Hornbeam from the full force of the driving wind and rain but, as they huddled together, sand blew over them and they were almost buried. The broomstick was lost, buried in sand or swept away in the wind they did not know which, but the result was the same. They could not find it anywhere.

They picked up the wounded elf and began to carry him over the dunes, hoping to find shelter on the leeward side but as they did this the first tremor of an earthquake hit the island. The sand between their feet began to move up and down like huge waves on a rough sea. The earth was heaving and the dunes were being levelled. Clumps of marram grass moved past them, flowing in rivers of sand down the beach to the sea.

Flocks of seabirds took to the air, shrieking in panic, and they wheeled away in all directions, some heading inland and some out over the ocean. Huge waves broke on the shore so that seawater ran right up the beach and over the dunes, levelling the sand even more quickly. Thick sandy mud now swirled around their feet and it was getting deeper by the second.

They trudged and fluttered inland very slowly, through this turbulent mud, carrying their delicate burden as the wind threatened to blow them back, across the newly made salty swamp, and out to sea, a sea that was boiling and steaming as if a volcano was erupting beneath the surface. They were battered by hailstones and icy sleet until their backs, arms and faces were cut and bruised.

Without his shirt Flum began to shiver uncontrollably. His teeth chattered and his face turned blue. They stopped and sheltered behind an uprooted tree. It was still warm with the energy from the lightning that had struck it before the wind had thrown it on its side. They pressed against the gnarled old trunk trying to extract the heat before it was dissipated by the relentless gale.

Pim took off some of his fine clothes, a warm velvety jacket and a soft wool waistcoat. Then, keeping only his silk shirt on, to protect his upper body from the hail, he made Flum dress in the other garments. He had to help because Flum's fingers were numb with cold and would no longer work properly.

Crouched behind the fallen tree they huddled together for warmth. They made Hornbeam a bed of leaves in the crook of a branch and sat on each side to try to protect him from the icy blasts. The two fairies felt that this could be the end.

"Sorry!" Flum croaked miserably.

"What for?" Pim coughed.

"For being a fupid stool."

"You and me both!" Pim groaned. "If anyone's to blame for all this it's me! I got myself captured in the first place by being a big-headed idiot!"

Pim's voice quivered with emotion.

There was a pause as the wind howled even louder and a fresh downpour drowned out their words. The tree trunk lurched and rolled from side to side. They checked on Hornbeam and moved in closer to him so as to support him more firmly while at the same time gripping their individual handholes even more tightly.

"I made it worse. I thought you were a traitor. I lost my head," Flum coughed, when they were settled again. There was a sob in his voice.

"I was just pretending. I got the idea from Cudlip," Pim sniffed.

"Poor Cudlip. I let him down as well. It's because of me he got exterminated." Big tears were now rolling down Flum's cheeks.

"How's that?"

"It was because of me that the rocket went off before it should."

"True," Pim sighed. "But you've been very brave ever since, trying to make up for everything. You've done some wonderfully courageous things. You saved me and that's for sure."

There was another pause because the tree was starting to float and the pair had to hitch Hornbeam further up so that he lay on top of the floating trunk, out of the water. The fairies fluttered up to sit beside him and found themselves a couple of convenient branches to hang on to. When their perches stopped rocking quite so violently and the wind subsided a little, Flum looked over at Pim and smiled shyly.

"Thanks for that," he snuffled, wiping with the tears away with the back of his hand.

"For what?"

"For saying I was brave."

"It's nothing but the truth," Pim assured him. Then he leant over and offered Flum his hand. "In case we don't come through this, will you say goodbye as friends?"

Flum was unable to answer, for he was very close to tears again, but he nodded vigorously and shook hands enthusiastically.

They were silent then because each had his own thoughts. What had happened to Tansy was uppermost in both of their minds but neither wanted to voice his concern. It would have upset and scared them even more to talk about her fate.

The tree was moving fast now, carried through the dark swirling waters by unseen currents. Sometimes they seemed to be moving inland but, at any given moment, their craft could be spun around and driven out sea.

Exhaustion began to take over and both fairies felt that their stamina was reaching its limit. Neither dared to close his eyes for more than a second for, if either were to fall asleep and slip into the water, he would not only sink out of sight but he could roll the others off the log and drag them down as well. None of them had the strength to survive for a moment in these raging waters.

The day wore on and both Pim and Flum hung on using nothing but stubborn will power. The column of fire had been blown away and gaps in the storm clouds showed that the sun was low in the sky now. It was back to its normal golden yellow colour and would soon set over the western horizon.

They could see now that they had been blown out to

sea and that they were floating a few hundred feet off shore. The island of Isolagloria was changed a great deal. The beautiful beach had gone and the sea water was now advancing over grassy fields to lap against the walls of the gem encrusted palace. Dark shadows moved across the once glittering walls interspersed occasionally by flashes of light which were produced when the rays of the setting sun broke through gaps in the clouds.

Something made Flum lift his head to look at Hornbeam. Was it a murmur or, more surprisingly, was it one of those soft chuckles so familiar to all of his friends in Mulberry Wood?

The old elf was lying on his back, eyes wide open, gazing up into the heavens with a blissful smile on his face.

Flum's face contorted with agony. He thought that he must be witnessing the death of this wise old creature and he sought desperately to find some noble words of farewell but, to his surprise, it was Hornbeam who spoke and in a clear voice too.

"You were right, Flum. You said that help was on its way!"

With tears in his eyes, Flum looked past the elf to see if Pim was watching too, which he was.

"Is he delirious, Pim?" Flum whispered. "I think he must be dear to neth."

Pim sat up without speaking and followed the elf's gaze with his own eyes but all he could see were the black clouds overhead and the grey sleet falling. Occasionally a flash of lightning would light up the sky but without revealing anything new.

"Perhaps he's leaving us," Pim answered at last.

Flum was sobbing silently now and Pim leant over to place a comforting hand on his shoulder.

"We should sing a fairy song of farewell," Pim said sadly. "If only Sylfia was here to sing to us!" he added with a sigh.

"I – I can't sing!" Flum wailed and then something broke inside him, the strings of his heart probably. He gave himself up to sobbing and, as he did so, he rested his head on the side of Hornbeam's chest. The mention of Sylfia had released a tide of grief within him. Would he ever see her again? Would he ever see Tansy again? What about his family? They would be so sad when they heard of his demise. His eyes closed and his head swam. His exhausted body shook with grief and he thought his heart would break with the despair and disappointment of it all. Then at long last he was overcome by exhaustion and passed out. Pim caught him by his waist band and with a mighty effort hauled him back onto the log. He let him sleep.

Flum was once more in a state of unconsciousness but this time it had been brought on by stress and exhaustion, not witch's spells. In his deep sleep he had a dream. He dreamt that Sylfia was sitting beside him on the floating tree, her arm was around his shoulders and she was singing softly telling him that everything was going to be alright. The strange thing was that it was not a song for Hornbeam's death but it was a happy homecoming song.

Hootsmon was there too and he was talking to Hornbeam saying wonderful things such as "My word, old friend ye've been in the wars," and "We'll have to get ye home and into a comfy bed," and "Ye shouldn't be floating about on the sea at your age, it's a wee bit bad for the lumbago!" and "Come on, old fella, up on my back. Gently does it. Snuggle in there. We'll soon be back in Mulberry Wood."

Flum opened his eyes at one point during the dream and shut them again quickly for he found himself looking into the penetrating yellow eyes of a huge bird of prey. That was the last straw. He knew nothing more for a very long time.

Chapter 32

When the witches had flown up to confront
The Sorceress Tansy was hiding beneath the wheels
of the chariot but after the transformation of the whole
rig into Grimlick this was no longer a comfortable
hiding place or even a hiding place at all. She was now
in full view of all the witches and ran the risk of being
taken for The Sorceress's apprentice or indeed
any type of accomplice.

Tansy did not want to share the same fate as
The Sorceress and she was in danger of being scorched
by the intense heat that radiated from the dragon's scales.
In addition, the flames that continually issued from the
mouth of the beast were a little too close for comfort.

The fluffy white Flying Cloud Carpet was still there,
thank goodness. Even though Macciovolio's controlling
power was gone, the little vehicle waited idly by, hoping
perhaps for another pilot and a new destination.

Tansy had no idea how to fly a cloud but it did provide

her with a hiding place. It had to be said, however, that this particular cloud looked a bit out of place now. All the clouds around about had become storm clouds and their shades ranged from dark grey to black. Fortunately, the witches and The Sorceress were too preoccupied to notice this detail and Tansy shuffled down into the fluffy white interior hoping to remain unnoticed.

She could follow the proceedings quite well. It was like looking through a thick net curtain but she could make out enough to know that the witches were taking no nonsense. She breathed a sigh of relief when The Sorceress was netted and led away northwards.

The next worry was that the sisters did not take the storm with them. It raged on and on above the island all day. Tansy could see that far below the beach was being eroded bit by bit and, since she assumed that her two fairy friends had taken Hornbeam there, she felt very worried indeed.

She herself was at the mercy of the squalls. Her hiding place blew about like a paper kite constantly ducking and diving like a stomach-churning fairground ride. She had to stay within the cloud because it would be suicide for her to attempt to fly anywhere in such a storm. A tiny, almost weightless fairy could not survive in such a turbulent atmosphere where it was also icy cold and very, very wet. She marvelled at the strength and endurance of Macciovolio's magic that had bound water vapour together in such a way that it became a resilient vessel for her survival in these conditions.

It was much later in the day that Tansy, sensing a brightening in the sky towards the west, raised herself up to look out over the rim of her craft. The clouds flying by in the upper atmosphere seemed to be travelling more slowly and, near the horizon, rays of sunlight were starting to break through the murky grey.

She nearly jumped out of her skin when a large bird of prey flew over her head for he was so near that she could have reached up and touched him. His bright eyes were an intense golden yellow and, as he flew past, he fixed her with a piercing, unblinking stare.

His head was snowy white with a speckled crown and the plumage on his front parts were also gleaming white. His back and wings were a dark dappled brown and a broad black stripe ran across his eyes and the front of his head making him look as though he was wearing a mask. For that reason his kind are sometimes called sea bandits.

Tansy gave a gasp of awe and amazement. These were the unmistakable markings of an osprey! The great fish bandit! The sea eagle! She had listened so often to stories about them but had never imagined that she would ever see one.

Her amazement doubled when a second osprey came into view, a female bird this time and they greeted each other with a soft creaking noise before soaring upwards together, to give a display of effortless flight on broad, angled wings.

"I wish Hootsmon was here to see this!" Tansy told the birds.

"Well, little lady, it's your lucky day!" came the reply.

There was a rustle of feathers and the little cloud swayed as the bulky form of the old owl plopped down beside her.

Tansy sobbed with relief as she hugged him and buried her face in the soft down that covered his front.

"Steady on there, ma wee friend. You're rufflin' ma feathers. Let me have ma dignity in the presence of those two up there."

"Sorry, Hootsmon," she sniffed. "I'm just so glad to see you! You came in time to see the ospreys as well. Aren't they wonderful?"

"Of coorse I can see the ospreys ya wee noodle! Ah brought 'em wi' me!"

Tansy had been amazed before but now she was absolutely gobsmacked.

"You brought them?" she marvelled.

"Och aye. Ya think, like all the rest o' them that ma stories are made up just for the wee bairns. Now ya know they're true!"

"Hootsmon you're fantastic!"

"Ah go on. It's a good thing they can't see ma blushes, ya funny wee lass!"

"But how did you know where to find us? How did you know that we needed help?"

Hootsmon did not answer her. He simply hooted at the male osprey who then landed gingerly on the cloud.

"I told him," a small muffled voice said. It came from deep inside the dappled feathers on the osprey's back.

There was a bit of a scramble and a few loose feathers floated down then the face of Sylfia peeped out. Tansy was beside herself with joy.

"I'll tell you everything later," Sylfia said as she smiled and hugged Tansy but almost immediately her face was wearing a frown again.

"Where are the others?" she asked and her voice betrayed her bitter disappointment at not finding them all together. "The magician's not here is he?"

"No he's gone. He's dead."

Sylfia heaved a sigh of relief but it was Tansy's turn to look sombre when she recollected how long it was since she had seen the others.

"The others are down there somewhere," she said, indicating the shrinking island far below. "I don't know exactly where and I'm scared to think about Hornbeam. He was badly hurt by The Sorceress."

"You two, never fear. We'll just pop down now and find them," Hornbeam spoke cheerily, trying to lift their spirits.

He hooted for the other osprey who landed on the cloud just as gingerly as her mate had done and Tansy carefully climbed up onto her back.

Then they were off, swooping down through the wind and sleet towards Isolagloria. Worried though she was, Tansy knew that this was probably the most exhilarating experience of her life so far. Under normal circumstances she would not have wanted it to end but she knew that this flight would finish when they had spotted the others and the sooner that happened the better.

For a long time they searched the storm-battered island and the grey waters around it. They began to be very worried indeed but they kept their fears to themselves. The ospreys were magnificent. With consummate skill they skimmed the waves, their feet often dangling in the swelling ocean. They were poised to grab and retrieve any precious body that their sharp eyes might see floating above or just below the waves.

The rescue party were close to giving up hope and with a heavy heart and tears in his big round eyes, Hootsmon was about to suggest that they turn for home when his acute hearing picked up a very high frequency whistle. He headed towards it through the wind and horizontal rain and gave a hoot of triumph when his sharp eyes caught sight of the three friends bobbing up and down on their floating tree.

Pim had seen the birds wheeling around the island and had recognised Hootsmon but he could not stand up or even wave because he needed his arms to hold onto the other two. Whistling like a pipistrelle, a skill he had picked up in his days as a bat-racer, was all he could think of but it had worked!

Hootsmon landed on the tree trunk and the skilful ospreys hovered nearby so that Sylfia and Tansy could fly down to join him. Flying is probably not the right word. They allowed themselves to be blown down onto the tree while fluttering their wings for stability. Once there they gently released Hornbeam from Pim's grasp and lifted him onto Hootsmon's back. While doing so they noticed how the old elf felt as light as a feather and how deathly pale he looked.

"I knew you would come," he croaked and miraculously managed a faint smile.

Tansy smiled back and squeezed his arm but she did not trust herself to speak. She quaked inside to see his ashen face and the weak condition of his old body.

Hootsmon took to the skies with his precious burden and then all three conscious fairies turned their attention to the rescue of the unconscious Flum.

Pim said that he was suffering from exhaustion and hypothermia.

"He needs a good night's rest and some home cooking. That'll put him right," Pim assured them. The other two looked unconvinced.

"I hope so. I really do," Sylfia told him. Her osprey landed beside them and she climbed on board, pulling Flum after her. She buried him deep in the feathers behind the head of the patiently waiting bird.

Then, seeing Pim's forlorn look, she jumped down again and gave him a hug.

"Whatever happens, thank you for looking after him, Pim. You've been very brave."

With that she leaped back up on the osprey's back and they took off for Mulberry Wood and safety.

Last to leave the floating tree were Tansy and Pim. They climbed onto the back of the female osprey and held on tight as she took to the air. Tansy was sick with worry and desperately wanted to ask questions. She wondered if Hornbeam or Flum or both might be dying but Pim looked so exhausted that she decided not to bother him just yet. In any case, now that the strain of hanging onto the other two had been taken away, he started to shake violently with exhaustion and with the cold.

"Who w-w-ould have th-th-thought it! O-o-ospreys coming to r-r-escue us!" he exclaimed through chattering teeth. "This is so ex-ex-exciting!"

"You can thank Hootsmon for that," Tansy told him.

"Really? W-W-Well I never. He's an in-in-interesting old bird."

Tansy looked at him without speaking.

"Wh-wh-what?" he asked.

"Come here you," she said and, grabbing him round the neck, she hugged him tight before planting a lingering kiss on his shivering lips.

"You're my hero!"

"Wow!" he gasped, as she relaxed her arms and leant back to look at him.

"It's almost worth getting half-drowned, mutilated and frozen to death. I might try it every day!"

"Just for a kiss?"

"No, for a ride on an osprey," he grinned.

"What?"

"Only joking! Come here!"

A second kiss would surely have followed if there had not been a deafening roar from the island. Looking back they saw that Isolagloria had been struck by a second earthquake many times more powerful than the first.

As they watched, the whole island shook like a jelly and the magnificent palace was struck by brilliant forked lightning that streaked the sky and shone with an eerie purple glow. It caused the building to shatter and the walls to tumble down. As the walls fell, the precious gems that had studded them flew off and were scattered far and wide, then an enormous fault tore the island in two. One half of the palace ruins shifted to the left and the other half moved to the right exposing the very foundations of the great marble building.

As they watched, storerooms and treasure chests were broken open and the vast wealth of The Sorceress poured out. Gold, silver, precious stones, all were scattered far and wide.

Sheet lightning came next. It lit up the sky and made the coins and jewels glitter so that the island looked like an enormous jewelled crown.

Finally, enormous waves crashed down on the ruins and the sea opened up like a cavernous mouth gaping wide to swallow them up. It was as though an ancient leviathan was rising from the depth of the ocean to consume the remains of The Sorceress's wealth.

In one great gulp the ocean swallowed up the treasure and it was gone, down into the deepest most inaccessible caverns of its rocky floor and hidden forever by the restless waves.

Then there was an ear splitting groan and each half of the island tipped on its side. For long moments both halves stayed still, pointing up towards the sky like the bows of two sinking ships. Then slowly and solemnly each half sank down, down and further down into the waves. There was a final resounding gulp and the last pieces of land disappeared from sight leaving a vast whirlpool of swirling black water that was more than a mile in diameter and many miles deep.

The ospreys and owl had stopped flying west and had been wheeling around so that they could watch the end of the island but now they resumed their course.

The storm had blown itself out. The rain suddenly stopped and the clouds drifted away. The moon rose, stately and serene, and its silvery beams illuminated the dark waters of the ocean.

A profound peace descended on the whole region. Only the dark forbidding whirlpool remained as a reminder that The Sorceress had hoarded her plunder there.

Tansy stopped looking back and turned to stare ahead, searching the horizon for a glimpse of her homeland. She could feel Pim's hand in hers. He was close beside her and he felt much warmer now, more relaxed.

It was good to have him back and she knew that this adventure had changed him. His pride had taken a severe knock but that was good because his experiences had turned him into a sympathetic and generous fairy.

She wanted to hear him say that they had won and that everything had been worthwhile, the danger and anxiety, the fear and the loss, everything that they had been through.

She wanted to look into his eyes and see fresh hope and new courage there because she was still very worried about her other friends and she wanted to be comforted by him saying that everything was going to be alright.

"Pim," she whispered and turned towards him, hopefully, expectantly.

He was fast asleep.

Chapter 33

Pim was right about Flum. It did not take him very long to recover.

As soon as they got him back home his mother, who could see immediately that he was suffering from cold and exhaustion, tucked him up in his comfortable old bed and left him to sleep for a very long time.

When he woke up she was ready with the best of her home cooking. All of her most nutritious and sustaining dishes were steaming and roasting in the kitchen. Within three days Flum was up and about again.

His mother was bursting to know what adventures had befallen her son but there was something in his eyes that told her not to ask too many questions yet. For the time being it was enough to see him recovering his health and cheerfully receiving his visitors. Tansy called in every day and she brought a beautiful fairy called Sylfia with her. Then Sylfia went home to see her family on The Chalk Downlands and Tansy brought the magnificent

Plimlimmon with her. Flum's mother was quite overcome with joy and pride when the aristocratic visitor told her that her son was a hero.

Hornbeam was more of a worry. Tansy practically took up residence in his parlour, except when her mother insisted that she go home to have a proper meal or to get some sleep.

Hootsmon flew far and wide to seek the advice of the best healers and each evening he brought back spells, potions and poultices. The Fairy King and Fairy Queen sent their own physicians to attend the old elf which showed their immense gratitude and tremendous respect for him.

Well wishers came from every corner of Mulberry Wood and Dingle Dell and many others came from even farther away. They knocked gently and asked softly, "How is he?" through the open windows or, standing at the open door; they would whisper, "No, I won't come in. I just wanted to leave this."

When they had gone Tansy would step outside to find that they had left provisions; a wooden box full of fruit, a churn full of fresh cream, a bowl of strawberries or a basket of freshly baked bread.

Before Sylfia left for home she spent time with Tansy in Hornbeam's parlour and they sat late into the night piecing together a complete picture of the group's adventures.

Sylfia told how she had been left behind when Hornbeam had flown off with Flum to chase

Macciovolio's cloud. When she had woken the next morning she had been terrified to discover that Sycodelia was in the Gaping Hole and had been watching her as she slept on Lummock's shoulder.

She had tried to make a bolt for it but found that she was unable to move. She felt the sycomagic again but this time, as she had gazed into the face of the witch, she discovered it was not evil and threatening but benign and reassuring.

Sycodelia looked like a lovely young fairy godmother dressed in her most beautiful clothes. Precious gems sparkling in her hair made a shining halo around her head. She smiled and spoke gently as she told Sylfia how she and her sisters were preparing to go after The Sorceress but she was worried that Hornbeam and the other fairies might get hurt in the conflict so she wanted Sylfia to fly to Mulberry Wood and fetch Hootsmon. She said that he knew other large birds that would also be willing to go to the rescue.

A few days after the top blew off the mountain a band of Mountain Pixies turned up at Bulzaban. Among them were Pimpernel and Bloomsbury who had seen a great opportunity for doing Outstanding Public Service. They and their new pixie friends worked day and night to clean up the mountain, and free the captive butterflies that were still alive. They returned Bulzaban to something resembling its natural form and, sometime in the future, the Gaping Hole will probably be mistaken by humans for an extinct volcano cone.

Some of the imps that remained had elected, like Pimpernel and Bloomsbury, to join the Mountain Pixies and try for rehabilitation, but Doris, Burt and most of what was left of the Imperial Guard marched off one dark night and have not been seen since.

Much later in the year and on an even darker night the boggles returned to their mountain, happy that most of the work had been done for them but disappointed to find that Cudlip had left a mess in the workshop.

The little Flying Cloud Carpet is still up there somewhere. Keep a look out for it. It is looking for a new owner. It could be you.

Spring turned into summer and Hornbeam regained some of his old strength. One day, during the first week of September, he could be seen sitting in the doorway of his house, swathed in blankets, shawls and woolly scarves, soaking up the dappled sunshine of late summer. He still looked very thin and frail but there was a contented smile on his wrinkled old face. Tansy came to sit beside him and hand him his cups of nettle tea. He laughed when Flum and Pim staggered into the clearing carrying a huge banner between them. The words on the banner read

"WELCOME BACK SYLFIA".

Next day the four fairies and their families assembled at the court of the Fairy King and Queen. The Golightly and Penumbra families rubbed shoulders with the fon Ffonfavors, something that had never happened before.

Everyone met the Mellifulas who, apart from Sylfia, had never been to Mulberry Wood. They had come up from the seaside and were staying at the fon Ffonfavor's mansion so that they could join in the celebrations and see their daughter honoured for her part in the Great Liberation Adventure.

There was tumultuous applause and the assembled throng broke into ecstatic cheers when Hootsmon flew in with Hornbeam on his back. The King himself helped to settle the elf on a pile of soft cushions and nobody but the Queen was allowed to pour his cups of reviving herbal tea and place them at his elbow.

When the formal presentations and citations, applause and congratulations had all been completed an uproarious party broke out. Fairy musicians played and sang joyously from dusk to dawn.

Tansy danced with Pim very elegantly, Flum danced with Sylfia very enthusiastically and Hootsmon taught Flum's mother how to do the Highland Fling.

Lummock arrived looking extremely bashful but absolutely thrilled to be among the beautiful fairy folk again. They completely surrounded him and some younger fairies were bold enough to fly up and stroke his huge shaggy head. They admired his strength, commended his gentleness and held up their babies to be kissed by him. They claimed him as a friend and called him a hero until he nearly swooned with pride and happiness.

Cudlip's part in the adventure had been told to the

fairies of Mulberry Wood and they had remembered him in a solemn ceremony on Midsummer Eve.

Now, on this evening of jubilation, as Hornbeam dozed on his cushions, he thought he felt the presence of his old friend.

"If you're ready I'll take you with me now," Cudlip whispered. "There's so much we can do together in the Land of Remembered Dreams. We'll have so many good times."

"Not yet, old friend, I've still two or three more things to do here," Hornbeam whispered back.

He turned to look at the familiar shadow of his friend. It was very faint, barely visible, but unmistakably Cudlip's and Hornbeam smiled a beatific smile.

"It won't be long, though," he whispered. "I'm almost ready."

THE END